To C.T. Newt
... "Todd"

MONSTROUS

C.T. Newsome

C.T. NEWSOME

MONSTROUS

This book is a work of fiction. Incidents, names, characters, and places are products of the author's imagination and used fictitiously. Any resemblance to actual locales, events, or persons living or dead is coincidental.

Published by

Book Design by E.R.I.N

ISBN: 0615903223
ISBN-13: 9780615903224

This book is dedicated to Lisa, my wife and my friend.

PROLOGUE

Jill Beckman burst into the abandoned Chamber Street subway terminal through a service door, her flashlight penciling forward in the darkness. The twenty-two-year old transit officer turned right and followed a graffiti-covered tile wall to an old relay room, the room where a woman's body had been reported.

The door was open. Jill stepped inside and jerked her flashlight around in the dark. The bright beam revealed a network of steel beams and rusted-out generators that filled the room. Somewhere among the labyrinth of metal conduits, a pipe hissed warm steam.

Near the back wall, the profile of a man wearing all black and kneeling suddenly appeared in her beam of light. Sprawled on the ground beneath him was a woman wearing pink running shoes, jeans, and a brown sweater.

Jill removed her service revolver and aimed the weapon. She moved closer—close enough that she could see the victim's horror stricken face and lifeless eyes staring up blankly. His black hair hung down, covering his face. He bowed slightly over the deceased woman, his right hand around her neck.

"Stand up where I can see you."

The man seemed frozen in place.

"I said to stand up …"

He withdrew his hand.

"Slowly…"

He stood up.

"My god," Jill gasped. She stepped backward and gazed up at him. His face was stark white. Everything about him was cold and lifeless except for his callous eyes that stared down, churning with a strange spectrum of colors, as one might see in an oily film on a wet surface.

"Don't, don't move…" Jill said. She reached for her shoulder radio and pressed the side call button. "Beckman…10-12…. Officer in distress."

There was a burst of static followed by a woman's grainy voice. "10-4 patrol, confirmed 10-12, officer in distress. Please specify your location and type of assistance."

"I need homicide and crime scene investigators to the abandoned east terminal. I'm on the main platform, inside the first relay room."

"Please advise if an ambulance is needed?"

"Affirmative," said Jill. "The victim is a white female. I have the suspect at gunpoint. The perp is a white male, approximately six-feet, three inches tall, 200 pounds, all black clothes, black hair, and eyes are…" She paused, studying the man's face. "His eyes are a strange mix of color—theatrical contact lenses or something…. I don't know."

"10-4, patrol. Stand by."

Beckman's radio beeped again. She heard a man's voice. "Officer Beckman, this is officer McCoy. Baker squad is on the concourse above you. We're coming down to you now."

"Copy that," Beckman said, tightening her grip on the handgun. She heard sound of police radios and footsteps moving up behind her.

1

NEW YORK, POLICE

DEPARTMENT COMMAND

CENTER

Barrier Isolation Room 3 was the homicide division's largest interrogation chamber. Measuring twenty-four feet across and twenty feet deep, the room resembled a white box with harsh lights and empty walls. A two-way reinforced mirrored window dominated the back wall.

Two muscular deputies escorted a handcuffed prisoner wearing all black into the chamber through a side door. The deputies sat the man at a metal table and left the room, sealing the door from the outside.

On the opposite side of the glass barrier, Chief Detective Ralph Tino and a group of agents waited for the prisoner's interrogation to begin.

"Jesus, what a freak," Tino said, staring at the prisoner through a tripod-mounted video camera.

An agent in the back of the room shifted uneasily. "Is someone going to fill us in? Who is he?"

"We're not sure," Tino said, looking up from the camera. "Neither he nor the victim had identification, and nothing's been verified yet."

FBI Special Agent Jason Rand entered the room. The thirty-year-old detective had thick brown hair and curious eyes. The lower part of his face was contoured in shadow from not shaving for a day. He wore a short black jacket and a white button-down shirt that was neatly tucked into a pair of khaki pants. He shook Tino's hand.

Tino checked his watch. "Well, you didn't waste any time, Agent Rand."

"Has he made a statement?" Rand said.

"No, he hasn't spoken to anyone. We just brought him into the interview room and were about to get started. I was hoping to get a quick comment from him before the lawyers get involved."

"Does he have a lawyer?"

"He hasn't requested legal counsel, nor has a defender been assigned."

Rand stared past Tino at the prisoner in the next room. *The killer is surprisingly young,* he thought. He figured the man was in his early to mid-twenties.

Tino said, "The victim had a pinkish-red inflammation on the left side of her neck, just like all the others; and as usual, we have no prints or physical evidence. We did, however, catch a break with the phone tip."

"That's encouraging." Rand said. He retrieved a small pad of paper from his coat and stared down at a page of notes. "What do we know about the caller?"

"She didn't identify herself, and unfortunately the call was made from a throwaway cell phone. She gave the time, location, and described the crime scene. The first to arrive was one of our transit officers, Jill Beckman. Apparently, Officer Beckman caught him in the act, with one of his hands still on the woman's neck."

"I would like to talk to Officer Beckman," said Rand.

"She's on her way up," said Tino.

"What about surveillance?"

"That's where it gets interesting," said Tino. "There's something you should see." He gestured toward a wall-mounted television monitor. The image was paused. It showed a grainy street level view of the Chamber Street subway entrance. He retrieved TV remote control from a side table and stabbed it in the direction of the monitor. The recorded image sped forward. "I'm going to take the video up to 11:35

PM," said Tino. "There, take a look," He paused the screen. "That's our victim."

The video had been shot from too far away for Rand to see any detail. He saw only a blurred, black-and-white outline of a woman standing on a street corner.

"How can you be sure that's the victim?" said Rand.

"It's her," said Tino.

"Can you clean up that image?"

"I'm afraid that's the best I can do for now. The footage was taken from an after-hours convenience store. This particular view and image quality are actually better than the recordings from the traffic monitors."

Rand read from his notepad. "The victim is a white female, aged twenty-five to thirty years old, 125 pounds, approximately five-feet, six inches tall, with dark brown hair, cut above the shoulders, brown eyes," He shrugged. "Not a lot to go on."

"I haven't given you everything," Tino said. He retrieved a manila folder from a side table and handed it to Rand.

Rand opened the file. He noticed two photographs paper-clipped to the inside cover. Both images were of the victim. One picture was from the crime scene and the other was from the morgue. Rand thumbed through several more pages of police data until he came to a single-page document that inventoried the victim's belongings. "Are these all of her possessions?" he said.

"Yes," said Tino. "It's everything she had in her handbag."

Rand looked up abruptly. "A Marston?"

"Yes. Interesting, huh? She was carrying a collector's antique four-barrel Marston handgun. They sell for around six grand. What's even more interesting is that we discovered two blue-tipped custom bullets chambered in the weapon. The boys in the lab are telling me that the shells are constructed with piezoelectric material."

"Some of your officers carry electric ammunition, do they not?"

"Yes, but the material encapsulated in this ammunition is unlike anything we're using. Our electric rounds are designed to save lives. The materials in these bullets are powerful enough to put a basketball-sized hole in a brick wall." Tino put his hands on his hips. "Are you certain that you're telling me everything about your investigation?"

"Yes," said Rand.

Tino shook his head. "Listen to me," he said, lowering his voice. "I've done everything you've asked. I've kept the murders off the press wire. But when this news eventually breaks, and it will, guess whose head will be the first one on the block?" He shook his head again.

"Just take it easy," Rand said.

"Take it easy? You haven't seen everything yet." He handed Rand a photograph.

"What's this?"

"The victim's belt."

Rand glanced at the photo. He recognized the silver military eagle insignia on the buckle. "Was there a hidden compartment?"

"There was a small slot underneath. We found a white pill."

Rand shrugged. "Drug dealers and addicts love those trapdoor belts. They're great for concealing contraband. And they're cheap—retail for around ten bucks at the Army-Navy store last time I checked." He placed the photograph in the file and handed the folder to Tino.

"We've had the pill analyzed. The chemical compounds are consistent with cyano group."

"Cyanide," Rand said thoughtfully. "A suicide pill."

Tino nodded. "Normal people don't carry this shit around—this is military or spy stuff."

"I agree," Rand said. "In any event, it shows that whoever she was, she didn't want to be taken alive, and she was facing something potentially more terrifying than death. Getting caught for something? I don't know. What else do you have?"

"The rest of her wardrobe was unremarkable: a brown button-up hooded sweater, white athletic ankle socks, blue jeans, white athletic bra, and a white tank top. And there's something else you need to know."

"Go on," Rand said.

"The anonymous caller phoned the murder in at 11:31 p.m. That's four minutes before the victim arrived."

"Interesting. Why wasn't any of this in your report?"

"It had to be verified," said Tino. "We're still collecting data."

"And are you certain about the timing, that she arrived after the call?"

"The events were cross-referenced. We're certain about the times."

"And your dispatcher was sure that the caller was a woman?"

"Without a doubt."

"Well," said Rand, "we can safely assume that whoever phoned in the tip wasn't a witness."

Tino nodded and pointed the remote back toward the television. "Now take a look at 11:42 p.m. Watch closely." On the monitor, the video showed a rough outline of two men wearing black, making their way down a sidewalk. They paused briefly at the top of the Chamber Street subway entrance before descending into the station.

"Anything on those two?" said Rand.

"No," Tino said. "But keep watching."

The video continued to run. Three black SUVs pulled up next to the curb. Several men dressed in plain clothes and armed with assault rifles stepped out of the vehicles.

"Are those your men?" Rand said.

"No, they're not," said Tino. "And they're packing some rather heavy automatic weaponry and driving unmarked vehicles. They set up a perimeter and secured an entire block. Care to speculate?"

"Not enough data," said Rand. "Didn't your men talk to them?"

"No, they bugged out right before our teams arrived."

"What about cameras inside the station?"

"Unfortunately not. That section of the tunnel has been out of commission for decades." Tino aimed the remote toward the television monitor and paused the screen.

"What happened to the other two men who entered the station?" said Rand.

"They didn't resurface from the Chamber Street entrance. It's a labyrinth down there. It's a multi-station complex with side tunnels and hatches leading everywhere. It also borders a large homeless encampment. They could have emerged from anywhere."

"I'm surprised your transit officer didn't see them," Rand said. "What exactly did she see?"

"You can ask her yourself. Here she comes now."

Jill Beckman entered the room. She was sipping coffee from a white paper cup. Tino waved her over.

"Officer Beckman, this is Special Agent Jason Rand of the FBI. He would like to ask you a few questions about what happened tonight."

Jill nodded and held out her hand. "It's nice to meet you."

"Likewise," Rand said, glancing her over. He shook her hand, and noticed that it was cold and trembling. Jill appeared to be visibly shaken by the incident.

"You had quite a night," said Rand.

"Yeah," Jill said.

"I'm glad you're okay. You did a fine job. Handled yourself well."

Jill nodded and cradled her cup of coffee with both hands.

"May I ask why you, instead of NYPD, were dispatched to the tunnel?" said Rand.

"I was closest to the scene when the call came through."

"Is the Chamber Street Terminal part of your normal patrol route?"

"Not the abandoned section," said Jill. "I patrol the J, M, and Z located at the intersection of Center and Chambers Street under the Manhattan municipal building."

"Are you familiar with that area of the tunnel?" said Rand.

"I've been on the abandoned platform a handful of times."

"I see," Rand said. "And how long ago, exactly, was the last time?"

"About a year ago," Jill said. "The stations had become a sanctuary for a large group of homeless. We relocated them, and walled the platform off, but it didn't take long for them to return. They're quite persistent, and have nowhere else to go. I haven't been in there since then. No one likes to go down there, and especially not alone. The station is bleak and known to be dangerous."

Rand nodded thoughtfully. "In your report you said that the suspect was crouched over the victim's body. You never saw the woman alive?"

"No. I didn't."

"Or see him strangle her?"

"No."

"Could he have been feeling for a pulse?"

"It's possible I guess," said Jill. "He didn't try to get away, if that means anything."

"You also said that his eyes were strange," said Rand.

"He appeared to be wearing these peculiar colored contact lenses. His eyes seemed to react to my flashlight."

"Were any lenses recovered?" Rand said, turning toward Tino.

"Nothing," said Tino. "We've had teams go over the entire area."

"Is there anything else I can do?" Jill said.

"Any more questions for officer Beckman?" Tino said.

"No, that's all for now."

Tino smiled. "Why don't you take off? Get some rest."

"Thanks," Jill said. She turned and left the room.

Rand glanced over his notes again. "No images of our suspect entering the station?"

"None," Tino said. "We're still going through the city surveillance archives, but it appears that our man was already in the tunnel, but for how long, we can't tell yet."

"Why do you think he waited around after he killed her?" Rand said.

"That's a good question. We should know more after we talk to him. Do you want to be in the interview room when we begin?"

"No, your men can handle it for now."

An agent stood to his feet and offered Rand his chair. The wheels were loose and it wobbled slightly as the officer started to push it in Rand's direction. Rand shook his head.

"The victim's wound appears to be a match," said Tino, "but we don't have any proof. Do you think he could be this serial or this ultra predator you've been hunting?"

Rand nodded slowly. "It's possible." He edged closer to the observation window. He studied the prisoner for a moment. "Start the interview."

Detectives Joe Goldman and Tom Leftner entered the interrogation room and waited for the door to close and lock behind them. Leftner lingered by the door while Goldman placed a small handheld recorder in the center of the table. He leaned closer to the prisoner's face, making note of the man's pale skin and the peculiar way his blue eyes seemed to mirror the light. The detectives introduced themselves. The prisoner stared forward, indifferent.

"You're very strange looking," said Goldman. "Has anyone ever told you that before?" He studied the man's clothing. The prisoner wore black pants and a solid black long-sleeve shirt that adhered tightly to his skin. He continued to stare forward with his eyes fixed on the far wall.

Goldman set a photograph of the strangled woman from the subway in front of the prisoner. "Did you know her?" he said.

The prisoner remained silent.

"You need to talk to us," said Goldman. "It's over, you were caught, and now we just need you to help us set the record straight. I'll ask again: did you know her?"

Goldman put his hands flat on the tabletop. "Well, I can tell you, my friend, that you are going to need a good lawyer." Goldman stood up and took off his jacket. He laid the coat across the table and rolled up his shirtsleeves. "I can see that it's going to be a long night. Why don't we all get comfortable? Let's get those cuffs off." He reached down and unlocked the prisoner's wrist restraints. "Can we get you anything? A soda, coffee, or cigarettes?"

Inside the observation room, Tino turned toward Rand. "It appears he's not quite ready to talk about it."

"It doesn't matter," Rand said. "Let him stew for a while."

"Okay, but think about this: he's been in custody for over an hour now, and unless we charge him, we can't hold him."

"You'd better start working on a detention warrant, then."

"We still don't have enough on him," said Tino. "Do you think a few extra hours will make a difference with this guy? I mean, look at him. He's a space cadet, for Christ sake. I don't think he's going to talk."

"By law, he has to identify himself. Otherwise it's obstruction, and grounds to print him."

Tino shrugged. "Still only a misdemeanor. He knows that we'll eventually have to let him go." Tino leaned over and pushed a yellow button on the intercom that allowed him to speak to Leftner and Goldman through their wireless earpieces. "Gentlemen, let's continue with his processing. Take him over and have him photographed and printed."

"Did you get that?" Goldman said.

"Damn strange," Leftner said. "We have barely started in on him."

Leftner came over and stared down at the prisoner. "Okay, time to take a break. Let's get your cuffs back on. We're going to take you down to central handling. After we photograph and print you, you can make a phone call and freshen—"

"No," The prisoner said softly. He slowly stood up. The florescent lights above his head flickered.

"No fingerprinting," Goldman said, staring up at the buzzing light with an odd expression. "Now why doesn't that surprise me?"

"Just take it easy," Leftner said. "Let's get those cuffs back on." He took the prisoner by the left hand and attempted to refasten his wrist restraints.

The prisoner seemed to cooperate at first, but without warning, he seized Leftner by his right arm and spun him around. The prisoner locked his arm under Leftner's neck and secured him firmly from behind.

"Let him go," Goldman said.

The prisoner stared forward defiantly, and tightened his grip around Leftner's neck.

"Okay," Goldman said. "It's got to be the hard way." He retrieved a phone from his belt and punched in a three-digit emergency code.

An instant later, two deputies burst through the side door with their batons drawn. The prisoner continued to hold Leftner around his neck, With his right hand the prisoner grabbed the first deputy by his face and slammed his head against the metal table. The stunned officer blinked his eyes several times before collapsing to the ground, his arms and legs twitching.

The second officer lowered his shoulder and charged the prisoner, in an attempt to break his hold on Leftner. The prisoner brought his right fist down hard on the man's back, knocking him to the ground. Goldman charged forward, but the prisoner brought his fist up, hitting him hard under his chin, knocking him backward over the metal table.

Inside the observation room Tino plucked a red emergency phone from the wall and pressed a series of numbers. The phone beeped and a man's voice said, "Go ahead, Watch Station 3."

"This is Tino in Barrier Isolation Room 3. We have a hostage situation in Interview Room 3. Agents need assistance. I repeat, we have a hostage situation in Interview Room 3."

"Captain Tyson's SWAT unit just finished debriefing," said the man on the other end of the line. "They're down the hall from you. Shall I divert them to Interrogation?"

"Affirmative," Tino said. "Remind them to check their weapons. Instruct Detective Brian's hostage team to stand by, and round up some medics on the double!" Tino hung up. "That idiot just made a big mistake," he said to Rand.

A four-man tactical squad in full riot gear entered the interrogation room. Each officer wore an armored vest, a face-guarded helmet, and carried a thick, Plexiglas riot shield.

Goldman, now recovered, stood up. He rubbed his mouth with his hand. His jaw felt broken. There was blood on his fingers. "Take him!" he shouted.

The four SWAT officers moved forward.

"Let him go," one of the SWAT officers said.

The prisoner released his grip from around Leftner's neck. The exhausted agent collapsed forward to the ground, coughing violently. He staggered to his feet and made his way over to the door, next to Goldman.

The four SWAT officers continued toward the prisoner with their batons and riot shields held forward. They stopped within an arm's length of the prisoner.

"Just stay calm," one of the officers said. "Reach down and put those manacles back around your wrists."

The prisoner stared down at the pair of handcuffs that dangled from a metal cable looped around his waist. He looked up suddenly, punched his left fist through the barrier of riot shields, and plucked a hexagonal tear gas canister from one of the officers' utility belts. He aimed the cylinder forward, his hand on the firing pin.

"You don't want to do that," one of the officers said.

Rand and Tino studied the situation from behind the glass.

"Is that tear gas?" Rand said.

"I'm afraid so," Tino said grimly. "Riot control with a built-in flash-strobe deterrent."

"What the hell is that?"

"It's like a flash-bang grenade, but continuously releases a burst of light every twenty seconds or so."

"What's on the other side of that room?" said Rand.

"A hallway and a secondary interview room, a supervisor's office, a lab, and lab storage."

"Where does the hallway lead?"

"A weather station on one end and a twelve-bay communication console on the other."

"Can it be sealed?"

"No, it's an open corridor," said Tino. "You honestly don't believe he can get out of that room, do you? It has a Superman-proof door that's sealed from the outside, and there are eight men in there with him."

"Five and a half men now," Rand said.

"I have second team already standing by."

"And if he sets off that gas grenade?"

"We vent the room and send in the second team with masks."

"I hope you're right," said Rand.

Inside the interrogation room, a SWAT officer threw his riot shield to the ground and lunged toward the prisoner. He locked his arms around the prisoner's wrist in an attempt to secure his hands.

"I can't hold him!" said the officer.

The prisoner pulled the grenade firing pin with a loud *ping*. He held the pin in his right hand and aimed the canister down. The officer struggled to keep him from releasing the strike lever.

The prisoner thrust the sharp end of the firing pin into the officer's neck. The officer screamed and collapsed onto the ground, clutching his blood-soaked neck. The prisoner aimed the canister toward the remaining SWAT officers. A white cloud of eye-burning vapor erupted from the canister's tip, blinding the onrushing officers.

The prisoner methodically swept the cylinder over the room and dropped it on the ground. The grenade struck the floor and flashed brightly. A poisonous fog slowly filled the room, whiting out the entire chamber.

"Unbelievable," Rand said.

The grenade continued to flash. With each burst of light Rand and Tino could make out the outline of the remaining SWAT officers as they struggled to subdue the prisoner.

Tino pushed the intercom button. Over the speaker came the frantic voices of the SWAT team as it struggled with the prisoner. There was a chilling scream, and the room fell silent.

"Damn!" Tino said. "Let's get that room vented and the second team ready to go in."

"Hold it," Rand said. "There's someone moving in there."

The vague outline of a man could be seen on the other side of the glass barrier. He came close to the window and then disappeared into the mist. The riot grenade flashed again, revealing his position in the middle of the room. He held a long, rectangular-shaped object over his head. The room went invisible again.

"Everyone get back!" Rand shouted.

A table hit the window with a loud crash. The corner of the table penetrated the impact-resistant glass, and tear gas poured through the breach.

Tino pulled out his radio. "Vent room three!" He started to repeat the order, but broke off, choked by fumes. "Everyone out!" he said.

They all moved toward the doorway. One of the agents crumpled to his knees and vomited on the floor. Everyone except Tino and Rand exited the room. Both men hovered by the doorway, taking in deep breaths of fresh air from outside. An officer came over and handed them a few wet towels.

Tino's phone beeped. "We're in position," a man's voice said.

"Stand by," Tino said, covering his eyes with a towel.

Rand wiped his eyes with the cool cloth. "Jesus, that shit burns."

"The room is starting to clear." Tino said, looking up.

Both men watched as the gas inside the interview room dissipated. The prisoner slowly emerged from the fog. He had Leftner in a stranglehold with the grenade firing pin aimed toward the side of Leftner's head. The tactical squad members lay scattered on the ground around their feet.

"Who the hell is this guy?" Rand said. "And can someone tell me how he is able to withstand that teargas? He's not even blinking, for God's sake!"

Tino walked over to the window and pressed the intercom button. "Now what are you going to do?" he said into the microphone. "Are you ready for round two? I don't think you're going to like what we send in next!"

Rand came up next to him. "Let's not be too hasty."

Several more officers entered the observation room holding rags over their faces. They came up behind Rand and Tino, staring past them.

"Everyone move back," Tino said. "Give us some room."

Rand pushed the intercom button. "What are your intentions?" he said. Several moments passed without a reply.

"We need to send in the second team," Tino said.

"Not yet," Rand said.

"I have injured men in there!"

"Injured, yes, but I don't think you want any more, and there appear to be no fatalities yet."

Tino's phone beeped again. "Brian team standing by," a man's voice said.

"Stand by, team two." Tino looked at Rand. "Well?"

Rand reached down and pressed the intercom button. "We can talk about this."

The prisoner turned and stared in their direction.

"What do you want?" Rand asked.

"Some of these men need medical attention," the prisoner said. His voice was soft and sympathetic.

"Tell us what you want," Rand said.

"To be left alone," said the prisoner.

"I'm afraid it's a little late for that. Now release that agent and we'll talk."

"We will talk first."

"No deal."

"The second team is ready," Tino said.

"Not yet," Rand said. "Let's find out what he wants."

"I think you will agree that this could go on much longer than those men in there can afford to wait," said Tino.

Rand shook his head. "Let's try to reason with him a moment more, and then we'll try it your way. We still don't know what he wants."

"He's obviously trying to keep us from creating a file, and he's not about to dictate to us."

Rand pressed the intercom button. "If we send in more men, they will be authorized to use deadly force."

"Then I will use lethal force," the prisoner said. "You have the ability to save these men's lives as well as those outside this room."

Tino turned around and looked at the agents behind him. "Can you believe this guy? That arrogant son-of-a—"

"Why don't we rush him?" one of the agents interrupted.

"No," Rand said, staring back at the officer.

More agents gathered behind Rand and Tino; their mood was growing more hostile.

"Detective Leftner is losing a lot of blood," the prisoner said.

"This doesn't make any sense," Rand said to Tino. "Your men brought him in without a struggle. I mean, if he can do all this to a tactical squad, then I can't imagine what he could have done to the handful of arresting officers. Resisting arrest would have been easy, and escape through all those connecting tunnels would have been even easier. Let's give him what he wants. I think we're going to have to make a deal."

"There is no way we're not going to process him," said Tino.

Rand nodded. "Tell him what he wants to hear. Let's just try to get those injured men out of there." He pressed the intercom button. "What exactly do you mean by wanting to be left alone?"

"No fingerprints, photographs, DNA samples, or iris scans," said the prisoner.

"Okay, you have a deal," said Rand. "Now let that man go and return to your chair."

"Send in a lawyer," said the prisoner.

Rand and Tino exchanged glances. Rand pushed the intercom button again. "You have my word."

"I will need a lawyer to broker the agreement between us," said the prisoner.

"I'm not opening that door until you're back in your seat with your hands restrained," said Rand.

"I have no desire to become a fugitive."

"Damn it," Rand said. He switched off the intercom and turned to Tino. "Well?"

Tino shrugged. "Well what?"

"I know it's late, but we're going to need a lawyer up here. Do you have one?"

Tino glanced at his watch. "Maybe Michael Glass. He's been practically living out of our officer's lounge since his wife filed for divorce."

"Glass?" Rand said. "Is he a public defender?"

"He's a private attorney working as a conflict counsel for the Public Defender Advocacy trial office."

"And he's available?"

"He's always in the station." Tino turned to the agents behind him. "See if you can find Michael Glass."

2

CONTRACT

"**O**verworked and underpaid," said Michael Glass. The fifty-five-year-old defense attorney entered the observation room, followed by two agents. Glass had the classic look of a hard-driving trial lawyer on the verge of a nervous breakdown. His hair was wiry and gray, and he wore a wrinkled, powder-blue-and-white striped seersucker suit. He stopped just inside the doorway and turned toward the two agents, seemingly unaware of the rest of the room.

"Do you guys have any idea how many cases I'm working right now? One hundred nineteen. Keep that in mind."

"Yeah, yeah, we all have heavy case loads," one of the agents said.

"I bet you're not over one nineteen, huh?"

"Not quite," the agent sighed.

"I didn't think so," Glass said. He turned abruptly and strode over to where Tino and Rand were waiting. "So what could be so important that you interrupted my sleep, gentlemen? I really need my winks. And I…" He stopped short, staring past them. He noticed the prisoner holding Leftner in the adjacent room. "What the hell?"

Tino folded his arms over his chest. "He asked for a lawyer."

"So I heard," said Glass. "He's a rather odd looking fellow."

"You noticed?" Tino said.

"Well, yes. Who is he?"

"We're not sure yet," Rand said.

Tino said, "Michael Glass, meet FBI Special Agent Jason Rand."

Glass held out his hand. "It's a pleasure. What exactly are you accusing our mystery man of?"

"Murder," Tino said.

"Could I take a look at the charging documents?"

"He hasn't been charged yet."

"I would still like to see his file."

"No time for that," Tino said. "We'll get you a discover package afterward, but right now we need you in there." He stepped over and put his hand on Glass' shoulder. "It's not that complicated. He killed a woman, he was caught, and now has gone berserk."

Glass nodded as he thought about it. "Yes…. Well, okay, I guess I could talk to him. Why wasn't he assigned a lawyer when he was brought in?"

"We haven't had him that long," said Tino.

"Do you have a confession?"

"Not yet."

"What did you do to get him all roiled up?"

"Absolutely nothing," Tino said, scowling. "He was unprovoked."

"I had to ask. How many officers is he holding in there?"

"Ten men."

"Impressive," Glass said. "Any sustentative demands?"

"He doesn't want us to ID him," said Tino. "He asked for a lawyer to negotiate it."

"Are you authorized to make deal of that caliber, Agent Rand?"

"We'll work it out," Rand said.

"That's not an answer."

"Yes I can. Now, are you ready?"

"Yeah, I guess so."

"Good," Rand said. He stared in at the prisoner, then pressed the intercom button. "Your counsel has arrived," he said into the microphone. "He's prepared to represent you."

"You may send him in," the prisoner said.

Rand turned toward Glass. "Okay, you're up."

Glass turned to leave, but Tino grabbed him by the arm.

"You better let him know that we mean business," said Tino. "If he so much as sneezes in there, we're going to mow him down."

Glass nodded. "Okay there Elliot Ness, just calm down, and let me work a little bit of my legal magic."

"Listen," Tino added, "if anything goes wrong, we will cut the room lights and send in a team with night vision. If the lights go out, move the hell out of the way as fast as you can."

"Send in the lawyer," the prisoner said.

"That's my cue," said Glass. "Now if you will excuse me, I'm going to try to fix all this." He turned and walked out of the room.

Tino's radio beeped. "This is Richards on Brian team. The medics are in position. And a Mr. Glass has arrived. He states that he has been authorized to enter Interview Room 3."

"That's affirmative," Tino said. "On my mark, Brian team." He turned back toward Rand and nodded. "Okay."

Rand pressed the intercom button. "We're about to open the door to your room," he said. "Do not attempt to leave. We are sending in your lawyer. We're also going to send in an emergency crew to evacuate those injured men."

"Only the lawyer," the prisoner said.

Tino leaned past Rand and pressed the intercom button. "Those men require medical attention."

"My terms will be generous," said the prisoner. "You will have your men back soon enough."

"What choice do we have?" Rand said.

Tino retrieved his radio and pressed the side call button. "Send in the lawyer."

The door opened. Glass stepped through and waited.

The prisoner stood in the middle of the room with his back toward Glass. Injured and unconscious agents lay scattered around his feet.

"They told me that you requested a lawyer," Glass said.

"Yes," the prisoner said, glancing over his shoulder.

"What can we do to end this? I haven't reviewed your file, so I have no idea what is going on. Were you mistreated or provoked?"

"My terms," the prisoner said.

"I'm listening."

"I will give them this man's life, and spare the rest of the men in this room, along with an admission of guilt."

"But are you guilty?" Glass said. He stared warily at the sharp firing pin that the prisoner held at Leftner's neck. "Why don't we wait and discuss this in private?"

"I have taken a life," said the prisoner. "I will confess, and will be tried, convicted, and there will be a death penalty."

"I see," Glass said, nodding as if the notion had just come to him. "A death penalty. I find it interesting that you say that. It's not necessarily true, you know. And what may I ask do you want in return for this confession and execution?"

"No fingerprints, photographs, or DNA samples. And I would like to be transferred to Florida, to a prison of my choice."

"You know that what you are asking is very peculiar," said Glass. "You're negotiating in the wrong direction. If you are truly guilty and are prepared to confess, then it is my duty to advise you that you should be angling for leniency."

"And I would like to retain you as my counsel," said the prisoner.

"Well, that's a lot to consider," Glass said. "Florida's a long way from here."

"If everyone will agree to the terms, your presence there will not be necessary. It will be a cinched conviction, and there will be no need for a trial."

"That's true," Glass said. "But if I agree to represent you, I would need and want to be there for the sentencing phase. And the approval of my representation of you there would be at the discretion of the Florida court." Glass stared in the direction of the observation room. "And there's an application fee. The cost can get pretty high in some states unless it's determined that you are indigent, at which point the court could decide to waive the fee."

"The Bureau will take care of the fee," Rand's hollow voice amplified loudly through the overhead speakers. "If the Florida court won't waive the fee, then we'll cover the cost of the out-of-state application."

Glass nodded thoughtfully. "Okay, then I'll do it."

"And we want to know his victim's name," Rand added. "*All* of his victims names."

"You don't have to answer that," Glass said.

"No," the prisoner said. "I'll answer no more questions."

"Fair enough," Glass said. He stared toward the mirrored window, his hands on his hips.

Inside the observation room, Tino turned toward Rand. "He's determined not to let us process him. He obviously has a record."

"Yes," Rand said "And he's negotiating in the wrong direction."

Tino smiled. "Who the hell cares? He's a nut case. So what if he has a death wish? It just means no appeals."

"And if we agree to his terms we'll have to wait for his DNA. But why would he care if we got it now or later? He has to know that we will eventually get it."

That's right," Tino said. "And we probably already have it. With all of the commotion in that room today, he's bound to have lost some hair or something. I'll have a team go over the entire room."

Rand reached for the intercom button. "Okay Mr. Glass, tell him that we accept his offer, and we'll have the agreement drawn up in writing."

Glass looked at the prisoner. "They will want a signed confession."

The prisoner stared down at Glass but didn't speak.

"And his name?" Rand said.

"Well?" Glass said.

"My name is Harold Fain," the prisoner said.

"His *real* name," said Rand.

Glass retrieved a pen and a business card from his front coat pocket. "Could you spell your last name?"

"F-A-I- N."

Glass wrote Fain's name on the back of the card, and slipped the paper into his pocket.

Fain released his grip around Leftner's neck. The agent fell forward into Glass's arms.

Fain dropped the firing pin on the ground and calmly retrieved an overturned chair. He placed the chair in the middle of the room. He refastened his arm restraints and sat down in the chair, staring forward as if nothing had happened.

3

ARLINGTON, VIRGINIA

"**A**rrested?" Jack Simons said with a phone to his ear. He sat up in a large black leather chair behind a hulking oak desk. He put his shoes on and stretched his feet out over the blue and gold Berber carpet of his spacious Pentagon office.

"Yes," a woman's voice said on the other end of the phone line. "It's him. He was apprehended in New York—an abandoned subway."

"That's impossible. What name was he booked under?"

"Harold Fain, and he was charged for Gelder's murder. They were found together. They have her listed as a Jane Doe."

"Damn it!" Simons said.

"The FBI is now involved," the woman continued. "Agent Jason Rand. He negotiated a confession, and they now plan to bypass a trial and go straight to sentencing."

"What did Fain want for this confession?"

"To be transferred to Florida—Cypress Supermax."

"Ricktor!" Simons said, standing up. "Gelder knew his location."

"Now you understand," she said. "Do you want Ricktor moved out of the prison?"

"I'm thinking," Simons said. He walked over to his open office door. The hallway beyond was crowded with Pentagon staffers hustling back and forth, on their way to various meetings. He loosened his tie and closed the door. "I want a timeline—from his extradition to sentencing to when he's due to arrive at Cypress."

"Without a trial it could be as soon as a few days. We could have Fain diverted to another prison, or we could attempt an intercept."

"Diverting him would mean overriding our friends at the Bureau, and that would raise too many questions. No, he's sacrificing himself to force our hand. He's flushing Ricktor out."

"Then we should initiate an intercept now and implement it upon Fain's transfer," said the woman. "Throw everything we have at him while we still have the resources."

"Tempting, but ultimately out of the question. That would play right into his hands."

"Then what do we do?"

"Let me think," Simons said. He stepped over to a small wet bar. He checked himself in a mirror that hung on the wall behind the bar. His short black hair was a snarled in the front where he had slept face down on his desk. He smoothed his hand down his black suit and picked a speck of white lint from his lapel. A clear plastic decanter of ice water sat on top of the counter. Condensation beaded around the sides of the carafe, forming a puddle on the shelf. He poured a glass of water, but didn't drink it.

"What are your instructions?" the woman said, breaking the silence.

"For us to salvage anything from this little venture, Ricktor must survive."

"Let's take Fain out!"

"How, like we've tried in the past? We can't afford to lose any more men. And now that he's in custody, we can't even consider a direct assault, and he knows that. We'll have to let it play out. At least we will know where he is."

"They won't be able to hold him."

"No, but he is confined for now. That gives us time. Time to scuttle what's left of the Legion Project, including the remaining Strategic Labs science teams. I want us to be the last two people to know where all the pieces go. You will need to watch Fain during his incarceration, but do not engage. We'll reconstitute once the dust has settled."

He turned off his phone and slid it into his pocket. He picked up the water pitcher and wiped the condensation with his left hand and combed his wet fingers through his hair. He frowned in the mirror and then turned and hurled the decanter of water across the room.

4

CYPRESS PENAL COMPLEX, EVERGLADE CITY, FLORIDA

Warren Ricktor's prison cell was a converted guard station located inside the main housing unit, above the fourth floor tier. A team of handpicked guards monitored him around the clock. No other prisoners were allowed on his row. His guards knew nothing about him, only that he enjoyed special privileges: he could come and go from his cell whenever he wanted to, and he got whatever he asked for. No one on the prison staff knew why he enjoyed such preferential treatment; they just did what they were told and they were told not to ask questions or else they might be fired.

A guard stood across from Ricktor's open cell with his foot on the rail, staring down at the inmates in orange jumpsuits mingling in the common area four stories below.

Two guards came up the stairs and walked over to where he was standing. The sound of crunching could be heard beneath their feet. They both looked down as they walked. Almonds lay scattered across the floor.

"Something wrong with Ricktor's almonds?" one of the guards asked.

"He threw them at me when he saw that they weren't organic, and they were bleached or something…. I don't know," said the other guard. "Ricktor's an asshole. Now, who's this with you Mike?"

Mike smiled. "This is Roger. He's on loan to us from A Wing."

Bill stepped off the rail and shook Roger's hand. "It's a pleasure. So what have you and your fellow guards heard about Ricktor over on A Block?"

"Nothing. I mean everyone knows something is going on up here, but no one knows what it is."

"Good," Bill said.

"Well," said Roger. "What's Ricktor's story?"

Bill frowned. "Rule one, Roger: never ask about Ricktor. It'll get you fired."

"You can't be serious."

"Dead serious. Did you sign the nondisclosure agreement?"

"I signed it, but I really didn't read it that closely. I thought that since I was going to be working over here, that I should ask some questions. Shouldn't I know something about the guy I'll be guarding?"

"Not about him," Bill said.

They all turned and stared into the cell. Ricktor sat in the middle of the room in a comfortable recliner, bundled in a plush white bathrobe, reading a newspaper. Next to him was a shelf of matching white hand and bath towels, and a full-length, stand-up mirror. The room's other furnishings consisted of a long table that was covered with a white cloth, and a second smaller wooden table that was set with a lamp and a well-stocked fruit bowl. A large flat screen television hung on the wall. The TV was tuned to a national news channel, but the sound was off.

Roger shook his head. "I mean, you read about this kind of stuff with old-school mobsters and shit, but this is ridiculous. Who the hell is he?"

"Again, I caution you," said Bill. "If you value your job here, you'll need to be careful."

"Take it easy. I'm just thinking out loud."

"Well, you can think it," Bill said. "But don't say it. And when you get back to A Block after next week, don't talk to your friends about it. Now let's go over a few things." He handed Roger a list.

"What's this?"

"Ricktor's daily requests. He e-mails his requirements to Warden Mangum every night."

Roger studied the list. "Six large 1.5-liter Fiji waters," he read aloud. "Twelve individual sized Fiji waters on ice." He looked, up shaking his head. "You have to be kidding me." He looked back down. "Tropical fruit assortment with wooden bowl to include organic bananas, plums, apples, and pears. Scented candles—seriously? Did he ask for all this today?"

Mike nodded.

"And he gets it," said Bill.

"This is outrageous." Roger handed the list back to Bill. "So basically everyone runs around this guy as if he's some kind of celebrity?"

"Yep. Think you can handle him? He's not easy to manage."

"He can't be more difficult than some of those nut jobs on A Block," said Roger.

"Yeah I guess," said Bill. "That is, if you don't mind being treated like someone's private butler all day. He also has a private nurse and a cook."

"That's amazing. And what does he do all day?"

"Mostly meditates," Bill said.

"He's not meditating," Mike said. "He practices acting like he's dead. That's what he told me."

"He plays dead?"

Mike nodded. "And he's good at it."

"Why?"

"Who knows?" Bill said. "He's bored. Yesterday he amused himself by watching a *Planet of the Apes* movie marathon."

"Why don't you gentlemen grab a cup of coffee for a minute." a voice said from behind the three guards.

They turned around and saw Roth Fredricks, the man in charge of coordinating Ricktor's security, standing at the top of the stairs. He was smoothing out his uniform.

"I need to speak to our guest alone," Fredricks said. He checked his watch. "I shouldn't be long. Say, ten minutes." He stepped aside as the three men came through and descended the stairs. He smoothed his hands down his guard uniform again and walked over to Ricktor's door.

Ricktor looked up from his newspaper. "What are you doing up here? You're supposed to be watching the lower stairs. And look at you, for Christ sake. Not even a hair out of place. And take off the Rolex—play the part. There's no guards wearing ten-thousand-dollar watches in here."

"Warden Mangum knows the deal," said Fredricks.

"He doesn't know anything," Ricktor said, looking back down at his paper. "What do you want?"

"There's been a development."

Ricktor continued to read his paper. After a moment, he looked up. "If it's regarding anything other than me leaving here, save your breath." He pulled out the business section of the paper and read above the fold.

"He's been located."

Ricktor laughed. "Well, thank God! Has he been neutralized?"

"He's in custody."

Ricktor put down his newspaper. "Then it's safe for me to leave this godforsaken place?"

"He was found, but not by us."

"What are you talking about?"

"He has been arrested for murder."

"Arrested—by the police?" said Ricktor.

Fredricks nodded.

"That's impossible," said Ricktor.

"It happened."

Ricktor shrugged. "I don't care about the details. If they have him, then it's as good as you having him. Just have Simons pull rank or something."

"It's not that simple," said Fredricks. "And he was charged for Gelder's murder."

"Gelder? That woman—so incredibly smart to be so stupid and…" He paused for a moment. "She knew my location."

"And now so does he. In fact, he negotiated a confession."

"Negotiated?"

"Part of his plea was to be transferred here."

"Jesus!" Ricktor said. He stood up and retied his bathrobe. "You've got to get me out of here."

Fredricks nodded. "It's in the works."

"Works?" When is he due to arrive?"

"Two weeks."

"I'm not staying in here."

"Of course not. You're too valuable to lose."

"Yes, so was Gelder. Now get me the hell out of here. Today!"

"In the morning," Fredricks said. "Simons is arranging it." He reached for his belt buckle. It was a silver rectangle, engraved with an eagle standing on a tree branch with its wings spread wide. Fredricks released a metal clasp, retrieved a small white pill from a hidden compartment, and held it in his open palm. "Just in case," he said, pushing the pill toward Ricktor. "Take it, you don't have much time." He checked his watch.

Ricktor took the pill and put it in the pocket of his bathrobe. He retrieved a bottle of water from a bucket of ice. His hands trembled as he unscrewed the cap. "He's going to kill us all," whispered Ricktor. He closed his eyes as he took a long sip and swallowed. When he opened his eyes, Fredricks was gone.

The next morning Ricktor sat down to his favorite breakfast: blueberry blintzes, eggplant omelet with caraway and coriander, half a grapefruit, and a tangerine mimosa. After he ate he showered and changed into a custom white Louis Vuitton suit and a powder blue shirt. He examined the blue and gold necktie that was delivered with the suit. He threw the tie into the trash. He checked himself in the long mirror and unfastened the second button on his shirt. *I look like a South Florida tourist*, he thought. Perhaps that's where they were moving him, someplace nicer this time. He stared around the prison cell as he thought about the relocation.

Roth Fredricks arrived outside Ricktor's open cell door dressed in the same white suit and tie. He noticed Ricktor's necktie in the garbage and removed his own. He retrieved a radio from inside his jacket. "Have the other two decoys remove their ties," he said into the radio.

"Is Simons here?" Ricktor said, still checking himself in the mirror.

"No," Fredricks said.

"How many men have been assigned to my relocation?"

"Enough. Now let's hurry. Time is wasting." Fredricks gestured toward the open door.

Ricktor followed Fredricks out onto the walkway. No guards were visible. Fredricks guided Ricktor to the end of the gangway, where they exited through an unlocked steel-plated door. They descended three stories down a dimly lit stairwell, where they came to a second metal door. Fredricks pounded his fist against the door and waited. A man in a black suit and sunglasses opened the door and motioned for them to step through. They emerged outside the prison, between a pair of ten-foot-high retaining walls.

Ricktor took a deep breath of moist Florida air and squinted at the bright blue sky. The main prison wall loomed behind him. He and Fredricks met up with his two decoys. Each man was the same height as Ricktor and wore an identical white suit. Four agents came over and paired up with each decoy. One of the agents passed around black hoods.

"Good luck," Fredricks said.

"Wait a minute," Ricktor said. "Where the hell am I going?"

Fredricks pulled on his hood. "Simons didn't say. And I don't want to know."

The second pair of decoys pulled on their hoods and waited.

Ricktor stepped to the end of the retaining wall and peeked around the corner. Four white limousines with tinted windows idled in the grass. He pulled on his hood, and felt a hand grab him by the arm and guide him toward the vehicles. He heard a car door open.

"Watch your head," a voice said.

Ricktor felt a hand on his shoulder. He was forced to crouch slightly as entered the vehicle. There was a rush of cold air, and the scent of new leather. Once the door closed he removed his hood. He noticed that he was in the third car. There were no other passengers in his vehicle, only a driver.

"What are you waiting for?" Ricktor asked.

The driver held up his phone.

"Are you armed?"

The driver held up his service pistol.

"Is that the only weapon you have?"

The driver pointed outside the vehicle. Across the field a black helicopter hovered above the tree line.

Ricktor breathed a sigh of relief and sat back in his seat. On the console to his right was a large manila envelope. He tore the packet open and dumped the contents on the seat. There was a passport, a California driver's license with a Malibu address, a cell phone, and a stack of new hundred-dollar bills. He picked up the cash and fanned through the notes. He retrieved the driver's license and glanced it over. The ID contained one of his older photographs. He recognized the picture from his employee file at Strategic Labs. His new name was Rick Smith—a common surname, he thought. The scientist in him wondered how many Rick Smiths were out there in the world. He made a mental note to look into it once he got settled. On the back of the ID was a yellow sticky note with the name of two bank accounts, each with usernames and passwords.

"How much longer?" Ricktor said, eyeing the driver through the rearview mirror.

The driver shook his head and held up his phone again.

Ricktor nodded and reached for the wet bar behind the driver's seat. He sorted through the rows of mini-bottles until he found a variety of vodkas. He picked out two Stolichnayas and shook up a martini and took a small sip. It tasted cold and dry and vaguely medicinal. He raised his glass in mock toast to himself, and tilted the glass all the way up, finishing the drink in one long swig. He reached for more bottles.

The two lead limousines moved off the grass onto a narrow road. The vehicles crossed a one-lane bridge and disappeared into the Everglades. Several moments passed. Ricktor finally felt his vehicle move into gear. The car eased forward and crossed over the bridge. Dense jungle lined both sides of the narrow highway, and a canal filled with shallow black water bordered the right side of the road.

Ten minutes into the route, the driver stopped the car.

"Why are you stopping?" Ricktor said.

"New orders," the driver said. He pointed through the front windshield toward a large plume of smoke on the road, a mile ahead. He initiated a U-turn, easing the car off the right shoulder.

Ricktor's new cell phone rang. "Hello…" he said.

"This is Simons."

"What, what's happening?"

"We lost contact with the two lead vehicles, and our helicopter is off radar."

"Damn it…" Ricktor said. "I told you people that this prison was a bad idea. There's only one road out of here. You should have flown me out of the compound."

"Don't let them take you," Simons said. The phone went dead.

"Take us back to the prison," Ricktor said.

"Yes, those are my orders," the driver said. The car jolted hard on the uneven pavement as they came back out on the road. They drove south toward the prison. The trailing limousine came to a stop in front of them.

"Why has he stopped?" Ricktor said.

"Its protocol. He'll maintain the original line. Wait for us to come past him." He pulled up closer to the other car, driving slowly. As they came closer, a single bullet shattered the fourth vehicle's front windshield on the driver's side. Blood spattered the glass from the inside.

With his driver dead, the panicked decoy exploded out of the back door of the vehicle. He pulled his hood off and came to Ricktor's back door and tugged on the locked handle.

"Put your hood on, you fool!" Ricktor said. Before he could open the door, a gunshot from a high-caliber, long-range rifle took the side of the decoy's head off.

"Go!" Ricktor shouted.

"Yeah," The driver said. He stepped on the accelerator. The driver's side window suddenly exploded inward. The driver slumped forward and the car careened off the right shoulder of the road and stalled on an earth embankment.

Ricktor opened the back door and stepped onto the grass. He cupped his hands around his eyes, staring down the deserted highway. The smoke in the distance was mostly gone now. A tractor-trailer was parked on the side of the road. Several men with fire extinguishers maneuvered around a disabled limousine. A black car came around the right side of the truck and slowly made its way toward Ricktor. *They won't kill me,* he thought, *not yet. They'll take me alive and make me wish that I were dead.* He retrieved the white pill from his coat pocket and held it in his open palm.

"I had the answer to life's mysteries," he said in a whisper. "I had the knowledge ... forbidden knowledge."

The black car came closer—close enough that Ricktor could see the driver's face behind the gleaming windshield. He put the cyanide pill in his mouth and climbed into the back seat of the limousine. He opened a small refrigerator and selected a bottle of champagne and pulled the cork. The sparkling wine bubbled over. He waited for the fizzing to stop before biting down on the pill. The acid exploded across his tongue toward the back of his throat. He lifted the champagne bottle to his lips and managed a single sip before he lost consciousness.

5

SIX MONTHS LATER

David Anslem held his visitor's pass toward a wall-mounted security camera. After a moment, the execution wing's main door opened toward him with a loud *clang*, revealing a long corridor of intense light. A young female guard wearing a gray uniform and mirrored goggles stepped through to greet him.

"Father Anslem?" the guard said.

"Yes."

The guard cocked her head to the side, glancing him over.

"Is something wrong?" David said.

"There's nothing wrong. It's just that you're awfully young and you certainly don't look like a priest—the jeans and black sweater, I mean. How long have you been a priest?"

"Ordained a year and a half ago at the ripe old age of twenty-three," he said. "And what would you have me to look like? Should I be wearing black-on-black with a grooved, raised white collar? Should I be older?"

"Yes, you're not like the others. You look to me like..." She stopped herself, looking him over again flirtatiously.

"Like what?"

"I don't know, but definitely not a priest."

David smiled. He knew that he didn't fit the mold of a priest and flirting from the opposite sex was something he had to get used to. Women were his greatest temptation—an attraction that almost kept him from entering seminary. He had nearly succumbed to temptation on more than one occasion. A few years back, he even grew out a beard to cover his jaw, and he wore a pair of thick, black-framed glasses to detract from the steely blue eyes that he had inherited from his mother. But it didn't work. Women still threw themselves at him.

The guard took his ID and compared it to a list of names on a small hand-held display.

"Are you permanently replacing Father Vest?" she said, gazing up from data pad.

"No. I'll be here through this evening—possibly longer. I don't know yet."

The guard appeared disappointed. She handed David back his ID.

"It's very bright," David said, staring up at the strange light tubes in the ceiling.

The guard smiled. "They're on timers, and they're just now cooling down from when we transferred Fain from his holding cell earlier. They remain very bright for a while." She pulled her goggles away from her eyes and stared around the corridor. "Much better," she said. She slid the goggles down around her neck and waited for her eyes to adjust.

"So what's it all about, the lights I mean? Why is it so bright in here?"

"Blind Light research wing, for violent prisoners," she said. "They're easier to transfer if you keep them sightless. The intense light has a neutralizing effect on our guest while we move them out of the prehold cells here, to the dead zone, down there." She nodded toward the far end of the corridor. "That's where we're holding him."

David stared toward the end of the hall. The walls had a strange white glow. He opened and closed his eyes several times, trying to force them to adjust. He stepped closer to the outer wall and ran his hand over the smooth, glossy finish. The surface felt padded from the thick layer of paint, and the coating sparkled like a multitude of tiny stars. "Interesting," he said. "It's like there's small mirrors in the paint."

The guard shrugged, disinterested. She motioned for David to follow her. "So when did you start?"

"About an hour ago," he said.

"Well you picked a good one. It's about to get real busy in here."

"So I've heard."

"And you're their last hope?" she said.

David stopped walking. "What do you mean?"

"Are you really a priest?"

"Yes, why do you ask?"

"I just wondered what they're up to, is all."

"You've lost me."

"Never mind," she said, flashing a mischievous smile. "I'll play along."

"I am a priest."

"I believe you," she said, still smirking. "Let's just get to it, shall we? Are you ready to meet Fain?"

"Yes, very much so."

The guard put her hands on her hips and shook her head.

"What's wrong?" David said.

"Are you going to save his soul?"

"I'm going to try."

"Well good luck with that one."

"Is there something wrong with that?"

She smiled sarcastically. "Just follow me."

There was a soft knock on Warden Mangum's office door. A young prison guard opened the door and leaned through. "You told me to let you know when the replacement priest entered the death line."

Mangum sat behind a modern metal-and-glass-topped desk with his arms folded over his enormous stomach. "Thank you Mr. Thomas. That will do for now. Keep me advised."

The door closed. Mangum turned his attention toward Special Agent Rand, who sat facing him on the opposite side of the desk. "What do you think, Agent Rand?"

"We'll see," Rand said.

"Fain hasn't uttered a single word in the six months that he's been in here."

"Maybe with it being this close to his execution, he'll be compelled to break his silence." Rand leaned forward and knocked on the corner of Mangum's desk. "In any event, it's now or never."

6

FAIN

David followed the guard past several rows of holding cells, all the doors were open, and the rooms were empty. The corridor ended at a shiny metal door that was mounted flush with the wall. There were no markings on the door, only a sealed shutter near the top and a narrow food slot on the bottom. Above the entrance, a section of dying light tubes buzzed and flickered intermittently.

The guard stepped forward and typed a code into a small data pad. The metal shutter slid open, revealing a four-inch-thick shatterproof glass window that was filled with quarter-sized air holes.

"Harold Fain," she said. She glanced at her watch and then pecked at her data pad.

"Can I go in now?" David said.

The guard shook her head as she continued to make notations in her log. "Authorized visits are all non contact."

"I work better if I'm face-to-face."

The guard looked up. "You'll be able to see him."

"But not inside the cell?"

"That's right."

David looked disappointed. He stepped closer to the cell door and peered through the small window. The room's lights were off, and he could see only the prisoner's outline against the back wall.

"How am I supposed to talk to him if I can't see him?" said David.

"Hold on," the guard said. She slid a plastic security card down the side of the data pad and entered a password. The sound of quiet machinery could be heard behind the wall and the door to Fain's cell slowly moved sideways, revealing a thick barrier of Plexiglas that stretched from floor to ceiling. "How's that?"

"It's better," David said, stepping closer to the glass wall. Fain stood motionless toward the back of the darkened cell with his eyes closed and his hands folded behind his back. He wore all black clothes instead of the traditional orange prison-issued clothing.

The cell's only amenities were a stainless steel toilet and a small concrete shelf that protruded from the wall. A small black box recorder sat on the shelf. The prisoner's last meal had been shoved through the feed slot and sat untouched on the floor.

"Harold Fain," David said. A red light flickered on the front of the black box.

Fain stood silent, with his eyes still closed.

"I need to ask you the most important question of your life. Your happiness or sorrow for all eternity will depend upon your answer." David glanced toward the guard over his shoulder. There was an awkward silence.

"Is salvation really an option for someone like him?" the guard said.

"Of course it is," said David.

"You probably don't even think he should be executed?"

"No, I don't think we should have to kill to show that killing is wrong."

"What about the Bible? An eye for an eye, and all that?"

"An eye for an eye and we're all blind," David said.

"Some Christian you are."

"Why do you say that?"

"It's just kind of odd hearing a Catholic priest quoting Gandhi, a Buddhist."

"Hindu," David corrected her. "Are you for Fain's death?"

"I think I'd like to kill that sick bastard myself. After what he has done, he deserves to die."

"We should all be thankful our God is a forgiving one. We all have sins and failings."

"Sins yes, but I've never killed anybody."

"God gives us a chance for grace."

"Even for him?" the guard said, nodding toward Fain, who was still standing motionless inside the darkened cell.

"Especially for him. I think you underestimate the extent of God's mercy. You see—" David noticed that Fain's eyes were now open. The guard began to speak, but he threw up a hand, waving her off. The guard frowned and walked back toward the opposite end of the corridor.

The light tubes above David's head suddenly returned to full brightness. The additional illumination allowed him to see Fain more clearly. He noticed Fain's pale complexion, and the odd way that his eyes seemed to mirror the light.

"Mr. Fain, I'm Father Anslem, David Anslem. I would like to talk to you." He paused, waiting for a reply. Several moments passed. "Because of what you have done, you've been condemned to death, but there is no reason why you should be eternally separated from God. You have but to ask for his forgiveness to receive the gift of salvation and everlasting life."

Fain stared forward in silence.

"Okay then," David said. He matched Fain's stare for a moment and then turned to leave.

The guard returned. "Is that all he gets?"

"Can you buzz me out of here?" David said, ruefully.

The guard nodded and reached for the radio on her belt. "Don't take it so hard. Fain hasn't spoken in the six months that he's been in here."

"Really?"

"Not a single—"

"Life everlasting," Fain said, softly.

"He spoke…" the guard said. She looked the prisoner over and stepped away with the radio to her mouth. "He's talking," she said. She glanced over her shoulder and then disappeared into a vacant holding cell.

David turned back toward the holding cell. "Will you speak with me?" he said.

"I will talk to you," Fain said, continuing to speak in a low voice.

"Well that's good. I would like to talk to you about salvation."

"You would struggle for my soul even after what I have been accused of?"

"You weren't just accused. You confessed and were convicted and sentenced."

"True enough," Fain said. He slowly walked across the room to the cell door, closer to where David stood. "But not everything is always as it seems."

"You have taken life, Mr. Fain. Life. God's most precious and wonderful gift to man."

"Do you believe that life is a gift?"

"It is," David said.

"If life is a gift, then why is it not meant to be kept? Why must it be returned?"

"Returned?"

"Yes. Life is a gift you will lose in spite of the fact that you cherish it and wish to keep it. The full measure of your existence is spent in fear of losing it."

"No, I disagree. Our life here may be short, but I like to think of it as a journey, and my existence a brief, but wonderful walk with God. The journey is my gift, and the many joys of life savored along the way."

"Joys?" Fain said. "What are life's pleasures under the constant threat of death? It's misery. And it's the brevity and loss of your joy that drives your despair. If life were truly wonderful then it would be offered in terms such that it could never be lost or taken against your will."

"Mortality is something every man has to come to terms with," said David. "We all die. But I understand how you feel about death, especially on a day like today."

"Death?"

"Yes," David said. "Your preoccupation with it comes as no surprise to me, since it is, after all, as I know you are aware, your final hours of life. Living under a death sentence can be difficult. And that is precisely why I am here."

"And how are you handling *your* death sentence, Father?"

"What death sentence are you referring to?"

"The one imposed by nature. You all are dying, aren't you?"

David smiled politely. "Maybe it is time to put aside your concern with death, Mr. Fain, and savor your remaining moments. I noticed you haven't touched your food. Would you like them to bring you something else? It's your last meal. They will bring you whatever you want. Tell me what you would like to have, and I'll ask them."

"Do you not think about death, Father?"

David stared down at the cold plate of food as he thought about the question. After a moment, he looked up at Fain. "Sometimes I do think about death, but I try not to dwell on the things I can't change. And a man of God has no reason to fear death. My life is God's, and my place is among his living creatures. I belong in his life."

"You belong to death, not life," Fain said, staring into David's eyes.

"I belong to God," David said, meeting Fain's stare.

"Of course you do. And do not all things come from God?"

"Yes that's right,"

"And life is his gift. Isn't that what you believe?"

"Yes."

"And so too is death."

"Death is a gift from God? No I don't believe that."

"You disagree?"

"Yes I do."

"But he allows it."

"Yes he does, because we are on a fallen world."

"Does death not taint your existence?"

"No," David said.

"You cannot escape death."

"No I can't. You're right about that. But through God's promise, I can escape the dread of it. God's guarantee of life eternal."

"You speak again of everlasting life."

"Of course," David said.

"Are you preoccupied with life?"

"No more than you. As it would appear, you are preoccupied with death."

"I have a long-lasting familiarity with death."

"Considering your conviction, that comes as no surprise to me."

"What do you know about it?"

"About the murder?"

"No, I'm interested in your knowledge of life—everlasting life. What can you tell me about it?"

"I can tell you that it's God's promise."

"To whom did God make this promise?"

"To everyone."

"To all who believe?"

"Yes," David said.

"I see," Fain said. "And what of death?"

"What of it?"

"You don't fear death, but you fear God. You don't fear death, because to you it is heaven. But then, that is precisely why you fear and envy God."

"That's preposterous. I don't envy God. And I don't fear death. I do fear God's wrath, as should we all."

"And what is his wrath? What are those wages of sin?"

"Death," David said, "and a death I have no reason to fear."

"Yes, but you should if you knew how permanent and how depriving it is. All those precious human traits, all the memories you've collected along the way, gone forever."

"I don't believe that."

"What if it's true?"

"I guess I will just have to wait and see."

"Yes," Fain said. "Time will tell whether it is your love for God or the fear of his flames."

"It's adoration," David said.

"You don't fear God's wrath?"

"It's about love. Worship."

"And why is that, Father? Is it for this faint trace of life you believe God granted you, or is it for the great possibilities that he has presented as lures of what might be? God tempts you, does he not?"

David shook his head. "Just what is that supposed to mean?"

God's offer of everlasting life is a strong temptation for good, Father. Wouldn't you agree?"

"No, I don't agree. And I'm sorry you feel that way,"

"But does God not hold immortality in his hand, and does life eternal not appeal to you more than anything? Is it not the prize you truly seek? I would even wager that there is nothing you would not be willing to do to have it."

David thought a moment, and then slowly shook his head. "That's not true."

"If given the choice, would you kill for it?"

"No," David snapped, appalled by the very thought of the question.

"Are you so sure?"

"Yes."

"Even if it meant everlasting life, Father?"

"I'm certain, yes."

Fain narrowed his eyes.

"You don't believe me?"

"Experience has shown me that when faced with the loss of everything, rational beings are willing to do just about anything to expand their duration in the breach between—"

"The breach?"

"Yes. The gulf between death, life, and death again."

"I disagree. It is my belief that there is only a beginning to this life, and an end."

"And eternal life after is the reward for your life well lived here. You're all too eager to sacrifice this life, postponing your pleasures in the here and now, for the promise of immortality?"

"Not just for everlasting life, but for heaven and eternity with our creator."

"I can see how that type of agreement would inspire you."

David nodded enthusiastically. "As it should you."

"But it doesn't."

"Well, then I guess I've done all I can for you. I said what I came to say, Mr. Fain. I have delivered the message and you can choose to save yourself from damnation."

"It's too late for that."

"But don't you see that it's not too late. You still do have a choice. That is why we have been created with understanding. We are unique among God's creatures, able to think and reason. The choice is still yours. "

"God's creatures," Fain said. He stopped talking, staring quietly into David's eyes.

"Yes, that's right."

"Human beings are matchless among God's living things. They are full of creativity, of vision, and are so passionate in their purpose. It's a waste to have such passions mingled with mortality."

"It is by God's design," David said.

"You would profess to know something of the province of God?"

"I am a priest. It is my duty to know."

"You dwell in his boundless universe, Father. You're an ephemeral being trapped in the everlasting and immeasurable edifice of your God. What hope have you of understanding any of it?"

"God speaks to me, as he does to all who will listen."

"And what does God tell you, Father?"

David thought for a moment and then said, "The most important thing of all, and what I have come to tell you."

"Go on."

"That whoever hears God's words, and believes that he sent his son, will have everlasting life and shall not come into a sentence of eternal damnation, but will be passed from death unto life."

"I see," Fain said thoughtfully. He brought his hands up to his mouth and shaped them into a steeple. "Is this what God told you?"

"Yes."

Fain turned his face down, staring harshly into David's eyes. "And do you think that God has told you everything?"

"No, but he has told me those things I need to know."

"No," Fain said. "I'm afraid he has not told you nearly enough. There is much more at work on this world than you know. More than you or anyone could ever hope to understand."

"It's not meant for us to comprehend," David said. "God has given us enough to piece together the truth of his word and his works. The evidence is all around us if we all open our eyes to it."

"I have observed it all, Father. The reality of it is that we are all forsaken." He fell silent, and again David noticed the peculiar way the light reflected in his eyes. It was a brief wave of color that lasted for a moment, and then it was gone.

The guard finished her phone call and walked up next to David. "I need to talk to you for a moment," she said.

David sighed. "What about?"

She motioned for David to step away with her. "It won't take long."

"Excuse me for a moment, Mr. Fain," David said, and reluctantly turned and followed the guard back toward the main entrance.

The guard glanced over her shoulder, gauging their distance from Fain's holding cell. Once they had reached the halfway point she stopped David and lowered her voice. "I just spoke to Superintendent Mangum. Evidently this is what they've been waiting for."

"They?" David said.

7

AGENTS

The execution wing's main door emitted a deafening buzz that was followed by the muffled sound of metal gears cranking behind solid concrete. The door opened, and David watched as Superintendent Mangum stepped through, followed closely by two men and a woman. Mangum was the only one not in a suit; he wore a white, short-sleeve shirt that fit tightly around his huge stomach. A colorful tie curved over his large gut and dangled well short of his belt line. David had only met Mangum once before. The superintendent had an honest face and, according to Father Vest, he was a fair man who ran a clean prison.

"Hello again, Father," Mangum said, holding out a thick hand. "I would like you to meet Detective Rand and his partner, Agent Mark Shullman."

"It's a pleasure," David said, glancing them over. Rand and his partner looked like twins. Although Rand was slightly taller, both men had thick, brown hair and wore the same black suits. Shullman carried a black leather briefcase.

"And this is Dr. Dana Parker," Rand said. "Dr. Parker is a forensic psychiatrist and has been consulting with our team. She is currently working on a new behavioral sciences book for the FBI Academy."

"Nice meeting you," Parker said, in a precise lawyer's voice.

David gauged her age to be in the midtwenties. She was attractive, with sandy blonde hair and piercing blue eyes. "You write books for the FBI?" he said.

Parker nodded. "For the intelligence community…among other people."

"What do you say we get out of this light?" Rand said.

"Of course," Mangum said. He guided everyone into an empty holding cell where the lights were softer.

Parker reached into a black leather bag and pulled out a stylish, chrome-colored compact. "Do you mind?" she said.

"What is that?" David said.

"It's a recorder. We would like to ask you a few questions. Would that be all right?"

"Yes, I suppose so. What's this all about?"

Mangum stepped forward and gave David a friendly pat on the back. "Well, I'll come right to the point, Father. The detectives feel we have an extraordinary opportunity. They were hoping that you could help them out."

"How?"

"What do you know about serial killer Harold Fain?" Rand said.

"Not much, I'm afraid. I pulled up a few headlines on him. There wasn't that much coverage. And from what I've read, there was no mention of a serial case."

Rand nodded. "Yes, I suppose that deserves an explanation. The case was brought to public attention, but not as a multiple murder. The trial and conviction moved so quickly, the media never really caught up. And after his sentencing, the press was more interested in the legality of Fain's extradition deal than the murder he had committed."

"What deal?" David asked.

"Fain agreed to confess if we transferred his case to Florida."

"Why?"

Rand shrugged. "It's the damnedest thing I've ever heard of. We really don't know."

"And who were the other victims he was charged for?"

"Fain wasn't officially charged with any other murders, just the one—the Jane Doe from the subway."

"Then technically he is not a serial killer?"

"I said he wasn't charged with any other murders, but believe us when we tell you that he is connected to other killings."

"What does this all have to do with me?"

"You somehow persuaded him to speak. He is talking to you?"

"Yes."

Parker said, "Others have tried and failed to make a breakthrough with Fain—clerics from several religions, the other prison chaplain, Father Vest, and several news reporters. Fain has thus far refused to break his silence."

"And out of everyone who has tried, Fain decides to talk to you," Mangum said.

David nodded thoughtfully.

"What was your impression of him?" Parker said, "What was he like?"

"He stands out from any other prisoner that I've ever encountered. He's surprisingly engaging. He didn't have the attitude of your typical inmate; he was articulate, finely tuned, and appears to come from some education. And something else that I found odd is how poised he is. I mean…he's strangely confident for someone who is about to be put to death."

Mangum smirked. "Let's see how that composure holds up once we have him strapped into the electric chair."

"Did Fain ask you to absolve him?" Rand said.

"No. In his first words, he regarded eternal life and I was hopeful that he was interested in saving his own soul, but ultimately his interest turned into an attack."

"Regardless," Rand said, "We've made a breakthrough. He broke his silence with you, Father. We're moments away from his execution, and this will be our last chance to get something out of him."

"Well I'm only interested in getting one thing out of him: repentance."

"Okay Father, but did you ever consider that perhaps some people on this planet go beyond redemption? I doubt seriously that he could be saved. I mean, are you going to tell me that after what he has done, that he can be forgiven?"

"Everyone is redeemable. It is a function of a priest to proclaim forgiveness. If I pardon his sins, then his offenses are forgiven."

Rand rolled his eyes. "You guys amaze me. It doesn't matter what anyone does on this planet. Fain is a proven killer and you're ready to give him a get-out-of-hell-free card. Honestly, if you think that will work for him, that's fine, but all we're asking is that you help us take advantage of this situation. You even said that he wasn't interested in being saved."

David folded his arms across his chest. "This is his moment of grace, not a time for interrogation."

"This is our last chance," Rand said. "And you're the last hope of a lot of victims' families out there. All we have is a confession to a single murder. As I said earlier, we have reason to believe he is a repeat killer. It's true this one case is closed, but when Fain dies, many of these open investigations could go unresolved—possibly forever."

"Take a look, Father," Shullman said. He opened a brown case folder and pulled out a two-page document that was attached to a small stack of color crime scene photos. He kept the photos and handed David the first page of the document. The top corner of the paper was crinkled, stained brown from an old coffee spill. Victims' names and address were listed alphabetically.

Rand said. "Many of these cases are already abandoned, and after today, any hope for their eventual resolution could be permanently lost. We are at a point now in our investigation where we feel that the only way these murders will ever be solved is with a confession."

"There must be fifty names on this list," said David.

Rand nodded. "And that's an incomplete list."

"There's more?" David said. "What makes you think he had anything to do with all these deaths?"

"Because of the manner of death," Rand said.

Shullman stepped forward and handed Rand a black leather briefcase. Rand opened the case from the top and retrieved a thick three-ring binder.

"Have a look."

David took the binder and flipped through the pages.

"What do you think?"

"You're not trying to tell me that you think he was involved in all of these?" said David. "They can't all be…I mean, he couldn't possibly be responsible for so many?"

"He is," Rand said.

Dr. Parker nodded. "This should give you some idea of the breed of killer that we are holding behind that door, Father."

"What kind of man…I mean, how could he be connected to so many? This serial killer—"

"Predator," Shullman said. "Fain's a monster."

"Is there a difference? I've never heard of anything like it."

"As far as serial killers are concerned, predators are rare," Rand said. "And Fain, without a doubt, is a whole new class of killer. A kind of ultra predator."

David said. "I've never heard of a serial case of this magnitude. Are you saying that one man could be responsible for all this? Even if he killed one a day, it seems impossible."

"Oh, but it *is* possible," Rand said. "And we suspect even more."

"Then why isn't it in all the papers? With that many people missing, there should be mass hysteria."

"That's why it's not in all the papers."

"Then he couldn't be acting alone, could he?" David said, shaking his head as he considered the enormity of Rand's shocking disclosure.

Rand said. "We believe there is another or, possibly, others. There are some overlaps in occurrences regionally where the place and time of death make it virtually impossible for one person to be in two places at once."

"An accomplice?" said David.

"We're not sure about that. What I mean is that yes, the style of murders are identical. However, we can't be certain that the killers know each other. If they did, it is our opinion that Fain would have divulged their names. Most often killers will give up their accomplices to save their own hides."

"Not if he wanted to die," Mangum said.

"There are easier ways to die, Warden," Rand said.

Mangum smiled. "Well, you caught him. Fain's behind bars and I think we will all feel better when he's in the ground."

"Naturally," Rand said. "Except that there is still one very disturbing factor. Since Fain's incarceration, the killings haven't stopped; they have continued. And even more distressing is that the murders have continued to grow in number."

David said, "Have you considered the possibility that you have the wrong man?"

"We have the right man, Father. Of that we have no doubt. Now we need to know about Fain's past murders, and find out what he knows about his continued style of murder. Can you help us?"

"I would like to help you," David said. "But you have to understand that my duty in this prison is a spiritual one."

"Father, you need to remember, first and foremost, that this is a prison and not a monastery. These prisoners are here for a reason; they've violated both man's and God's laws. You tried to save Fain. You said that he wasn't interested. Fain is a lost cause—a lost soul. You have to accept the fact that you can't save everyone."

David nodded. "Yes, I know you're right."

"Then will you assist us? Will you talk to him again?"

"Just what the hell is going on here?"

A bitter voice broke in from behind them. They all turned and saw Fain's lawyer, Michael Glass, standing outside the open door, his hands on his hips. His long gray hair was combed back. He wore a tattered black suit and carried a weathered brown leather bag over his right shoulder. He swept past the guard and approached the group. He sat the bag on the table and rubbed the muscles in his shoulder. "Well?" he said.

"Just calm down, Mr. Glass," Rand said. "Fain has every right to talk to a priest."

Glass frowned. "No contact means any contact—priests included. You have to honor that."

"You deprived the victim's families of their hope for closure, and now you're going to deprive Fain of his chance for salvation."

"Oh, give me a goddamn break! I'm not denying him anything. You could have at least tried to find someone who *looks* like a priest."

"He has credentials," Rand said.

"FBI credentials?"

"He's a priest."

David moved out of the group as the quarrel escalated. It all suddenly made sense to him—why Father Vest had taken a leave of absence from the prison so suddenly. "Father Vest wasn't really sick, was he?" David said.

"What do you think, Father?" Glass said.

"It was busy in the death chamber over the last two weeks," Mangum said. "Having an execution and four arrivals in fifteen days had taken a toll on him. He needed the break."

"I don't appreciate being part of your little conspiracy," David said. "It appears that you gentlemen have some things to work out, and they don't involve me."

"Please, Father," Rand said, "hear us out."

Everyone was quiet for a moment. Rand, assuming that David would stay, switched his attentions back to Glass. "What's the harm in a few questions, Mr. Glass?"

"Still trying to figure it out," Glass said. "Have you confirmed Fain's name yet?"

"No," Rand said.

Glass laughed. "Really?"

"That's right," Rand said.

"But how can that be?" David said. "How can you not know who he is? You're the FBI!"

"We are not able to confirm his identity," Rand said.

David shrugged. "Then who is Harold Fain?"

"Just a name," Rand said. "It never checked out."

"A false identity," Mangum said. "Now that's interesting."

"And you can still execute someone without knowing who they are?" said David.

"Oh yes," Rand said.

Mangum nodded. "He still did the crime."

"We've been down this road before," Glass said. "This is all for naught, a waste of everyone's time. Nothing will change the fact that my client still isn't talking."

"Oh, but he *is* talking," Mangum said.

"Really?" Glass said.

"He's ready to spill his guts," Rand said. "We need this."

Glass waved his hand dismissingly. "My client will have a chance to have a last word before the execution. If he has something to say, he can say it then."

"Look at these," Rand said. He handed Glass a neat stack of crime scene photographs.

Glass glanced at the image on top of the pile. It was a photograph of a murdered elderly man lying in an alleyway. Glass didn't look any further. He passed the photographs back to Rand. "Who did Fain talk to?" he said.

"Just the priest."

"Well, you have no guarantees that he will continue talking."

"That is a possibility."

Glass turned toward David. "Do you want to help them, Father?"

David nodded. "I have to admit, at this point, I am a bit curious."

"Good!" Rand said. "Let's get started."

"Wait," Glass said. "I haven't agreed to anything yet, nor has the priest."

"It's okay," David said. "If you agree to make the exception, I'll talk to him, but on one condition."

"Which is?" Rand said.

"I maintain my own agenda. I'll agree to ask him a few additional questions, but that's all. I'm not going to push him. It's not going to be an interrogation."

"That's fair enough," Glass said.

"I think it's a good idea," Rand said. "We don't want to change your approach. Whatever it is that you were doing, you should continue. So...are you ready?"

David took in a deep breath and exhaled. "As I'll ever be, I suppose."

There was a whirling noise, and they all felt a vibration beneath their feet. The lights dimmed and returned brightly.

"That's the first death drill," Mangum said. He checked his watch. "It won't be long now."

They all looked at David. He seemed lost in his own thoughts.

Shullman opened his jacket and pulled out a black ink pen. "Would you have any objections to us wiring you, Father?" He handed David the pen. "This is a transmitter."

"A body wire?" said David. "I don't know that I would be comfortable with that. It somehow doesn't seem appropriate. You already have a recorder in the cell." David handed the pen back to Shullman.

"It would help us," Parker said, "if we could hear your conversation. This is a two-way device. We can listen, and we can communicate with you, directing you with the right questions."

David looked uncomfortably at Glass.

"It's your call, Father," Glass said.

"It's very small," Parker said. "Fain will not know you have it."

Rand stepped forward and held out a skin-colored ear implant. "All you need to do is put this in your ear. Here, give it a try." He placed the earpiece into David's open palm.

"Which way?" David said. He rolled the receiver around in his hand, carefully examining each end. The device was slightly larger than a pencil eraser.

"It's designed to work either way," Shullman said. "May I?" He took the small receiver, reached up, and inserted it in David's ear. He held out the pen transmitter. "Just put it somewhere on you."

"Does it matter where?"

"Not really. The pen is a simple amplifier that boosts the signal." Shullman retrieved three over-the-ear headsets from his bag. He kept a headset and handed the others to Rand and Parker. Rand put in his earpiece and activated a battery pack on his belt. David heard a loud click in his ear, followed by static. He instinctively reached toward the right side of his head and pulled at his ear lobe.

"Can you hear me?" Rand said.

"Yes," David said. "But there's a disturbing echo."

"That's feedback. We're standing too close to each other. It should cease once you're in front of his cell." Shullman took a step backward and spoke again. "How's that?"

"Much better," David said.

"Good," Rand said. He switched off the microphone.

"Are you sure you're okay with this?" Glass said.

"I suppose," David said. He took a last look at the pen transmitter and slid it into his front pants pocket. "I should probably have my head examined."

Parker handed David her business card. "That might not be a bad idea, Father. When this is all over, and you feel that you need—"

"I was kidding," David said.

"I didn't mean it like that. What I meant was if you ever wanted to talk about what comes out in there. I expect that you will hear some disturbing things. It can have an effect on you."

David handed back the business card. "I think I'll be all right."

"Just keep it," Parker said. "You never know."

David gave her a courteous smile and put the card in his pocket.

"Father," Rand said. "We need certain information from Fain. Most importantly, we need to find out who he really is. Uncovering his identity would break the case wide open. We need to know what he did with the real Harold Fain. What device he uses to incapacitate his victims. We need to know about the locations of the other victims. We also need information as it pertains to the continued style of murder. Those are just a few of the questions we need answered, but try not to come straight out and ask him—at least not at first. Early on, we will want to keep it as informal and as unstructured as possible. He has a story to tell and needs to be listened to. Show compassion and care."

"I do care," David said. "I care a great deal."

"I know you do, Father. I know you're sad for him, and want to help him, in spite of what he has done. Just remember that he has taken many lives, and by such action has ruined countless others, and now we need him to tell you about it."

"I'll give it my best shot."

"Thank you," Rand said. "That's all we can ask."

Glass chuckled and shook his head.

"What's so funny, counselor?" Parker said.

"I think you could be in for a big disappointment. Fain isn't interested in helping anyone, and especially not the people who put him away and are about to pull the plug, or flip the switch, rather."

"You could be right, Mr. Glass," Rand said. "But it's my belief that with Father Anslem asking the right questions, our chances are more than good that Fain will cooperate." He gave David a confident smile and squeezed his shoulder. "Just remember my rule of thumb."

"What's that?" said David.

"Talk less and listen more," Rand activated his headset. "Let's do it."

"Okay…" David said. He stepped out into the corridor and walked down to Fain's holding cell.

Fain stood motionless, with his eyes closed, behind the thick barrier of Plexiglas. David's heart pounded in his chest as he reflected on what Rand had told him about the cold-blooded killer. *What if it were all true?* he thought. He imagined for a moment all of the horrors Fain was responsible for, and the awful things he had done to so many innocent people. He looked away briefly, attempting to suppress from his awareness the visions of those unthinkable crimes.

"Back so soon, Father?" Fain said, slowly opening his eyes.

"Yes," David said.

"Do we have more to discuss?"

"I thought that we might continue our earlier conversation."

"What more is there to talk about?"

"I'm here to offer you a glimmer of hope."

"*And you care about what's going to happen to him,*" Parker said.

"*Yes,*" Rand said. "*Tell him that this will be the last chance for him to clear his conscience. Then ask about the victim from the subway.*"

David could hear the agents' voices in his head seemingly at once. Their transmission came in skips and was heavily distorted by static. He fought the urge to answer them and thought to himself that this must be how someone who suffers from schizophrenia must feel.

"Is there something wrong, Father?" Fain said.

"No," David said. Nothing is wrong. I wanted to ask you about the woman in the subway."

"The woman?"

"Yes."

"Ahh," Fain said. A slight smile formed on his lips. "Perhaps you no longer serve your God, but now work for 'them.'"

"Them?" David said.

Fain didn't answer. He turned his gaze toward the recorder on the table.

"Yes…you're right," said David. "Since you were willing to speak to me, they thought perhaps you would be willing to talk to them. They need your help resolving some of their cases. They feel that there are many other crime—uh, murders that are unsolved, and with your help, many of those unexplained deaths could now be understood."

"I'm afraid that I can't help them."

"You can't or you won't?"

Fain swept his eyes back toward David. "I'm unfamiliar with their investigations."

"*Father*," Rand said, "*ask him if he will agree to talk to us.*"

"The agents wanted me to ask you if you would be willing to speak with them?"

"No, Father, I would much rather talk to you."

"*Damn it!*" Rand said. "*Ask him if he will at least agree to look at the photos in our case files.*"

"They have some photographs that they would like you to look at," said David.

"Of the dead?" Fain said.

David nodded. "Would you be willing to take a look?"

"No," Fain said. "There is no need for any of that."

David heard a collective sigh of disappointment from the entire group.

"*Well, you tried, Father*," Rand said. "*I guess it will all have to depend on you. Let's see what you can get out of him. You need to begin maneuvering him toward additional admissions. Talk to him about the subway victim. Let's see what comes out.*

"You already confessed to murder, Mr. Fain. You admitted to the agents that you killed the woman in the subway, but are you prepared to confess to me?"

"*Easy, Father,*" Rand said. "*That's too direct.*"

"Do you need me to confess again, Father?" said Fain.

"*Or maybe not,*" Shullman said.

"*Tell him yes, Father,*" Rand said.

"I would like to hear the truth," David said.

"Are you asking, or are the agents?"

"It's for me," David said.

"And why does it suddenly matter to you?"

"I just need to know. Tell me about the subway. Tell me about the murder."

Several moments passed without an answer.

Rand's gravely voice once again crackled into David's ear. "*Rephrase your question, Father. It's best if you don't hesitate. When he pauses like that, hit him quickly with another question. Let's not let him harden on us.*"

"Did she suffer?"

"*Better...*"

"Will you tell me?" David said.

"I've told you everything."

"*Ask him who he is. Ask him about his name, Father.*"

"Who are you, really?" David said.

"I am Harold Fain."

"*Where was he born?*"

"Then will you tell me Mr. Fain, where are you from?"

"Am I not from God, David?"

"Yes, as are we all, but what of your earthly parents? What I want to know is, where in this world are you from?"

"Later, David. We'll talk of it later."

"Time is of the essence."

Fain slowly shook his head. "Not for me."

"*He's jerking you around,*" Rand said.

"We're running out of time, Mr. Fain. Will you help them?"

"Perhaps we could make a deal."

"A deal?

"For another victim."

"What did you say?"

"*Be very careful, Father,*" Rand said.

"What about the victim?" David said.

"*And the others,*" Rand said.

"What about the others?"

"Will they bargain?"

"*Not for one name,*" Rand said.

"They will," David said. "Just give them what they want. Give them all the names. Tell them where they will find the others and who knows…they could even—"

"Stay my execution?"

"I don't know about that. It's possible, I guess. Is that what you would want?"

"No. That is not what I want. I'll give them the grave if they will execute me now."

"What?"

"*We can do that,*" Rand said.

"I don't understand?" David said.

"*Don't worry about it, Father. Just get the gravesite. This could be all we get.*"

"And something else." Fain said.

"Go on."

"A phone call."

"*Now that's interesting,*" Parker said. "*Ask him whom he wishes to call. No, wait, don't ask him. Simply agree.*"

"They will grant you a phone call and an early execution," David said.

"It's agreed, then. You can tell the agents that they will find what they are looking for in Virginia."

"Who will they find?"

"The first."

Rand said. "*Father, ask him again about the other victims. Ask him for more locations.*"

"You said the first, but how many are there?" David asked Fain.

"Will they execute me?"

"Yes."

"Will they execute me now?"

"They will," David said. "I give you my word."

"Your word?"

David nodded. "I know for certain that they will agree to your terms. You have to trust me."

"Then come closer, forgiver."

David cautiously stepped up to the glass door.

Fain also moved closer to the door. "Give the agents the coordinates 44JC308. It's a place called Carter's Grove."

David pulled out a pen and wrote the cipher on the back of Dr. Parker's business card.

And there is something else." Fain said.

"What?"

"You must go with them, David."

"Why would I go?"

"I would like for you to be with them."

"I don't think I'll be going along."

Fain made a slight bow, showing David that he understood.

"I mean that I don't know why I would. It really has nothing to do with me."

"If you will agree to go with them, I will give them more."

"*Agree, Father,*" Rand said.

"Okay…. Okay, I'll go."

Fain leaned in and positioned his face in front of David's. His mouth was inches from the air holes. He spoke in a whisper. "Come closer, David, and I will tell you, and only you, where to look. But first you must promise me that you will wait until you arrive there before you give them the final piece of information. Will you give your word?"

"I don't know," David said. "Why can't you just tell them?"

"*I don't know what?*" Rand asked. "*What did he ask? What don't you know?*"

"I want to make sure they take you with them, and the information I give you will provide you with the leverage that you will need if they refuse your company. They will try to talk you out of going and, most likely, even order you not to go."

David shrugged. "That is certainly within their right."

"*What's going on?*" Shullman said.

David glanced down the corridor toward the agents. Rand pointed at his headset.

"Are you ready?" Fain said.

David turned back toward the cell. He nodded and leaned in, angling his ear closer to the door. Even with the four-inch glass barrier between them, he felt uneasy being so close to the prisoner.

Fain stared at David through the small holes in the glass. "You mustn't tell them until after you arrive. Will you agree?"

"You have my word."

"Martin's Hundred," Fain said in an even lower voice. "37° 23' 29" north, 77° 4' 53" west."

David wrote the information on a separate piece of paper and slipped the note into his front pants pocket. He glanced at the agents again. Rand threw his hands up in the air.

"The gift of God," Fain continued.

"What does that mean?"

"The detectives will know," Fain said, speaking in a normal voice again. "Oh, and I almost forgot to ask, did your agent friends ever find out the name of the woman from the subway?"

"*No,*" Rand said soberly.

"They didn't," David said.

"Her name was Rory Gelder."

"Gelder?"

"Rory Gelder worked for the Justice Department—Central Intelligence."

"*What the hell?*" Rand said.

"The CIA?" David said.

"*She was an agent? Mark, cross check Gelder's name. Father, ask Fain how he obtained that information.*"

"How did you know Gelder?" David said.

"Gelder said something to me before she died."

"What?" David said.

"'Legion.'"

"Legion?"

"Yes. It was an odd thing to say, don't you think?"

"What does 'Legion' mean?"

"Tell your agent friends to direct their inquiries to Jack Simons. Perhaps he will be willing to help them from here on."

"*Who the hell is this guy?*" Shullman said.

"Tell them to hurry, David," Fain said. "I grow tired of waiting."

"Are you that eager to die? Will you choose death and eternal damnation?"

Fain folded his hands firmly behind his back. "I believe we have a deal."

"Yes, yes we do."

"Tell them to make haste, David."

"I will tell them. Is there nothing else I may say?"

Fain fell silent again.

"*That's it, Father,*" Parker said. "*Why don't you come on back with us? You've done all you can.*"

When it became apparent that all appeals were for naught, David turned and took a few steps toward the group. He stopped and looked back at Fain one last time. "I'm sorry," he said, and he continued down the corridor toward Rand and his team.

Mangum shook David's hand and gave him a conciliatory pat on the back.

"You did great, Father," Rand said.

"You think so?" David said.

Rand said, "It wasn't a lot of information, but should be enough. Just the break we needed."

"Do you think the woman Fain killed in the subway was really a CIA agent?"

"I don't know," Rand said.

Shullman stared down at his phone. "Nothing. There's no record of an agent Gelder or mention of a Legion file or project."

"Maybe it's above your pay grade," Glass mused.

"Wait a minute," Shullman said. "The name Gelder doesn't check out, but the other name he gave us does—that is, if I have spelled his last name correctly. Jack Simons, Department of Special Circumstances. It's a small classified division."

"I've heard of the DSC," Rand said. "Anything else on Simons?"

Shullman continued to read the notes on his phone. "Well besides the DSC, he also oversees the case monitors for Special Investigations."

"Is there a contact phone number?"

"Just the standard CIA line."

"That's no good. I want a direct line to Simons' office. It's imperative that we talk to him before Fain's execution. Fain killed one of their agents. I want to know why."

"Got him…" Shullman said. "Simons is working out of an office in the Pentagon." He pecked at the keys on his phone. "I'm sending you the number."

"So you believe Fain?" David said.

"No, not until the information has been verified," said Rand. "Speaking of which, Fain did a lot of whispering to you over there. We weren't able to hear all of it."

David shrugged. "He said something about Carter's Grove."

"Yes," Rand said. "I heard that part, but there appeared to be more that he was telling you."

"Yes he did. Fain whispered a second sequence of numbers. I didn't get all of it." David handed Rand the business card with the incomplete numbers.

Rand glanced the card over and then passed it to Shullman. "See what comes up on these numbers, Mark." He turned back to David. "And you're certain there were two series of numbers?"

"Yes, I'm positive. I'm sorry, but he relayed the figures too quickly. My mind just went blank. Do you think the recorder was able to pick it up?"

"It's doubtful," Mangum said. "The cell has a built-in recorder that's not functioning at the moment, and when it is working, the voice activation feature is a bit twitchy. That's why the agents have the little black box recorder in there."

"The black box is more sensitive than the built-in recorder," Rand said. "But it would be limited to what you could hear at normal range."

"Got it," Shullman said. "44JC308 is an archeological site number for Carter's Grove," He looked up from his phone. "It's near Williamsburg, Virginia. The number is a basic survey marker. For it to be useful, we'll need a geo-coded location."

"Well, Father?" Rand said. "That second part?"

David exhaled. "I don't know. A similar series of numbers, I think. What do you think it means?"

"My guess is that he was giving you the precise location."

"Amazing," Glass said. "An actual latitude and longitude of a gravesite. Well, he was thorough, I'll give him that."

"Have you ever seen anything like this before?" David said.

"No," Rand said. "Not with coordinates, if indeed that's what they turn out to be. They usually remember landmarks. I had a case once where a killer left a trail of bread crumbs using the victim's finger bones." He turned toward Mangum. "We agreed to execute Fain early. Is that going to be a problem?"

Mangum looked at his watch. "No, it shouldn't be, but I'll need to get moving. It will take time to round everyone up. If you'll excuse me, I'll go ahead and get started."

"By all means," Rand said. He stepped aside and allowed Mangum to come through. "Now let's see about this Simons character." Rand pulled out his phone and dialed Simons' number. The phone rang twice before the line connected.

"Please hold," a woman's automated voice said. There was soft beep followed by the same automated voice. "Your call is being routed to the office of Jack Simons." Another beep sounded, and was followed by a woman's live voice.

"Jack Simons' office. This is Deborah Jacobs."

"Ms. Jacobs, this is Jason Rand. I'm an agent with the Bureau. I need to speak to Mr. Simons if he's available."

"Mr. Simons is not in his office at the moment, but I'll check his schedule." There was a click and silence. After a moment, Deborah Jacobs came back on the line. "Mr. Simons is between meetings at this time and has a moment to speak to you. I'm going to conference you through to his mobile." There was silence again.

"Jack Simons," a serious voice said on the other end of the phone line.

"Yes, Mr. Simons, this is Agent Jason Rand."

"My secretary said that you're with the Bureau."

"That's correct."

"What can I do for you, Agent Rand?"

"I thought you should know that I'm in the middle of a murder investigation, and it has come to our attention that one of the killer's victims, whom we have currently listed as a Jane Doe, could possibly be one of your agents."

"One of my agents? Well, I can assure that all of my agents are accounted for."

"I see…. I would still like to ask you a few questions, if you have the time."

"Certainly, Agent Rand. What would you like to know?"

"For starters, what can you tell me about a project or file code named Legion?"

"Legion?"

"Yes. What can you tell about it?"

"I'm afraid that I'm not at liberty to discuss the particulars of any of our programs with you. How did you hear about it?"

"I heard it from a condemned killer named Harold Fain. Don't you find it unusual that a confessed murderer—a serial killer—knew about one of your classified projects?"

"Classified?"

"Well since you're not able to discuss it, I naturally assumed—"

"Well you shouldn't. And yes, I do find all of what you're saying to be very peculiar."

"Is Harold Fain familiar to you?"

"No," Simons said. "I'm sorry, but I haven't heard that name before."

"Fain also divulged the name of his last victim as Rory Gelder. He claims that she worked for Central Intelligence."

"He told you that?"

"Yes, but we've been unable to confirm it."

"I'm accessing employment records now," Simons said. "Wait just a moment. Yes, yes, it does appear that a Rory Gelder had worked for the Justice Department.

"Had?"

"Agent Gelder is retired, and has been for some time."

"When did she stop working for the CIA?"

"Now, that information is classified, Agent Rand," Simons said.

"Was Gelder involved with Legion?"

"I can't answer that."

"I understand," Rand said. "Fain also mentioned you by name. He even asked that we call you."

"Hmm…how odd. Now Agent Rand, perhaps you could answer a few questions for me?"

"I'll try."

"What else did this murderer…what was his name?"

"Harold Fain."

"Yes, well…what else did he tell you?"

"Mr. Simons, I'm not at liberty to discus the particulars of the case at the moment, but I can tell you that we have the location of what we believe is Harold Fain's first victim."

"I see. And this serial killer only gave you one victim?"

"I'm afraid so," Rand said. "The bastard had no conscience."

"Well nevertheless, great work, Agent Rand. Would you mind keeping me in the loop on your progress?"

"It's hardly a special interest case."

"Well, if his victim, the Jane Doe does turn out to be Rory Gelder, even if she was retired, I would like to know the details surrounding her death."

"Fain's being executed tonight. Are you okay with that?"

"Why wouldn't I be?"

"Well—"

"I'll be in touch, Agent Rand."

The call ended.

"Damn...." Rand said. "That was very strange."

"What is it?" Shullman said.

"Simons. He hung up on me. He said that he would be back in touch."

"What are you thinking?"

"It makes me wonder even more who the hell this Fain character is? Simons confirmed that Gelder was retired CIA, but claims that he knows nothing of Harold Fain."

"So Fain was telling the truth."

"But for all we know, it was just a coincidence," Parker said. "If Gelder was retired, it could have been a simple case of her being in the wrong place at the wrong time, and not job related."

"No," Rand said, "I don't think so. I think Gelder's death was job related, and I think this adds a whole new wrinkle."

"What do we do about Simons?" Shullman asked.

"Nothing for now."

"Wait to hear back from him," Parker said. "I'm sure that your phone call caught him unaware, and he will need to verify what you disclosed about Gelder. He did say he would be back in touch with you."

Shullman said, "If Fain is significant, then surely Simons would intervene in his execution. Wouldn't he want his shot at Fain?"

"One would think so. It's damn strange."

8

DEATH CHAMBER

"**W**here the hell is he?" Mangum said. "We can't do an execution without a physician."

Chief Correctional Officer Mike Taylor ran his fingers through the bristly hairs of his crew cut as he stared up at the wall clock. "I know that we agreed to execute Fain early, but his request basically falls into our regular schedule. Is an hour going to make that much of a difference?"

"Yes. To me it does. We have an agreement. Have you tried Lathem at his practice?"

"Yes. His office closed two hours ago."

"Try his mobile again. Start calling everyone in…and see if you can get an alternate."

"On such short notice?"

"Are *you* going to pronounce him?" Mangum said.

Taylor laughed. "I'll pronounce him if you'll forge the death certificate."

"What's so urgent?" A voice broke in from behind them. Dr. Frederick Lathem came through the door holding a Styrofoam carryout box and a bottle of Diet Coke.

"Thank God," Mangum said. "We were starting to worry."

"Well, what the hell?" Lathem said. "I was just being seated at Cloons. He held up his to-go box. "After an hour wait." He sat the box down on the electric chair. The aroma of barbeque filled the chamber. He turned the cap on his Coke bottle with a loud hiss.

"We're going early," Mangum said.

Lathem took a sip of Coke. "When?"

"We're calling everyone in now."

"Well, I'd better hurry then." Lathem sat down in the electric chair and opened his box of food. He looked up at Mangum. "Hush puppy?"

"No thanks. Just eat it quickly."

9

EXECUTION

David entered the death chamber and found Rand and his team already waiting inside. Mangum stepped through the main door with Paul Strickland, the head of prison security. Strickland stood out among Mangum's staff. He wore a tailored black suit and wire rim eyeglasses. Mangum motioned for David to come over. Rand, Shullman, and Parker followed behind him, completing the group.

"Father, I don't believe I've had the opportunity to introduce you to our prison security chief, Paul Strickland."

"Nice meeting you," David said.

Strickland gave a slight nod and flashed a cordial smile.

"And the gentleman with the crew cut over there is Mike Taylor, the prison's second-in-command and my right hand."

Taylor stood next to the electric chair control panel with two technicians. When he heard his name, he stopped talking and waved in their direction.

"Are we ready, Mike?" Magnum asked.

Taylor gave a thumbs-up sign.

Mangum turned toward Lathem. "The only one missing, doctor, is your medical assistant. Does he know that were moving ahead of schedule?"

"I left him a message. I still haven't heard back from him, and I wouldn't count on him making it before nine."

Mangum frowned. "Is it okay with you if we proceed without him?"

"It doesn't make a difference, really. The ambulance attendant is qualified if I need help."

A tall highway patrol officer came over. "Where do you want my men?"

Mangum said. "Everyone, this is Captain Francis with the Highway Patrol. The captain has agreed to assist us with additional manpower tonight. I think you all know how I feel about this prisoner. He's not to be taken lightly, and it goes without saying that we're going to be playing this out with the utmost caution."

Mangum turned his attention to Strickland. "I want half of our extraction platoon to stand by in one of the vacant holding cells. The other half will need to form two lines outside of Fain's door. Captain Francis, your men will wait outside the death chamber main entrance. We'll be keeping that door open. I'll need you to instruct your men to move around out there so Fain can see them. I want him to understand that we mean business. Father, we will put you in front of Fain's holding cell alongside Mr. Strickland. Normally one of Strickland's men would handle the escort duties, but I would prefer it if you would make first contact. You can pass Fain off to Mr. Strickland once he enters the death chamber."

"Have his clothes been delivered?" Lathem said.

"Yes they have," Mangum said. "But he doesn't seem interested in changing into them."

"Maybe he doesn't like short pants," Glass said, laughing. "Electrodes don't work through clothing, so I guess you'll just have to cancel the execution."

"Well strip him naked if it comes to it," Strickland said, bitterly.

"No one is touching him until he's strapped in," Mangum said. "Let me worry about his shorts."

Glass folded his arms and stared around the room. He noticed that Captain Francis' troopers were carrying shotguns. "You have a lot of firepower here, Warden. Isn't it against prison policy for guards to be armed inside the compound?"

"We're bending the rules today," Mangum said. "But not to worry, this is a detached facility, not part of the main prison complex. The risk is minimal."

Glass shook his head. "With this type of prisoner, tensions are naturally high. Fain has a history of lashing out, and your men appear to be a bit on edge, to say the least. I doubt it would take much to get those trigger fingers moving."

Francis said, "My troopers have been briefed on Mr. Fain's history and Mr. Mangum has given us wide latitude."

"Like what?" Glass asked. "Shoot first and ask questions later?"

A broad smile formed on Captain Francis' face.

Mangum shook his head. "Francis' men have been instructed to give one verbal warning, followed by a warning shot, before opening up on him. I don't plan on getting caught flat-footed. I don't believe Fain will give us trouble, but we have to be prepared. As the old saying goes, 'Hope for the best, but plan for the worst.' The last thing I want is an incident. That prisoner and I had a deal. I've kept my end of the bargain, and so far, so has he. But if he should lash out, I want the resources nearby to deal with him swiftly and severely."

"Resources?" Glass said sarcastically. "You've turned this place into a militarized madhouse."

"It does seem excessive," David said.

"They're ready to blow him away," Glass said.

"I don't think it will come to that," Mangum said. "Besides, we have the proper measures in place." He pointed toward a guard who was standing by the door holding an odd looking transparent shield. "Have you tested that equipment today, Mr. Myers?"

"No, sir."

"You better give it a test."

The guard walked over to where they were all standing. "Eighty thousand volts of restraint, ladies and gentlemen." He held the shield away from his body. The shield sparked loudly and bright blue coils of electricity radiated horizontally across its surface. The electricity suddenly stopped and then started again with a much louder and brighter electrical flash.

Glass stood off to the side, shaking his head.

"And you say that thing isn't lethal?" David said.

"No," The guard said. He deactivated the shield. "The device has a ten-second stun cycle that totally jams the prisoner's nervous system. The recipient will typically fall to the floor with a loss of bladder function, and occasionally they'll shit in their pants."

"Lovely," Parker said.

"You would think that having all this technology would render supervision with live ammunition unnecessary," David said.

"Just a precaution," Mangum said. "He needs to know that we mean business. If Fain believes that we are prepared to use lethal force, he might think twice about trying anything."

"He dies tonight regardless," Glass said. "You're flaunting lethal force to ensure that he cooperates so you can just use deadlier force. I'm not sure, but I think that if I were in his shoes, I might choose a firing squad over a frying pan. You might be inviting trouble here, Warden."

"I don't think so," Mangum said, glancing at his watch. "Two minutes, ladies and gentlemen."

With Mangum's warning, the staff began to move around the death chamber with sudden urgency. David tried to stay out of everyone's way. He found an open spot behind the electric chair. He noticed that the floor surrounding the chair was made of rubber. The chair was constructed from solid oak. Thick rubber belt restraints were built into the arm and leg rests, and a sponge-lined electrode helmet hung from the backrest. A small plaque on the back of the chair read, J. A. MARSHTRICO AND ASSOCIATES ASSUMES NO LIABILITY FOR THE INTENDED OR ACTUAL USE OF THIS DEVICE. David shook his head as he read the absurd warning.

The executioner came into the room, smiling. He was a tall man in his midthirties. He had short black hair and wore a black jumpsuit. "Any special requests tonight?" he said. "Deep fried, barbequed, or perhaps my specialty, the slow roast?"

"Knock it off," Mangum said. He walked over to the first of the two mirrored observation windows. A heavy black curtain covered the window from the opposite side. He knocked on the glass. The curtain parted slightly, and a guard peeked through. Mangum stepped back and twirled his fingers in the air and waited for the curtain to open. A second guard stood toward the front of the chamber. Twelve state witnesses sat in metal chairs behind him.

Mangum said. "I'm going to ask that everyone in the witness pool please remain seated throughout the execution. There shall be no shouting out at the prisoner or addressing him in any way. Let's keep it professional." He walked over to a small table and picked up an older model cordless phone. "Mr. Glass, this station phone has a dedicated line and will remain open and clear as protocol requires." He handed the receiver to Glass. "I need you to verify that for me, if you would please?"

Glass listened, nodded, and returned the phone to its dock.

Mangum retrieved a second cell phone from his front pants pocket. "We'll let Fain make the call that he requested on this one." He handed the phone to Glass and turned and surveyed the room. "Are there any final concerns from anyone before we get started?"

"Yes," said Lathem. "What do I do with this?" He held up a clipboard with a partly completed death certificate. "There's a lot of empty blocks on this form. We don't have a place of birth or names of the birth parents. What would you like me to do?"

"We have his name," said Mangum. "Just stamp the rest 'unknown.'" He glanced at his watch. "Let's get this moving. Where's the transporter?"

A skinny paramedic stepped forward, wearing a white t-shirt and a yellow baseball cap with a swordfish on the front.

"You're the driver?" Mangum said.

"Yes, sir."

"Where's your burial removal transit permit?"

The driver handed Mangum the authorization form.

"Our doctor is short a medical tech. Would you mind standing in for him?"

"Do I have to do anything?"

"All you have to do is co-sign the state warrant and death certificate."

"Sounds easy enough. Count me in."

"Thanks," Magnum said. He signed the removal permit and passed it to Lathem. "Father Anslem, if you would, please take your place up front with Mr. Strickland."

David came past Strickland and stood directly in front of Fain's holding cell door.

"Okay," Mangum said. "Open the death chamber holding cell."

There was a loud buzz and Fain's cell door opened slowly. Fain stood by the open entrance, staring at nothing.

David's heart raced as he stepped forward. "Mr. Fain, the time has come."

Fain stood silent and aloof, staring past David, observing those who were charged with his destruction.

"Mr. Fain," David said. "If you would, please?"

Fain turned his eyes back toward David. He stepped through the doorway. The light in the holding cell flickered behind him and then returned to full power.

"Mr. Fain, I would like to caution you. Warden Mangum has commissioned the help of several well-armed state police officers. I urge you to give them your full cooperation. I will be taking you back to meet Mr. Strickland now. He is the man the state of Florida has charged with the task of administering your punishment." After a short pause, David turned, walked back, and took his place next to Strickland.

Fain lingered a moment by the entrance and then walked over to where Strickland and David were standing.

"This is Mr. Strickland," David said. "He'll be taking you from here."

"Mr. Fain, your death warrant has been signed," Strickland said. "Please state your full name for the record."

Fain remained silent.

"Bring him over," Mangum said.

Strickland guided Fain over to the electric chair and turned him so that his back was facing toward the seat.

Lathem moved behind the chair. He uncapped a syringe filled with Thorazine. The needle dribbled, leaving small puddles of sedative on the floor.

Strickland said, "Mr. Fain, I will ask you once again to address the witness pool. State your full name for the record."

Fain continued to stare in silence.

"Let's skip the formalities," Mangum said. "Mr. Fain, please be seated."

Fain eased into the electric chair.

A technician came over and looped a leather harness around Fain's waist and then fixed thick belt restraints around both wrists.

Lathem recapped his syringe and breathed a sigh of relief. Everyone seemed more at ease.

"Leave one of his arms free," Mangum said.

"Sir?"

Mangum didn't bother to explain. He stepped over and freed Fain's right arm. "As was promised, Mr. Fain, you're due a final phone call. Mr. Glass, would you give your client the phone?"

"Oh, yes," Glass said. "The phone." He walked over and held out a small black handset.

Fain took the phone and dialed a long series of numbers. He put the receiver to his ear and listened but didn't speak. After a moment he pressed a single digit. He deactivated the phone and handed it to Mangum.

"International," Rand said. "Fain dialed an international number." He came over to Mangum. "Warden, may I see that phone?"

"Is there a problem?"

"I need to check that number before you proceed." He took the phone and pressed the redial button. The phone's memory activated and quickly rotated through the last number dialed. Rand nodded thoughtfully as he watched the numbers scroll across the display. It was, as he suspected, a thirteen-digit international number. He put the receiver up to his ear and waited as the phone established a connection. The phone rang four times. There was a click and then a soft beep like that of an answering machine. Rand held the phone away from his ear and shook his head.

"Did someone pick up?" Mangum asked.

"An answering machine or recorder," Rand said.

"Are you sure?" Parker said.

"Positive."

"What does that mean?" Mangum said.

"I'm not sure yet."

"May we proceed with the execution?"

"He's all yours," Rand said. He moved to the chamber entrance and met with Shullman on the other side. "I need you to ID a number."

"Not a problem."

Rand pressed the redial button. The thirteen-digit international phone number scrolled across the display. "Do you recognize the country code?"

Shullman's eyebrows tensed as he considered the series of numbers. "I'm fairly certain that 39 is Spain."

"And the city?"

"The city code is 91. I don't know it off the top of my head." Shullman held out his cell phone. "If I could get a signal, I could look it up. There's something about this area that's blocking my reception."

Parker walked up next to them. "They're getting close in there. Any luck with the number?"

"No," Rand said. "Phone issues. We'll have to get it later." He turned and walked a short distance back to the entrance of the death chamber. He watched as a guard took a pair of stainless steel scissors and attempted to cut the pant legs off Fain's trousers. The guard placed the sharper edge of the scissors under the pant cuffs and squeezed as hard has he could. Nothing happened.

"Damn," said the guard. "It's as though the fabric is made of Kevlar." He made another attempt to cut the pant legs, and finally gave up.

"Don't worry about it," Mangum said. "Roll it up high enough that we're able to place the electrodes."

The guard folded the pant fabric midway up Fain's calf and secured each leg with a strap. He centered a metal contactor over each ankle and gave Mangum a nod.

"How much does he weigh?" the executioner asked.

"We didn't weigh him," Mangum said. "What's your guess on his weight, doctor?"

Lathem eyed Fain carefully. "He's tall. I'd guess that he weighs around two hundred pounds."

"Did you get that, Mr. Bowder?" Mangum said.

"Got it," Bowder said. He stepped behind a control station with a sloped metal console. "I'll add twenty percent. I'll keep it just under six amperes, and I think twenty-four hundred volts should be about right." He made the necessary calculations and held his hands away from the console.

An electrician in a red jumpsuit moved behind the chair and checked the power connection. He knelt down and pulled on a thick black electrical cable that snaked out from the back of the chair. "Current regulator circuit and line breaker connections are secured," he said.

"Very good," Mangum said. "Power up the chair, Mr. Bowder. And let's get that witness room curtain all the way open. Mr. Glass, if you would like any last words with your client before the helmet goes on, now would be the time."

Glass stared down at Fain for a moment and then waved his hand.

"Let's get this over with," Mangum said. "Get that helmet ready." He smoothed his hands over his stomach. "Everyone to their stations, please. Harold Fain, you took life. Now you lose your claim on life. For the crime of murder, the people of the state of Florida have sentenced you to die by electrocution. Do you have any last words?"

Fain stared forward.

"Okay...." Mangum said. "Secure the helmet link. And since we're not shaving his head, make sure you have good contact with his temples and forehead."

A technician moved forward and placed the saline-coated helmet over Fain's head.

The executioner moved into position behind the control panel. The system's green power light reflected on his face.

Mangum said, "The time is now twenty twenty-eight. Engage the chair and carry out the execution."

"I've got a problem!" Bowder said.

"What are you talking about?" said Mangum.

"The system is charged but I'm not able to activate the current."

"Why not? You had a green light."

Bowder shrugged. "Not anymore. There must be a short in the panel."

"That's just great…" Mangum said.

"Do you want me to run a console test?" Bowder said.

"No. Reset the system and see what happens."

"Okay," Bowder said. He turned off the switches in reverse order. He reactivated the main disconnect and turned on the circuit breaker to the power supply. He looked down at the unlit electric chair energizing lamp, and shook his head.

Mangum stepped over and tapped the light with his middle finger. "Damn strange. Deactivate the failsafe. We'll just have to do it by hand."

"What seems to be the problem?" Glass said.

"Our electronics are out on the console."

"Should we delay the execution?"

"No, we'll be running the chair manually. Get your stopwatch ready, Mr. Bowder."

"What about the EEG?" Glass asked.

"It's off," Bowder said. He continued to make adjustments behind the control panel.

"How will we know when his heart stops?"

"The old-fashioned way," Lathem said, holding up a stethoscope.

Mangum looked up at the wall clock. "The time in the log will be changed to offset the delay. The time is now twenty thirty-five. He clapped his hands. "Let's try it again with thirty seconds on, ten seconds off, on my mark…."

The executioner stepped up next to Bowder.

"Now!" Mangum said.

"Here it goes," the executioner said. He turned the connector switch all the way to the right. The current activated with a loud jolt. Fain's body reacted stiffly to the 2,400 volts of electricity that now flowed through his body.

Bowder reached toward the control panel. "Current off in ten, nine, eight, seven, six, five, four, three, two, and one."

Fain's head moved slightly.

"Damn it," Mangum snarled. "Raise the voltage to 2,640 volts."

"That's beyond the saturation voltage point we set. It will trip the—"

"Just do it!" Mangum snapped.

"Give me a second to bypass."

Mangum took handkerchief and dried the beads of sweat from his forehead.

"Okay, it's ready," Bowder said.

"Give it to him again," Mangum said.

"Power on and repeating," the executioner said.

An electrical hum could be heard, and the lights flickered. Fain sat rigidly in the chair as the electricity poured into his body. Smoke and flame erupted from Fain's right leg manacle. Toward the back of the room, an electrician's toolbox spilled over on the floor, The metal contents, wrenches, screwdrivers, and bolts moved as if magnetized toward the electric chair. The lights suddenly went out, plunging the room into darkness. Fain slumped forward in the electric chair, his body highlighted by a faint blue electrical corona. The emergency lights came on.

"Shut it off!" Mangum said.

Bowder coughed and waved his hand through a cloud of gray smoke that poured from the control panel. Just as he reached for the emergency switch, the front panel exploded, showering him in a torrent of sparks. An electrician grabbed him and moved him away from the control console. A second technician moved in behind the electric chair and whacked at the power cable with a rubber baton. The input circuit breaker came free from the back of the chair with a loud *ping* and the hum of electricity slowly diminished.

"What the hell happened?" Mangum said, staring down at the base of the electric chair. The two power coils were melted into the rubber floor, and a mixture of metal tools lay scattered around the base of the chair.

Bowder came over. "The build up must have been off the charts."

"How much?" Mangum said.

"My guess would be over ninety amperes, but we didn't get an actual reading because the computer's off. The fail-safes should have kept this from happening."

"The current regulator has failed on this chair before," Mangum said.

"And when that happens, the over current breaker will trip. The output contactor resets when a spike is detected. All connections to the power supply should have been severed."

"So what?" Glass said. "You blew a fuse."

"Didn't you see it?" Bowder bellowed.

Glass shook his head. "See what?"

"Electricity. It fed back through the console."

"I saw it," David said. "I saw little pink and blue speckled flashes. Has this ever happened before?"

"It can't happen!"

"Obviously it can," Glass said.

Mangum said, "What I would like to know is, how could it happen?"

"No," Glass said. "I don't care about your equipment. I would like to know Fain's condition."

"He should be a pile of ashes," Bowder said.

They all stared at Fain, who sat motionless in the chair with his body slumped forward, supported by the chair's restraints.

"Doc," Mangum said, "do you want to go ahead and check his heart?"

"Sure," Lathem said. He walked over and stood next to Fain. He was just about to begin his examination when he felt the hairs on his right arm bristle. He rolled back his shirtsleeve. The hairs on his arm were raised. "Are you sure everything is switched off?"

"The power's off," Bowder said. "And the chair's disconnected."

Lathem nodded uneasily. He reached out toward Fain but was unable to touch him. "That's odd," he said, pulling his hand back. It was as if some unseen force repelled his hand. After a moment Lathem leaned forward to try again. This time he successfully placed his hand on Fain's shoulder. He felt a tingling sensation. The feeling wasn't unpleasant at first, but when he tried to withdraw his hand, he saw a blue flash of light and felt a painful burst of electrical force explode into his body. It was as if he'd struck by lighting from within. The jolt knocked him backward to the ground, where he laid curled in a ball, clutching his right hand.

"What the hell was that?" Mangum said. "Are you okay, Doc?"

"I think so." Lathem said. He sat up on the floor.

"The power is off," Bowder said. "Maybe some kind of static charge."

"Static electricity?" Glass said. "That was more than static. It nearly tore the doctor's arm off. Have you ever seen anything like this before?"

"No, I haven't."

"How do you explain it, Mr. Bowder?" Mangum said.

Bowder pulled a red pen from his shirt pocket and drummed it on his lips as he reflected on the incident. "It's my belief, as crazy it might sound, that Fain somehow drained off an extremely high charge of electricity. In essence, he picked up a voltage gradient and became a human conductor."

"Well, let's put it all to rest now, shall we?" Mangum said. He motioned for the paramedic to join him and Lathem. "How's the arm, Doc?"

"My hand is still a bit numb," said the doctor. He flexed his fingers and closed his hand into a tight fist. "And now my shoulder is starting to hurt."

"We still need someone to pronounce Fain," Glass said.

"Give us a minute here, will you, counselor?" Mangum said. "Are you able to continue, Doc?"

"I think so." Lathem stood and stepped slowly over to the electric chair. "You're sure I'm not going to get zapped again?"

"Not to worry," a technician said. He stepped over to the electric chair and held out a black box volt-ammeter. "As you can see, we have a zero potential level."

Lathem took a deep breath. He slapped Fain's legs with his hand and winced. Nothing happened, and he breathed a sigh of relief. His hands trembled as he moved the stethoscope in a circular pattern around Fain's chest.

"What's the good word, Doc?" Mangum said.

"I don't know."

"What the hell does that mean?" Glass said.

"Give me a second."

"No need to give him a physical over there," Mangum said.

Lathem glanced uneasily over his shoulder toward Mangum. After a moment, he turned back and moved the stethoscope higher on Fain's chest.

"What are you doing?" Mangum said impatiently. "Let's hear it."

"I think he's dead."

"Think?" Glass said.

"What's wrong?" Mangum said.

"Lathem shook his head. "I don't know. I thought I heard something." He continued to listen to the area around Fain's heart. He took a deep breath and immediately felt stabbing pains shoot through his chest.

"Just pronounce him, for Christ sake!" Mangum said.

"He's dead," Lathem said, finally. The pain in his chest continued. He felt light-headed.

Mangum said, "This is Florida CMSP. The time is now twenty-one hundred and we are standing down from this operation." He walked over to the witness room. "The sentence of death in the ruling of the state of Florida versus Harold Fain has been carried out. I invite all the official observers to exit at this time." He swept his eyes over the cluttered death chamber.

Two technicians began undoing Fain's restraints.

"It's very strange," Bowder said. He was staring at Fain's legs.

"What are you looking at?" Mangum said.

"Fain's legs. There's no evidence of high-voltage burns."

"Let me see that," Mangum said. He knelt down on one knee. A melted electrode lay on the floor behind Fain's right foot. The electrode's contactor was fused to the manacle. "The contacts are completely melted and yet there is no hyper-thermal effect to the skin," said Mangum. "No marks whatsoever."

Bowder knelt down beside Mangum. "Well, he's dead, so we obviously had an uninterrupted flow of electricity into his body. It's just the first time that I've ever seen it happen without damaging the skin." He poked at Fain's ankle with his pen. "The electricity went right through him, without a mark. Electricity always leaves a mark. And with the overload, there should be holes through to the bone." He glanced toward the busted console. "Damn strange."

Mangum stood up. "Well I want to know exactly what went wrong tonight. I want a complete test run on all of this—the control console, power supply, and the electric chair."

"Tonight?" the chair technical supervisor said.

"Immediately."

"That could take a while."

"I don't care if it takes all night," Mangum snapped.

"My team will need comp time."

"Run the tests and let me know what you find." Mangum turned to Lathem, who was leaning against the wall, rubbing his chest. "You going to be okay, doc?"

"I don't know," Lathem said. He felt a tingling sensation in his left hand and he found it difficult to breathe. He clutched his chest. It felt as though his lungs were being squeezed in a vise. "I might be having a heart attack," he said.

"A heart attack?" Mangum said. "Are you certain?"

They all stared around at each other with a look of panic on their faces.

Glass finally said, "What do you want us to do?"

"Nothing yet."

"Well, you sound pretty calm about it," Mangum said. "Do you want us to call you an ambulance?"

"No. The symptoms can last a number of hours. Can someone get me some aspirins from my medical bag?"

Mangum looked around.

"By the door," Lathem said. He turned toward the ambulance driver. "Where are you taking Fain's body?"

"The morgue at St. Mary's Hospital."

"Do you mind if I tag along?"

"Not at all. You're aware, though, that it's about a twenty-minute drive?"

Mangum handed Lathem a bottle of aspirin. "We're a long way from town," said Mangum. "I could phone in an air ambulance."

"Not necessary," Lathem said, popping two aspirins into his mouth.

"Okay. You're the doctor."

Lathem turned toward the paramedic. "When are you leaving?"

"As soon as they load the body, we'll be underway."

"What about our samples?" Rand said. He watched as two technicians unbuckled Fain's body from the electric chair and placed Fain in a shiny black vinyl pouch. "Hold up, gentlemen."

Glass said, "Just get some hairs from his cell."

"We checked his cell. There wasn't any tissue or hairs. Evidently he doesn't shed, so it looks like we'll need to get a DNA sample from him now."

"I'll swab his mouth," Shullman said.

"We can get it at the morgue," Parker said. She nodded toward the two technicians. The two men zipped the body bag closed and locked it with a tamper-proof seal.

10

DEPARTURE

David waited to rendezvous with Rand's team outside the prison's main entrance. As night fell, the wall and tower lights switched on, bathing the prison perimeter in harsh white light.

Rand came out of the door behind David. "Good," said Rand. "I was hoping you were still here, Father. I have a few more questions."

"Hello again, Agent Rand. I was actually waiting for you. I have something to ask you as well, but you first."

"I was going to ask you if you remembered any more details about what Fain told you—the additional coordinates, I mean."

"I'm sorry, no. But there was something else that I forgot to mention to you. There was something that Fain asked me to do."

"I'm listening."

"Fain wanted me to come with you to Carter's Grove. He was rather adamant about it. I thought that his request was rather peculiar. I can't imagine why he would want me to come with you. Can you think of a good reason?"

"Not any good reasons come to mind. Fain was a manipulator, Father. I'm sure he had his reasons, and none of them were rational."

"I see. And how would you feel about me tagging along?"

Parker came out of the prison entrance. She'd overheard the conversation. "It wouldn't be a good idea, Father. It's still an open investigation and—"

"I thought that, perhaps, considering the muddled location... maybe if I had time to sleep on it, or perhaps by being there, it might help me to remember."

"I doubt it. And besides, if you do suddenly recall the information, you can always call us."

"Let's not be so hasty, Dana," Rand said. "I mean, I agree with you. It's certainly against protocol, but I might be willing to make an exception if Father Anslem can promise me that he will keep what he witnesses confidential."

"Of course," David said.

"And you really want to go with us?"

"Want? No. I don't. I am as opposed to going as you are having me go. I made a promise and I mean to keep it. And who knows? Perhaps when we're on site tomorrow, I'll remember more, and with a little luck, maybe you'll be able to piece it all together."

"Okay Father, you're on."

"When do we leave?" David said.

Rand looked at his watch. "As soon as you're ready."

"Tonight?"

"I'm afraid so. We will need to be on site in Virginia by daybreak. Where are you staying?"

"I have a place on Marco Island."

"We have a branch office on Marco. You can follow us there and drop your car at the FBI compound."

The main gate opened. The ambulance carrying Fain's body came slowly through. The vehicle crossed the parking lot and disappeared into the dense jungle of the Everglades' Big Cypress National Preserve.

Inside the ambulance, Lathem shifted uncomfortably in his seat. He felt queasy. He rolled his window down. A breeze came through and he leaned back, angling his face toward the current of fresh air.

"I didn't catch your name earlier," the driver said. "You're a doctor, right?"

"Fred Lathem, and yes, I'm a doctor."

"I'm James Peachtree, but my friends call me Jimmy. Should I run hot?"

"No sirens. When we get to the Monroe turnoff you can throw your lights on."

"Monroe's in two miles. I'll go ahead and turn them on."

"That's fine," Lathem said.

The ambulance hit a pothole with a loud jolt.

"Blasted road," Lathem said through clinched teeth.

Jimmy gave Lathem a nervous glance. "I'll get you there." He pushed his foot down on the accelerator. "Just hang on." He reached for the ambulance radio and punched in his transport number code.

The radio beeped softly, and then a woman's fuzzy voice sounded on the frequency. "Go ahead, transport 124."

"This is transport 124 en route, heading west on US 41. I have a passenger, a Dr. Fred Lathem. He's the staff doctor from Cypress Ultra-Max. He has diagnosed himself with having a heart attack."

"Ten-four, transport 124. Please advise patient's status."

"Stable, I think." He sounded unsure and eyed Lathem up and down. "Doc, anything to add?"

Lathem shook his head.

"He appears to be stable," Jimmy said. He released the side call button. The radio beeped and erupted with a continuous burst of static. He clicked the button several more times. "That's strange," he said. He placed the handset back in its holder and turned the volume down. "Hold onto something, Doc. The washout is coming up."

Lathem knew the area of road that Jimmy was referring to. A quarter mile of the two-lane highway had been stripped for repairs the year before, but the job was delayed when it was determined that the entire road needed to be overhauled. Without the protective layer of pavement, the exposed section of highway had crumbled away, leaving a strip barely wide enough for two cars to pass side by side.

Lathem fumbled in the dark for his seatbelt. He finally gave up and braced himself with his right arm against the passenger side door.

"Wow, there it is," Jimmy said. "It snuck up on me."

The asphalt just ahead of them dropped away, revealing a mangled track of road that resembled the surface of the moon. The front end of the ambulance dropped off the pavement with a jolt.

"I have it down to a science," Jimmy said. "The key is to look straight down, watch the road directly in front of you. The bigger ruts are along the edges. We'll shoot straight through."

"Jesus—slow down!" Lathem said.

"See, that wasn't so bad."

"Says you. Try it while having a heart attack."

"You've got a point…oh *shit*!"

"What?" Lathem said. And then he saw a man dressed in all black, standing in the middle of the road. There was a sudden scrape of rubber, and Jimmy jerked the steering wheel to the right. The ambulance skidded sideways. The wheels caught in a pothole, flipping the vehicle onto its left side, sending Lathem into the driver's side door. He felt a sharp pain in the back of his neck, and then everything went dark.

11

WRECKAGE

"**N**ow what?" Rand said. He tapped the brakes and steered his Suburban onto the right shoulder of the road. A mix of police cruisers and rescue vehicles blocked the narrow two-lane highway. Two highway patrolmen directed traffic around an overturned ambulance while a second pair of officers set flares down each side of the emergency pull-off lanes.

Parker sat next to Rand. "That's the ambulance from the prison." She said.

Shullman leaned forward from the back seat with his elbows on the backrest.

"Is Father Anslem still with us?" Rand said.

Shullman glanced over his shoulder. "He's with us. He's already out of his vehicle." He rolled down the left passenger-side window and waved David over.

"Why are we stopping?" David said, walking up to the driver's side of the car.

"That's the ambulance from the prison," Rand said. He turned on his dashboard strobe lights and stepped out of the vehicle. "Let's have a look." He walked over to the closest officer and flashed him his badge. "Who's in charge?"

The trooper eyed Rand's FBI credentials with raised eyebrows and then pointed an orange cone-tipped flashlight at a group of officers standing next to the overturned ambulance.

A black helicopter circled low in the air above the accident scene. The aircraft's powerful blades whined, and sand swirled up from the road, churning through the bright beam of its searchlight.

"Stay close, Father," Rand said. They walked over toward the overturned ambulance. Rand held out his badge. "Who can tell me what happened here?" he said.

"We were hoping maybe you could tell us," a trooper said.

They immediately recognized Captain Francis from Fain's execution.

"Know anything about that helicopter?" Francis said. He took off his hat and wiped the sweat from his brow.

"I thought it was one of yours," said Rand.

"No," Francis said. "There's no markings, and they're not answering our hails."

"What about a registered flight plan?"

"Negative."

The helicopter aimed its searchlight in their direction as it moved higher into the night sky. The aircraft banked right and slowly disappeared over the tree line.

"What do you think?" Shullman said.

"Damn strange," Rand said. He watched the helicopter disappear over the horizon. After a moment he turned his attention back to Francis. "Any idea as to what happened to the ambulance?"

"It appears that they were attempting to avoid something in the road. There's evidence that hard action was taken by the driver. The ambulance made impact here." He pointed down. Shattered glass and a twisted front bumper lay scattered across the road.

"Is all of this wreckage just from the ambulance?" Rand said.

Francis glanced over his notes. "By the looks of the debris field, it appears that there were no other vehicles involved. We have lots of wildlife through here, but there was no blood or animal fur in the grill. And there's something else you should know."

"I'm listening."

"Fain's body is missing."

"Damn it!" Rand said. "I hope your men understand that—"

"Oh they do," Francis said. "Nothing has been touched. We've treated the entire area as a crime scene."

"Have roadblocks been set?" Shullman said.

"Yes. Unfortunately it was initiated too late. There has been no activity on the road since the incident."

"Who discovered the crash?" Rand asked.

"An off-duty prison guard was the first to come upon the scene," said Francis. "His name is Tenny. Michael J. Tenny."

"What did he see?"

"Nothing remarkable. His statement will be in the crash report. I'll get you a copy."

"Thanks," Rand said. He walked behind the ambulance. The back right door was open wide, bent all the way back, against the vehicle. "Odd," said Rand. "The door hinges are bent inside out." He borrowed a flashlight from one of Francis' men and shined it in through the back door. The medical cabinets were open, and most of the contents, medical equipment, and several blankets were scattered against the left side. The gurney that had held Fain's body was locked firmly into the floorboard, empty. Rand exchanged glances with Shullman and Parker.

"What the hell happened here?" Rand said. What's the status of the ambulance driver and the doctor from the prison...what was his name?"

"Lathem," Francis said. "He's DOA. Fractured skull, and the EMTs aren't certain, but they suspect a crushed vertebra. They won't know for sure until after an autopsy."

"What about the driver?"

"James Peachtree," Francis said. "We found him in the woods. I'm afraid he is dead too. Pierced torso."

"Pierced from what?" Rand said.

"We found him in the marsh about hundred yards from here. He fell or was pushed off an embankment into shallow water. Got himself mangled on some jagged cypress roots. We discovered several shoe prints around the scene, and there is evidence of pursuers on foot leading into the marsh.

"Can you believe this?" Shullman said.

"But who would want Fain's body?" David said.

Rand didn't answer. He slipped on a pair of rubber gloves and walked to the front side of the ambulance. Broken glass crunched under his feet as maneuvered close to the shattered windshield. He crouched down and aimed his flashlight through a large hole in the windshield, making a mental note that the glass was busted from the inside. He came around to the underside of the ambulance and used the axle as a footstep to climb up. The passenger side door was missing. "What happened to this door?" he said.

"It broke off." Francis pointed his flashlight toward the canal. "And somehow ended up all the way over there."

"That's strange," Rand said. "The door's location is against the momentum and skid pattern." He shined his light into the front cab. The back wall was pushed forward and dented in the middle. The dashboard was pushed down, and the steering wheel ring was bent forward. The glove box was smashed open, and the housing unit containing the in-car recording device had been removed. Rand climbed back down to the road.

"See anything?" Parker said.

Rand nodded slowly. "It's what I didn't see that matters."

"Oh?"

"The vehicle's recording unit has been removed." Rand turned toward Francis. "Have any of your men tampered with this scene?"

"No one has touched anything. Keep in mind that early on we had no idea this was going to become a crime scene. The crash was a routine MVA as far as we were concerned. It wasn't until after we discovered that Fain's body was missing that we suspected foul play."

Rand glanced at his watch. "Shouldn't your detectives be on site by now?"

"They have been dispatched, but we're isolated out here. The nearest sheriff's substation is in Everglade City."

"Do you want me to stay behind?" Shullman said.

"No," Rand said. We'll continue on to Virginia tonight. We can turn this over to our local branch office for now. I would like for one of our men to go back over the crime scene in the daylight." He handed Francis a business card. "When your detectives arrive, have them call this number so they may coordinate their efforts with our branch office on Marco Island."

"Understood," Francis said. He placed Rand's card into his pocket. "And what about the people who caused this, and took Fain's body? This is more than just a murderer's fan club here, am I right?"

Rand nodded. His phone rang. "Hello. Leeds, this is Rand," he said, turning from the group.

"We've traced the international number Fain called," Leeds said.

"What did you find out?"

"The number he dialed had a country code 39 for Spain, and a city code of 97. That's a town called Andratix. He called a room in a small inn there called the Avila. A Doctor James Farrell rented the room on a long-term lease. His name hasn't checked out. It appears to be an alias. We discovered a phone relay unit in the room that rerouted the call to an apartment in New York City. We checked the apartment rental records and discovered that the residence was also obtained through long-term lease and that there's no information on the occupant—just a name, Charles Henning. Henning was bogus too. And just like the room in Spain, a relay phone unit received the call and forwarded it to a motel in Everglade City. The motel is about twenty miles from the prison and seventeen miles from your current location. I'm afraid that is where the trail ends. Our Marco field agents swept that last motel room, and they discovered only a phone answering machine with its memory purged. They took the device with them, but said that it's fried and they won't be able to recover anything useful. Sorry."

"Yeah, me too," Rand said. "Thanks for the quick turnaround. I'll be in touch." He slid his phone into his pocket and turned back toward the group. "That was Leeds regarding the phone call."

"Any luck?" Shullman said.

Rand frowned. "More questions than answers—more unknowns. Fain's phone call was rerouted to Florida. Not too far from here, actually."

"No doubt setting this little abduction in motion," Shullman said.

David shook his head. "I don't understand why someone would want his body."

"It probably gave Fain some final degree of sadistic pleasure knowing that his friends would make off with his body, and make us look like fools in the process."

"Fain is dead," Parker said. "He can do no more harm."

"True," Rand said. "But someone like him is still on the loose, and we're powerless to stop him…or them."

12

CARTER'S GROVE, VIRGINIA

6:45 a.m. Two sheriff's deputies bundled in yellow raincoats directed Rand and his motorcade off the road into a fence-lined pasture. A middle-aged couple stood on the front porch of their colonial two-story house, watching nervously as the convoy of black SUVs rolled past their driveway.

David accompanied Rand's team in the lead vehicle. He sat in the back seat with Shullman and Parker. He stared out the tinted right side window, awed by the number of agents and local officers who had assembled in the large field.

"Stop here," Rand said. He opened his door and stepped out of the vehicle.

A group of local police officers wearing identical tan and brown uniforms came over to greet them. The lead officer was a tall, well built man.

"Where can I find Sheriff Jeffery Cole?" Rand said.

"You're looking at him," Cole said.

Rand stepped forward and shook his hand. "Thanks for the extra manpower."

"Don't mention it. Just let me know what you need from us."

"Well, for starters, maybe you could take a look at our maps?" He looked at Shullman. "Let's have a look at those most recent surveys."

Shullman unrolled a map on the front hood of a police cruiser. "This is a topographic map of Carter's Grove."

Cole glanced at the map. "The GPS lines are in blue?"

Shullman nodded, activated the screen of a small GPS computer, and pointed to an area on the map. "This is us, here."

"Is this field part of the historic property?" Rand said.

"No, the meadow is private property, the mansion too. It was recently closed to the public and sold to a private owner, along with roughly seventy-six acres. The owner lets visitors use this field for parking overflow." Cole traced his index finger along an uneven red line on the map. "Everything south of the road and all the property outside the fence line—around four hundred acres—is still held by the Virginia Department of Historic Resources."

"What about the mansion?"

Cole pointed toward the woods. In the distance a large Georgian-style manor was visible through a break in the trees. "By noon, this place will be full of people: backpackers, campers, and university students."

"Not today," Rand said. "The tourists will need to be kept out. We will need to close this whole area off until we conclude our operation."

"What about the residents?" Cole said. He gestured toward the house that Rand and his team had passed on their way into the pasture. The couple was still on the porch, and the husband was now brandishing a pair of binoculars.

Rand frowned. "The locals can stay, as long as they remain on their property. Tell your team leaders to coordinate with Detective Leeds. We will need to visit each resident with a passive diversion alert."

"What did you have in mind?" Shullman asked.

"I don't know. How about a gas leak or something? I'll leave it up to you. Think of something good. I want to avoid a media circus."

"I think it's too late for that," Cole said. He pointed toward the road, where three local news vans were parked on the grass. A reporter emerged from the first van and attempted to talk his way through the police line.

"What did you expect?" Cole said. "A sleepy tourist town invaded by an army of investigators? Just give them the truth."

"In time," Rand said. He turned his attention back to the map.

"It's a large target search area," Cole said. "I hope you plan on being here for a while."

"How long?" David said.

"Relax, Father," Rand said. "You'll be back on a plane to Florida in a few hours."

David nodded and nervously studied the coordinates on a small piece of paper that he concealed in his hand. He stepped closer to Rand and stared at the map.

Cole said, "Per your earlier request, Agent Rand, my men have set up around the outside of the pasture. They're standing by for your search requirements."

"Thanks," Rand said. "We will be combining a free search and grid search approach to cover the target area. We will also combine our three K-9 units with your dog teams. How many dogs do you have?"

"Six bloodhounds and five German shepherds, all trained to find people, dead or alive."

"We also have a K-10 unit," Rand said.

"It will be useless in this terrain," Cole said. "There are too many hills and ravines for it to be effective."

"What is a K-10 unit?" David asked.

"Robotic dog," Rand said. "They're unloading it now." On a nearby tractor-trailer two FBI agents rolled a cumbersome black metal box down the back ramp.

"It's has a computer sensor that simulates a dog's nose, Father," Shullman said. "The K-10's sensor is much more sensitive than the real thing."

Cole said, "You still have to find what you're looking for before you can even use that thing."

"No offense, Sheriff, but your dogs can't talk. The K-10 is able to successfully describe what it smells—odors as faint as a few parts per million. We'll just have to let the real dogs find the body first."

"If someone is out there, they'll find them," Cole said.

The K-9 squad leader came over. "The dog units are all acclimated and waiting to deploy," he said.

Rand turned his attention back to the survey map. "Begin your search on the main grounds, focusing initially on the buildings and outer structures. And what are these?" He asked, pointing to a group of black squares on the map near the tree line.

"Stables," Cole said.

Rand said, "Start with the stables and work your way into the woods. Cover every square inch. I don't care how long it takes."

The K-9 unit leader nodded and rejoined his squad. All of the dog teams slowly spread out and moved into the woods beyond the perimeter.

Rand looked down the hill toward the far end of the pasture. He noticed that a cluster of pine trees on the opposite side of the fence was marked off with yellow tape, and the ground was covered with hundreds of small red and orange wire flags. "Who authorized those markers?" he said.

"Those are not ours," Cole said. "The colored pin flags belong to the diggers. There are excavation sites all over the property. The students mark previously explored and potential search areas with flags."

"I would like to speak with the students," Rand said.

Cole's radio chirped. "We have civilians in the woods," a man's voice said. "Two males and three females."

Cole glanced at his watch and pressed the side call button on his radio. "Round them up."

"Who are they?" Rand asked.

"Over there," Shullman said, pointing down the hill toward the right side of the meadow. "Near the tree line."

On the opposite side of the fence, a group of young adults, outfitted with camping gear, were talking to one of Cole's officers.

"Come on," Rand said. "I want to talk to them." He retrieved his radio and gestured for one of Cole's officers to collect the map. "Sheriff, tell your men to hold them there. We're coming down."

"What have we done?" one of the female students asked.

"Nothing," Rand said. "We just need to ask you a few questions. Are there more people in your party?"

"Yes, there are students spread out all over, between sites F and G."

"What's your name?" Rand asked.

"Sidney."

"Well, Sidney," Rand said. "What's the nature of your business?"

"Archeology. We're students."

"Do you have a permit?" Shullman said.

"Are you serious?" one of the other girls asked. She took out a can of bug repellent and sprayed her legs, then passed the canister to the young man standing next to her.

"Yes, we're quite serious," said Rand.

"We don't have it here."

"Who's in charge of your little expedition?"

"Dr. Butler," said Sidney.

"Is he here?"

"That's him over there." She pointed at a narrow path in the woods. A thin, middle-aged man with flowing gray hair made his way toward them through a wooded ravine. He wore a backpack, a khaki long sleeve shirt, and a pair of brown cargo pants with the cuffs tucked into a pair of mud-covered hiking boots.

"He looks like a skinny Ben Franklin," Shullman said. "But younger."

"Yeah, thanks," Butler said, walking up to where they were standing. "About the younger part, I mean." He saw the large group of officers assembled in the pasture. "What seems to be the problem?"

"We're looking for something," Shullman said.

Butler took a sip of water from a stainless steel bottle. "What exactly?"

"That's confidential," Rand said. "How many of your students are in the field today?"

Before Butler could answer, Rand's radio beeped from inside his coat. He retrieved the radio and pressed the call button. "Rand here. Go ahead."

The radio beeped again, followed by a man's voice. "This is Agent Hardy. Both dive teams have checked in. They just finished clearing the lake, and I'm afraid there were no signs of any human remains."

Rand held the radio to his mouth. "Remember it has been over six months. We're not looking for intact bodies at this point. What about sonar?"

"No bones or body parts. A couple of nice images of an old car, a bicycle, cables, a couple of old sunken boats, bottles, and lots of mud. It's Friday, and the Department of Transportation divers have been at it since midnight. They were wondering if you needed them to stick around, or can they go."

"Not yet. Tell them to stand by."

"Body parts?" Butler asked with raised eyebrows.

"That's right," Rand said. He slid the radio back into his coat. "What can you tell us about the Carter's Grove excavations?"

"I've been working this site off and on for the last ten years. The main sites have been fully excavated for some time now. They were first excavated in the early 1970s."

Rand held out a blurry photograph of Harold Fain. "Do you recognize the person in this picture?"

"I've never seen him before."

"You're certain?" Rand said.

"Yes. What did he do?"

"Murder."

"And you think he concealed the body of his victim here?"

"It's a possibility."

Butler shook his head. "Well, he wasn't very smart to conceal a body on a property crowded with a bunch of archeologists who were running around with shovels and pick axes."

"This is all protected property," Rand said. "If he has hidden a body on an excavated site, that could mean that it wouldn't be checked again. It's protected, am I right?"

"Protected, certainly, but hiding a victim in a significant and previously excavated site—especially one that yielded important artifacts— would be a mistake because the location would certainly be revisited in time. He would have been wiser to conceal the body in an area that was previously searched and deemed not to contain anything of archeological value."

Parker said, "Who has participated in the excavations?"

Butler rolled his eyes. "You're talking about years, and a lot of people from all over the country. The site is worked by joint summer field school teams from several universities. My school, for instance, is the University of California, Berkeley. The participating schools are all coordinated through the Colonial Williamsburg Foundation, which is under the direction of a group of PhD candidates. I can provide you with a list of names. Do you think this murder is somehow tied to one of the universities?"

"Possibly," Shullman said.

"The victim or the killer?" Cole said.

Rand waved his hand dismissively. "We'll be focusing on the excavated sites first, and then we'll cover the surrounding grounds."

"Well…" Butler said.

"What?" Rand said.

Butler shook his head as he rolled up both shirtsleeves "The excavated areas are miniscule compared to the size of Martin's Hundred—"

"Did you say Martin's Hundred?" David said. "Fain mentioned that name to me last night. And he told me something else. Let's see now, what was it? Oh, now I remember. It was the *Gift of God.*"

Rand frowned. "Why didn't you mention that before, Father? What is this Martin's Hundred?"

"The Martin's Hundred Society," Butler said. "Named for the shareholder Richard Martin. He was a seventh-century entrepreneur who was granted this tract of land you're standing on. The *Gift of God* was their ship. It appears your source is a historian. This whole area was granted to the Martin Hundred Society in 1622."

"And the hundred—who were Mr. Martin's hundred?"

"A 'hundred' meant a tract of land large enough to sustain a hundred people."

"Just how big of an area are we talking about?" Rand said.

"Just shy of twenty-two thousand acres."

"That's enormous," Shullman said.

Cole said, "You're going to need more men."

"And your source didn't tell you where to find the victim's body?" Butler said.

Rand exhaled, exasperated. "No details. All he gave us was the archeological site number for Carter's Grove."

"It's a lot of area to cover."

"You're going to need a lot more men," Cole said again.

"I suggest we get started," Rand said. "Let's have a look at that map again."

One of Cole's men spread the map out on a picnic table.

Rand waited for everyone to gather behind him. "I'll take a group down to site A, here," he said, pointing to an area in the bottom quadrant of the map. "We will actually pass close to site B in the woods here, so why don't we check it first. Shullman, you and Parker take some men down to site C here."

"I'm afraid you will all be going in the wrong direction," David said nervously.

"Oh?" Rand said. "What makes you say that?"

David held out a small piece of paper. "I was supposed to wait until we got here to show you this."

"What is it?" Rand said.

"The missing coordinates. I promised Fain that I would wait until we arrived before showing it to you. I took the liberty of studying your map earlier. I think these numbers will make more sense to you now."

"So, we've just been spinning our wheels here?" Rand scowled. "You know, Father, that borders on obstruction."

"I know, and I'm sorry, but I gave Fain my word."

"Why would you do that?"

"As I mentioned before, Fain wanted me to come with you and I don't know why. All I know is that he wanted me to come with you and it was his belief that you would be unwilling to bring me along."

"You persuaded us to let you go," Rand said.

"I did. And if you had refused, Fain wanted me to use the information as leverage to ensure that you would change your mind. Fain wasn't going to give me the final coordinates unless I agreed. I've kept my word, and now you have the information. I hope it proves useful."

"Well, in that case, you made the right decision," Rand said. "Let's have a look at that satellite map again, Mark."

Shullman opened his computer and everyone gathered around him, staring at the screen. A satellite view of the historic property came into view. Shullman entered the new coordinates, and soon a series of numbers emerged, overlaying the computer-generated topographical map.

Rand pointed at the screen. "If these contour numbers are correct, the transect line should meet right about here."

"It's actually nowhere near Carter's Grove," Butler said. "That's mostly a wooded area. It's about five hundred yards from site B. That area has been carefully surveyed on more than one occasion. It was found to have nothing of archeological value."

Rand flashed a triumphant smile. "It's about to become a crime scene." He entered the new coordinates on his GPS and handed it to Shullman. "Lead the way."

Shullman stared at the screen and waited while satellite synchronized with their location.

"Come on," Butler said. "It will save time if I just show you where it is. You students stay here. I'll be back in a few minutes. Follow me," he said, and started off toward the tree line. When Butler realized that no one was following him, he stopped and turned back toward the group. "Are you coming?"

They all stared at Rand. After a moment, he nodded, and everyone fell in behind Butler as he headed into the woods.

Rand turned to Shullman as they walked. "Have Sheriff Cole's dog team diverted to those coordinates," said Rand. "Tell him that we will rendezvous with him there."

A long procession of FBI agents and law enforcement officers followed Butler down a narrow ravine. After a quarter mile, the woods opened up into a small tree-lined meadow. The group made its way up and down a long series of wooded gullies, and finally emerged into a strip of thick forest where the ground leveled out. Mixed with the larger trees were lush patches of foliage. Waist-high saplings covered the ground, and ferns and vines tumbled down from the higher tree branches.

"This should be very close," Butler said.

Rand scrutinized the area with a quick glance. "Everyone fan out. Mark, let's get the GPS locked onto those coordinates."

"I'm working on it," Shullman said. "We should be close." He looked up from the GPS, studying the forested landscape.

Cole's K-9 unit arrived and began moving in a grid pattern around the site. Several investigators worked their way in from the perimeter, tapping around in the grass with their feet, searching through the vegetation.

A red light on Shullman's GPS flashed intermittently. "It should be right about here." He took a step backward and pointed to a small boulder that protruded from the ground. Next to the large rock was a massive oak tree that was flanked by two small earth mounds.

"Bring the dogs over," Rand said.

The K-9 team commander held up four fingers, and the officers with German shepherds released their animals. The four dogs burst forward and explored the area around the oak tree. The animals anxiously probed through the plants and dead leaves with their noses, sniffing back and forth as they went. After a few moments, they stopped and stared back at their handlers.

"There's nothing here," Cole said. "Are you sure this is the right area?"

Shullman glanced at the contour codes on the GPS. "Yes, this is the right spot. We should be right on top of it."

Rand folded his arms and looked at David. "Was there more, Father?"

"That's all of it," David said.

"It appears that you all got played," Butler said. He took a sip of water from a silver canteen. He leaned his head back and drenched his face and hair with water from the canteen. While looking up, he noticed something odd about the branches higher up in the oak tree. He dried his face on his shirtsleeve and stepped back, looking up at the top of the tree again. The limbs were trimmed off on one side.

It wasn't natural, he thought. He stared down at the boulder with a puzzled expression. A layer of dead vines clung to the stone like old fingers. The exposed right side of the boulder was almost perfectly round. The top and left side of the rock were covered with earth and overgrown with thick patches of green moss.

"What are you looking at?" Rand said.

Butler shook his head. "I don't know. It may be nothing." He knelt next to the bolder and rubbed away the thin layer of dirt and moist lichens. "Or maybe there is something after all."

"What is it?" Rand said.

"There's a mark—possibly an inscription—on the side of this rock." He produced a small paintbrush from his back pocket and continued sweeping around the side of the stone. Soon an engraved pattern emerged.

"This stone is a marker," Butler said with finality. "The inscription is too worn to read."

"What are you talking about?" Rand said.

Butler stood up. "We're close to something." He took a step backward and surveyed the ground around the base of the tree again. "Here," he said, pointing to the soil a few feet to the right of the boulder. There was a slight crater-shaped indentation in the ground, measuring eight feet in diameter. "I didn't notice it at first glance due to the dense layer of underbrush," said Butler. With his foot he pushed aside a layer of dead leaves and undergrowth, exposing the soil at the edge of the circular depression. "Can you see how the dirt changes colors? The soil inside the circle is a tarnished color. I don't know how our field teams missed this before."

"What do you think it is?" Parker said.

"What makes you think it's anything?" Rand said.

"That's easy," said Butler. "We have two indicators: the engraved boulder and the sheared-off tree limbs."

"Who would go to the trouble to climb all the way up there?" David said.

"They wouldn't. Those limbs were cut off when this tree was a sapling."

Rand looked skeptical. He held out his arms in semicircle, gauging the width of the tree trunk. "That tree would have to be over two hundred years old," he said.

"I would guess that it's closer to four hundred," Butler said.

"Why would someone need to trim off the tree limbs?"

Butler said, "That would depend on what the hole in the ground was used for. Early settlers would commonly dig a hole next to a tree so they could use the trunk as a platform. They would attach a wooden support to the trunk, along with a rope and bucket, that they would use to hoist material in and out of the hole they dug. It could be a well, or—"

"A grave," Rand said. "Let's start digging. Let's see who Fain has put in here."

"Now wait just a minute," Butler said. He stepped into the indentation and began clearing away leaves with his feet. "It's fairly obvious that there is something here, but even a layman can see that this ground has not been disturbed for a very long time."

Rand shook his head. "We will need to see what is underneath that stain."

Butler frowned. "It will need to be excavated."

"We'll take care of that for you." Rand motioned for his men with shovels to come over.

Butler stepped in front of the officers. "You can't just start digging. Boundaries will need to be established, topography charted, a site map will need to be drawn up, and a control pit needs to be dug. I'll need to define the site conditions."

"No time for any of that," Rand said. "Gentlemen, let's get those shovels moving."

The officers brushed past Butler and formed a semicircle around the perimeter of the crater.

"This is federal land," Butler said, pointing a finger in Rand's direction. "You're violating the law."

"Hold up, men," Rand said. He turned to Butler. "We have strong evidence that a known murderer has tampered with this site."

"And from what I've observed," said Butler, "it's my professional opinion that it would be impossible."

"We have to be certain."

"Then let *me* start the dig," said Butler. "If we find that there is no sign of recent human habitation, my students and I take over the site; and if we discover a victim, then you can have it."

Rand thought about it for a moment and then nodded. "Fair enough, and we take over even if the victim's remains are commingled with artifacts?"

"Agreed," Butler said, smiling.

Rand motioned for his men to move back.

Butler said, "I'll just need to make a quick grid reference." He took off his backpack and retrieved a small camera. He placed a scale stick on the ground and took photographs from several angles around the perimeter of the depression. He retrieved a bundle of foot-long metal spikes and twine, measured a square around the site, and carefully placed the metal spikes and string to form a grid around the open area.

Butler then moved into a roped-off quadrant near the edge. He unfolded a small hand shovel and began to scrape away the upper levels of soil. He removed the first layer of surface debris and piled it neatly outside the rope. He made a quick sketch and a notation in his field logbook, and continued digging. He probed at the wet soil with the tip of his shovel and dug a thin trench, stopping between each scoop of dirt to examine the sediment on the end of his shovel. The subsoil was thick and damp. It had a rust color with dark gray marble swirls mixed throughout the layers.

Butler continued to dig for a while, pausing periodically to check his shovel and wipe the sweat from his face. He crouched down on one knee and examined an area on the sidewall of the pit. He looked puzzled. A strange pipe-like tentacle protruded from the earth.

Parker stepped closer. "Is that a human arm?"

"Is it?" Rand said. He stepped closer and handed Butler a plastic water bottle.

"Thanks," Butler said. He took a long sip of water and coughed. "Relax, it's just a root." He took a moment to catch his breath, then resumed the excavation. After several moments of digging, he reached the one-meter mark. The soil was now a pinkish brown color and was becoming more difficult to dig through. He stabbed the end of the shovel into the dirt again. Something thumped just below the surface. He laid his shovel to the side and knelt down and began sweeping away the next layer of clay sediment with his bare hands. He suddenly stood to his feet, smiling.

"What is it?" Rand asked

"Unbelievable," Butler said. "It's absolutely remarkable."

"Why are you smiling?" Parker said.

"Nothing short of scholarly ecstasy, my friends. There's no other thrill quite like it. Take a look." Butler reached down and wrestled with something in the earth. After a moment there was a sucking sound. He pulled back and held up what looked like a rusty, dirt-encrusted salad bowl.

"What is it?" Rand said.

"A helmet," Parker said.

Butler smiled. "Good eye. That's exactly what it is. And it's still attached to the owner's head."

"Is there a skull in that helmet?" Rand asked.

"No. I noticed the top of the skull when I pulled the helmet out. I'll have to dig the skull out. And by the look of the gash in this helmet, and the hole in the skull, I might just have my own murder mystery to solve—a four-hundred-year-old murder. The coordinates were just too precise. It's absolutely amazing. Do you have any idea what we have found here? I really have to talk to your source. I have to know how he knew about this place. Do you mind if I talk with him?"

"That might prove to be a difficult proposition," Rand said, "since he was executed last night."

"Oh," Butler said, disappointed. He retrieved a towel from his bag and wiped the dirt from his hands. He took several photographs of the partially excavated crater and made another entry in his logbook. He stared at the hole in the ground, trying to decide how to approach the dig next. After a moment he crouched down and began working on the cranial remains.

"Could anyone else have known about this location?" Parker said.

Butler laughed and held up a dirt-encrusted skull. "The only one who knew about this place...well, you're looking at him."

Rand looked agitated. "How old is that skull?"

"Older than your investigation," Butler said.

"We will need to verify that. I think it's time for my men to get back involved here."

"What are you talking about?"

"I think it's time for us to take over this dig. It was by no coincidence that we found this site. A known killer knew of this place. Just like you said, the coordinates were too precise. I'll need a list of every student and all the teams involved in the exploration of this site and the neighboring ravines. My men will continue the dig. They will photograph the site and you can reconstruct the entire pit once we're satisfied. Dr. Parker is a forensic pathologist. She can supervise the dig."

"Is that true?" Butler asked. "You're a pathologist?"

"Yes," said Parker.

Butler handed her the skull. "Could you tell Agent Rand here that the age marker in this skull predates his investigation? Predates America, even."

Dr. Parker examined the skull. "It's old," She said. "There's no doubt about that, but what we're interested in is what else is in there with it. You could be upsetting potential evidence by being in there."

"I thought we agreed that this ground has never been disturbed. This is a historic site and is ultimately protected by historic preservation."

"Not when it interferes with a federal investigation," Rand said. "This is a crime scene."

Butler stepped between Rand and the pit. "You will be permanently upsetting this site."

"Move aside Professor, or you'll be up on charges for obstructing justice. I'll have you arrested and you can read about how I bulldozed the whole area from a jail cell."

"How about a little help here, Sheriff?" Butler said.

"It appears you boys have reached an impasse," said the Sheriff. "It's not my call, but can I suggest a compromise? I really don't see the harm in letting Butler's staff participate in the dig. It is their expertise and they will be under your supervision. And if we have to wait for a court decision…well, that could really slow things down."

Rand stared thoughtfully at the indentation in the ground. Time was wasting, he thought, and it didn't appear that Butler was going to budge.

"Well?" Butler said.

"Okay," Rand said. "But I want it expedited. I want it dug out today."

"You can't be serious."

"Today," Rand said.

"Well, if I agree to a quick dig, then I want to take a look around under the surface. What kind of soil scanning equipment do you have?"

"You name it," Rand said. He looked at the investigators who had assembled behind him. "Mark, do we have the ground radar here yet?"

"It's on its way over."

"We're wasting daylight," Parker said.

Rand said, "Doctor Butler, you may continue the dig, but under the supervision of the FBI. As long as you understand that this site holds clues to resolving a murder, and that the artifacts you wish to protect are secondary to that aim."

Butler nodded. "Agreed, and it will be my pleasure to prove that you've all been wasting your time."

Rand pointed past Butler. "Here comes your ground scanner."

An agent on a four-wheeled ATV came up the hill, towing a small trailer. "Where do you want it?" the agent asked, raising his voice over the sound of the four-wheeler's engine.

Rand gestured toward the partially excavated pit.

The agent gave a thumbs-up sign and switched off the ATV. He opened the door of the trailer and rolled out the radar unit. The device looked like a futuristic lawn mower with oversized rubber wheels and two antennas. The name INTELLIDAR INC. was stenciled in large yellow letters on its side. Two officers helped guide the device over the uneven terrain. They waited while a group of officers removed Butler's framework of ropes and spikes. Once the area was clear, they eased the radar unit into the shallow crater.

An agent wearing a backpack attached a data pad to the handle bar, converting the tablet into a hands-free control station. Rand and Butler waited for the system to boot up.

"Use red, green, and blue," Rand said.

"Red has been preprogrammed for bones," said the operator. "I'll set green for metal and blue for the surrounding soil. Do you want any other variables?"

"No," Rand said. "Let's see one meter. Professor, drop that skull back into the hole for a reference marker."

Butler reluctantly stepped closer to the pit and placed the skull back into the hole. He stood next to Rand and watched the radar monitor. The skull showed up on the display as dark red circle and contrasted sharply with the bright indigo background.

"One meter," the agent said. "Let me refresh the screen."

Shullman, Parker, and David watched as the monitor changed color. The display remained all blue, except for the red sphere that represented the skull and a small wedge of green at the bottom right corner."

"That's a shard of something metal." Rand said. "Switch to a magnetic scan."

"I was just about to do that," said the operator. "Here it goes." The agent pushed a button on his keyboard and waited. Several more green colored fragments appeared on the monitor screen.

"What do you make of that, Professor?"

"Probably a pottery kiln or a smith," said Butler. "I'm seeing a lot of pieces of armor and weapons. Those long shafts appear to be musket barrels and armored breast plates," he said, pointing toward the bottom of the screen. "And some iron links. They appear to be chains. See all the circles?"

"Lots of them," Parker said.

"Are you satisfied yet?" Butler said.

"Go deeper," Rand said. "Go down another foot and switch off the magnetic sensor. All that metal is playing havoc with the frequency."

The technician nodded and programmed in the coordinates. After a few moments the image reset with new colors.

"Red," Shullman said.

"More bones," Rand said. The screen resembled a tie-dyed shirt, a series of coconut-sized red circles mixed with multi-shaped patches of blue and green. The screen changed again. More red circles appeared.

"Set a marker on that coordinate," Rand said. "Drop down one more meter and switch to a higher resolution. I want to see an actual image."

The agent nodded and pushed another button. The background faded to white, then slowly came back into view as a grainy, dark image that resembled an ultrasound.

"Oh my God!" Parker said. "Those are all—"

"Skulls," David said soberly.

The grisly find seemed to have no effect on Rand. "Keep going down," he said. "Set it for one-meter increments. Capture each image."

"We can only go five meters," the technician said.

Rand nodded. "Go ahead."

The screen changed again.

"It's packed with bones," Parker said.

Shullman nodded. "A mass grave."

"This is absolutely amazing," Butler said. "And I'm very sorry, gentlemen."

"For what?" Rand said.

"It should be apparent to you by now that these bones have nothing to do with your investigation. I'm sincerely sorry for that. However, I am delighted that your source was able to pinpoint this location. This has the appearance of a mass execution—larger and possibly predating the Wolstenhome Towne massacre of 1622. This is an extraordinary moment for academia."

"Is that what you think?" Rand said.

"Who would have put all of those bodies in that hole?" David said.

Butler thought for a moment. "It's my guess that this hole was once a well, and was later converted into a mass grave. I find it to be most peculiar, though, because this kind of practice is unprecedented between the colonists and the Indians. The colonists would never have stuffed the dead into their water supply, and I can't imagine the natives doing it. From the radar image, there appear to be bits and pieces of Indian objects commingled with colonial artifacts. If it is determined that there are Indian remains in there, then there are other variables at work here."

"How can you tell from those images who is buried in there?" Parker said.

"Or how old the bones are?" Rand said.

"Well, of course I'll need to make a closer inspection, but from the images that I've seen on the monitor, there were several native Indian weapons buried in there. I saw several tomahawk heads, and arrows mixed in with the early colonial artifacts."

"Wonderful," Rand said.

"I'm sorry it didn't work out for you, Detective."

Parker turned to Rand. "You didn't think it was going to be that easy, did you?"

"This time I was kind of hoping it was," said Rand. "I have a feeling we're right back where we started." He looked at his watch and slapped at an insect on his wrist. "I'm going to hop a flight back to New York."

"You're not coming back to Florida?" David asked.

"No," Rand said. "I have to be back to New York tonight. I'll see that you get a flight home."

"What about the dig?" Butler said. "May I continue here with my students?"

"Yes," Rand said. "You can continue the dig, and I want it dug out today."

"That's impossible," Butler said, frowning. "It will take months."

Rand shook his head. "It will have to be today. I'm going to leave an agent behind to supervise. I will need a mineralization scan of each bone fragment that comes out of there to determine the time since death. I'm still not fully convinced that Fain wasn't able to get something into that hole. There's something not adding up here. And if it's okay with you, Father, I'm going to have an agent from our branch office on Marco Island watch you for a couple days."

David looked worried. "Do you think that I'm in danger?"

"No, I don't." He put his hand on David's shoulder and guided him a short distance from the group. "Don't be alarmed, Father, it's strictly routine. You can decline the offer, but I would like you to think about letting us keep an eye on you. Fain seemed to take a special interest in you, and with his body being abducted...well, there appears to be an unforeseen element at work." He handed David his business card. "I'm sure you have nothing to worry about. We'll have you watched for a couple days, and if you ever need to contact me, you have both my mobile and office number. I would also like us to agree on a safety word that we'll keep between the two of us. An object of some kind— something that's easily remembered."

"Let me think," David said. "I'm drawing a blank."

"It can be anything."

"How about a tree? That's the image I use for my online banking account."

Rand smiled. "A tree is fine. And remember to keep it just between the two of us. If you find it necessary to contact me or my team, we'll know it's you, and vice versa."

"You guys think of everything."

Rand smiled cheerlessly. "If only that were true."

13

THE PIT

Two floodlights mounted on six-foot-high tripods illuminated the large hole in the earth. Insects fluttered in and out of the bright lights. Dr. Alan Butler stood next to the pit, holding a mud-crusted rope that disappeared into the shaft. He swatted his hand through the swarm of insects. The bugs parted briefly and then returned in a frenzy.

On the opposite side of the pit, a gas generator shuddered loudly and a large yellow hose ran beside it, siphoning out a dark mixture of mud and water.

"Okay," a man's voice said from deep within the hole.

Butler felt a tug on the other end of the rope, and he began to pull up the line. After a moment, a large sludge-filled crate came into view. Butler sat the wooden box on the ground, unhooked the muddy twine, and examined the finds. Mixed with the wet earth were a variety of skeletal remains, armor plates, and two metal fin-shaped helmets. He handed the packed container to one of his students and lowered another empty crate into the hole. He wiped his hands on a mud-caked towel and then turned and angled the floodlight closer to the hole.

Not far from the pit, four additional floodlights illuminated a twelve-by-twenty-foot blue canvas tarp that was covered with more than a dozen piles of partially excavated bones and early-seventeenth-century artifacts. A tall FBI agent with blond hair stood a short distance away, sipping coffee from a thermos and watching over the students as they sorted through their finds.

Butler walked over to the tarp and supervised the student excavators as they worked. *The students are exhausted*, he thought. They had been digging all day, and the excitement they had all felt earlier from making such an extraordinary discovery was gone. "There's a treasure trove of artifacts here," he said under his breath. He shook his head and exhaled, exasperated.

"Are you talking to yourself now, Dr. Butler?" a female student said, walking up next to him. Her white T-shirt was smeared with mud and both of her arms were covered in thick, red clay up to each elbow.

"Just a little frustrated is all," Butler said. "This is a magnificent find, and the dig shouldn't be rushed. This site deserves our constant attention and months of careful excavation."

"I've never seen so many bones," said the student.

Butler nodded. "A mass grave. Most of the skulls exhibit evidence of blunt force trauma."

"Do you think it's an Indian and settler clash like the evidence we've seen over at site C, the Wolstenhome Towne massacre?"

"No, this is different. This was a massacre of both Indians and settlers, with the slaughter of men, women, and children. I've never seen or heard of anything like it."

One of the young men came over. "Dr. Butler, how much longer will you need us tonight?" He stared down at his wristwatch, angling it toward the light. "I mean, I'm not complaining, but we've been at it all day, and now we're cutting into my Saturday night, and the pressure canister is almost out of rinse water."

"Someone will just have to go back down to the lake and refill it," Butler said.

"Do you know how far the lake is?"

Butler nodded. "Well, until we can get a waterline out this far—"

"I know, I know. I'll refill it, but I'm going to need help this time."

A muffled voice came from deep within the hole. "Dr. Butler...I think I've found something,"

Butler stepped to the edge of the pit. "What is it, Thomas?"

"I've hit something," said Thomas. "It's wooden, or wood of some kind." His voice sounded muted, absorbed by the long tunnel of mud. "I don't think I can dig through it."

Butler peered into the hole in the ground. He could make out the light on Thomas's hard hat moving around in the dark, twelve feet below. "Make sure you mark that spot," said Butler. "What do you think it is?"

"I don't know, but when I hit it with the shovel it sounds hollow, like a trunk or something. It could possibly be an aquifer."

"Not out of wood," Butler said. "You better come up. I want to have a look."

"There's something else."

"What is it?"

Several more students came over and stared into the hole.

Butler held his hands out. "Not too close, guys. The edge is very slippery. I don't want anyone falling in." He picked up a rope that was tied off around the base of the oak tree. He looped the line around his hand and yanked on it several times, testing the slack. He carefully leaned out over the hole and aimed his flashlight down. He could see Thomas's outline working at the bottom of shaft. "Thomas?" he said.

Thomas looked up. "Oh, hi, Dr. Butler." He pushed the yellow hose into the mud. There was a loud slurping sound. After a moment the floor cleared, revealing a hard surface. "Listen to this," he said. He picked up his shovel and struck it against the ground. The impact made a loud wooden drum sound. "Did you hear that?" he said.

Butler nodded. "Yes, that's very interesting."

"And take a look at this."

Butler watched as Thomas stepped backward and angled the light on his hard hat toward the sidewall.

"Dr. Butler, can you see?"

"No, not from this angle.... What is it?"

"I'm not exactly sure, but it looks like a door."

PART II

IMMORTAL

Destiny is but a phrase of the weak human heart—the dark apology for every error. The strong and virtuous admit no destiny. On earth conscience guides; in heaven God watches. And destiny is but the phantom we invoke to silence the one and dethrone the other.

—Edward George Earle Lytton Bulwer-Lytton (1803–73)

14

THE GIFT

David Anslem's church, the Victory, was a small white building in a tree-lined meadow, thirty miles south of Naples, Florida. A white, three-rail stable fence bordered the church, and rows of floodlights angled up from the ground, illuminating the structure's cross-topped bell tower.

Inside the church, David stood behind the pulpit in the dim light of the empty worship hall, reflecting on the bizarre events of the past twenty-four hours. Being back in familiar surroundings helped him to smooth out his cluttered thoughts. He glanced at the long stained-glass window that dominated the wall behind the altar. The window's multicolored panes portrayed images of heaven and earth with a host of divine angels in between. *Everything is in its proper place*, he thought.

He turned his attention to the small organ to his right. He smiled as he thought of sweet, elderly Ms. Janes, who had already lain out her composition and had opened the music to one of David's favorite pieces. He swept his eyes over the sanctuary. The hymnals were perfectly spaced on padded pews. Below the altar, new candles had been set, and the servers' white robes were pressed and hung in perfect rows, ready for the next day's communion.

David took a breath; the air hinted of fresh cut flowers and was slightly musty. *It's good to be home.* He came down and sat on the front pew. He placed his cell phone and car keys on the seat and stretched his legs out. It had been a long and bumpy flight back from Virginia, and he was exhausted. He was just about to doze off when he suddenly became aware of someone moving down the aisle behind him.

A man dressed in black passed close to David's pew. He stopped just in front of the pulpit and waited with his back toward David. For several moments, the man stood in the dim light, looking up at the stained-glass window.

"May I help you?" David said.

"I like this window," the man said. "God's angels ascending...heavenward. And the silver cross, ever a reminder of God's victory over sin and death."

David got to his feet. There was something about the man's voice that struck him as familiar.

"Is the church closed?" the man asked.

"Confession was from five to five-thirty, and vigil was at six. The last service ended at eight o'clock. I don't mean to be rude, but it has been a long day, and—"

"I can only imagine," the man said. He turned around.

"Fain..." David gasped, and staggered backward, staring up at Harold Fain with an expression of disbelief. *It's not possible*, he thought. The man standing in front of him was an exact copy of the prisoner he had seen condemned to death the night before. He wore the same black metallic clothing and had the same face: ashen skin and unnatural eyes that swirled with color like some nightmarish kaleidoscope.

"I thought that we might continue our earlier conversation," Fain said. He walked over to where David was standing.

"You're dead," David sputtered.

"I'm alive."

"It's not possible. You were condemned to death."

"But you see...I am fated to life."

"You, you died. I saw you die."

"I cannot die."

"Impossible!" David said, and he immediately turned and ran toward his office, pausing briefly by the door to steal a glance over his shoulder.

"You have nothing to fear, David," Fain said, still standing in front of the sanctuary.

David lunged into his office and bolted the door behind him. He dug in his pocket for his cell phone…and remembered that he had left his phone and car keys in the front pew. He went to his desk and picked up the phone. There was no dial tone.

Frantic thoughts ran through his mind. He went to the treasury safe and retrieved an old Colt .45 caliber handgun. He chambered a bullet and returned to the office door. He waited and listened. He heard only the sound of his own anxious breathing.

Several moments passed. Finally David mustered the courage to go back into the sanctuary. He cracked the door and peeked through. Fain stood near the altar, waiting. He turned his gazed toward David.

"I mean you no harm, David."

David opened the door wider. "Who are you?"

"I'm Harold Fain."

"Harold Fain is dead."

"I am the same man you met yesterday.

"That's impossible."

"Not for me."

"We'll just ask agent Rand what he thinks about this."

"Rand," Fain mused. "What will you tell him and his ruthlessly skeptical band of detectives? What do you think they will say?"

"I don't know."

"Don't you want answers?" Fain said. "It will be in your best interest to hear me out. But if you wish for me to leave…"

"Wait," David said, stepping out of his office. He paused briefly and then walked over to where Fain was standing. He made sure to keep his distance, and held his weapon forward, so Fain could see it.

"A gun," Fain said sedately. "And what do you propose to do with that relic?"

"It was my grandfather's. It might be old, but it still fires, and it has a hair trigger, so stay where you are." David felt weak, and his hands trembled as he tried to keep the gun leveled in Fain's direction.

Fain took a half step closer and raised his hand in a nonthreatening manner. "You are in no danger from me, David; but if you were, do you believe that your gun could do any better than the thousands of volts produced by the electric chair?"

"I don't know, but if you come any closer, we're going to find out. Tell me who you are?"

"I am Harold Fain."

"And I saw Harold Fain die," David said, and he jumped suddenly as the gun unexpectedly went off in his hand with a loud report. A bullet discharged and struck the empty pew behind Fain, sending shards of wood and pieces of cushion into the air.

"Oh my God!" said David. "I didn't mean to do that."

Fain nodded. "Do you recall our earlier conversation outside my cell, when you told me that you would not be willing to kill for everlasting life?"

"Yes."

"It appears that you were not telling the truth."

David shook his head. "My feelings regarding that have not changed."

"Yet here you are, prepared to kill me now to preserve your own life. You would kill me to protect your remaining years."

"It's different," David said, staring down at the weapon. "How can this be happening?" He lowered the gun and looked up. "How can you still be alive?"

"I'm not like you, David."

"I don't believe you."

"Is my presence here not undeniable proof?"

"I watched them pronounce Harold Fain....Harold Fain is dead!"

"And I'm telling you that I cannot die."

"What do you want?"

"Come, I want to show you something." He motioned for David to follow him toward the back of the church. They walked down the right side of the sanctuary and came to a door that led outside.

"Have a look," Fain said, gesturing toward the exit.

"Outside?"

Fain nodded.

David turned the lock and opened the door. He glanced at Fain suspiciously before turning his gaze outside.

"That's our cemetery," said David.

"Farther out," Fain said.

David opened the door wider and stared into the darkness. Beyond the field of tombstones a single streetlamp illuminated a vacant gravel parking lot. Next to the gravel square was a narrow tree-lined dirt road. A white sedan was parked on the grass shoulder. The driver's side door was open, and a man's body hung halfway out of the vehicle, the upper half of his torso slumped on the ground.

"One of Rand's men," Fain said. "Left here to watch you."

"Protect me," David said.

"He failed."

"What have you done?"

"I did nothing to him. I found the agent as you see him now."

"Then who?" David said.

"Have a look closer in."

David looked around in the dark. "I don't see anything." He flipped a switch on the wall and an floodlight illuminated a cement path that led into the cemetery. Two men in black lay motionless on the ground beneath a long row of gardenia bushes.

"If I had not intervened, you would not be alive now," Fain said. "It would have been easy for them...with you being isolated all the way out here in the country."

David stepped away from the door. "Could someone please tell me what is going on here?"

"You are in great danger, David." Fain closed the door and turned the bolt. "They were coming for you, and they will again."

"Who are they, and why me?"

"I'll tell you everything if you will listen and believe me."

"I'm listening."

"Very well," Fain said. "When I met you in prison, you appeared to me to be an honorable man, a man I could trust. I sensed the conflict in you as you wrestled for my soul. In your heart you truly wished to save me, a man whom the world believed to be irredeemable. You even helped me by agreeing to partner with the agents."

"I thought I was helping the agents."

"And you *were* helping them. It was an equal exchange. Did you not gain information from me that proved useful to agent Rand's investigation?"

"Information? Are you referring to Carter's Grove? They didn't find a body there."

"Did you give them the location?"

"I did. They found some old historic grave site, but discovered nothing related to their investigation."

"I see," Fain said. He turned and walked back into the main worship hall.

David followed behind him. "Why have you involved me in your affairs?"

Fain stopped in front of the pulpit and turned toward David. "I needed someone to broker the deal for my early execution."

"A deal that didn't make any sense," David said. He looked at the gun in his hand and placed it on the pulpit. "It was a bargain that no one understood and still doesn't understand: the early execution, the phone call to Spain, the wasted trip to Virginia, and your victim turning out to be a CIA agent. Is it true? Was Rory Gelder an agent?"

"Yes."

"And you knew that when you killed her."

"Yes."

"Why?"

"Dr. Gelder had information that I needed."

"So you just killed her for it?"

"It was an act of mercy. If I had not taken her life, her associates would have."

"Another CIA agent would have killed her?"

"Yes. Gelder reported to a man named Jack Simons. Do you remember me mentioning him to you in prison?"

"Yes."

"Simons assigned Gelder control of a government-sponsored laboratory specializing in bioweapons called Strategic Labs. The lab was privately owned, but the CIA funded and managed it. Gelder oversaw a classified program code named Legion—a 'super soldier' program. There is also another player, a hidden controller who manipulated both Gelder and Simons. His name is Pan. He provided Gelder with the genetic blueprint for an advanced human."

"Is Pan a scientist?"

"No. Pan and I are similar in nature. We are adversaries. It was by his direction that the Legion project was initiated. And it was by his mechanisms, or manifestations if you will, that Gelder's chief geneticist Warren Ricktor was able to achieve a most astonishing scientific breakthrough. Pan and Gelder conspired to lure Simons in with the promise of a superior human being; they produced several viable prototypes. They created a false file on me. They told Simons that I was their prime example. They ransacked their own facility and killed all witnesses, claiming that I escaped with their formula. With such lies they were able to easily convince Simons to commit his CIA resources to hunt me. Simons, ignorant of the truth, believes me to be nothing more than a genetically altered rogue agent on a murder spree, bent on destroying my creators and ultimately purging all evidence of my ominous origin. They were correct on one account: I do mean to kill them all."

"Why?"

"The echelon of life must be enforced."

"I don't understand."

"Suffice to say that no human will ever obtain our DNA."

"If Pan is like you, then why would he give it to Simons?"

"To provoke me."

"Why?"

"Because we are adversaries, and in our war he continues to direct Simons against me. Pan is unpredictable, and a master manipulator, whose methods are beyond Machiavellian. His own means are vast, but rarely does he commit them. And why should he, when he can easily control another's resources? *Human* resources. In Simons' fervor to obtain this new science that Pan has provided, he ignores an all-important military axiom: 'Never create a weapon that you have no defense against.' Simons tampers with knowledge beyond his comprehension, never truly under his control. What he seeks is impossible to manage, and if left unchecked, would create a great deal of chaos in your world and, in time, even mine. Gelder was seduced by power and overcome by greed, and in the end she betrayed both Pan and Simons."

"And this Pan character?" David said. "You said that the two of you share the same ancestry…then you are related?"

"We are similar in physiology, but that is all."

"Does he share the same unique abilities that you do? Your ability to cheat death?"

"Yes."

"How is it accomplished?"

"I can only tell you that life is a mystery and I simply have more of it than most."

"That's not an answer."

"That's all I can tell you at this time."

"Will you tell me who the dead men are out on the church lawn?"

"They were agents, David. You are one of the few remaining loose ends, and Simons sent them to kill you."

"Then because of you I am involved, and in danger of losing my life."

"That's why I'm here," Fain said. He walked over to the left side of the sanctuary where a small door led outside. He checked the lock and peered through a four-pane window in the top of the door.

David could see Fain's reflection in the series of glass frames. "What are you looking at out there?"

"It's not safe here, David."

"What can I do, abandon my church and go into hiding? I don't think so. I think I should call Rand or the police."

"They can't help you," Fain said, still staring out the window. "Only I can help you now."

"You're the one who caused all of this. What can you do?"

"I can remake you, David. You can become like me."

"Like a cold-blooded killer?"

"Not a killer…. Invincible."

"Invincible?"

"Immortal," Fain said.

"Just when I thought it couldn't get any crazier."

"Why do you look so surprised?" Fain said, turning from the window.

"You can make me live forever?" said David.

"Yes."

"I'm not saying that I even believe you, but why me?"

"I involved you in this, and I feel compelled to watch over you," said Fain.

"Rand can offer me protection," said David, "once he sees what happened to his man here tonight. The FBI can protect me. I'll change my name or whatever I have to do."

"How can Rand safeguard you, when he can't protect himself? The clues I've provided bring him ever closer to the truth—a truth that will ultimately prove his undoing. Now that you are part of his investigation, you have been targeted."

"But you partnered me with him before. You even said yourself that it was to keep me safe."

"It is true that if I had not given you information vital to their investigation, and insisted that you stay close to them, you would not be alive now. But now you are no longer useful to them. They sent those two men to deal with you. And now that I've helped you, they will be even more eager to interrogate you. If you want to survive, it will be necessary for you to become like me. Think of it as a parting gift."

"Listen to me," said David. "I'm not sure about this private war that you, Simons, and whoever is waging here, but it doesn't involve me, and I want out."

"I'm afraid that it's too late for that. The question now is, do you want to live or die?"

"I want to live, of course."

"Then I will help you. I will save you from Simons and the one he ultimately serves."

"What would he and Simons want from me?" said David.

"They will have to make certain that I haven't influenced you."

"But you haven't."

"They will need to make certain of that," said Fain.

"How?" said David.

"I can assure you that it won't be pleasant. But I can prevent that from happening. I can save you."

"And if I agree, what then?"

"You would be immortalized, and in time, it will be within your power to save yourself." Fain paused. "What is your answer, David?"

There was a moment of silence as David thought about Fain's offer.

"They will kill you, David."

"I'm in God's hands," David said. "If it's his wish to have my life back, then who am I to argue?"

Fain folded his hands behind his back and stared up at the stained glass. "Your faith is courageous, David. When Simons finds you, there will be no reward for such loyalty. You will never see heaven. You will never know if your faith was warranted. It will be out of mine, yours, or God's control." He turned, facing David once again. "One or more of Pan's Relaters will accompany Simons. They won't care about your faith or your beliefs; they will only want what is inside you. They will want your soul."

"What?" David stammered. "Soul? What are you saying? I mean, if this is all true as you claim, then you and your kind compete with God as if you are somehow *like* God. To take what you offer would make my faith void, and all of God's promises nullified."

"And to decline my offer is a betrayal of reason," said Fain. "I'm offering you everlasting life. I can't tell you what will happen after death; no one can. But I can assure you that it won't be what you expect or can even imagine, and there is the potential that resides outside your faith and hope that nothing exists at all. What I can say for certain is that within me exists power more potent than mortal life."

"What of God's commandments?"

"God's apocalyptic code does not apply to me."

David shook his head. "Then you claim to be sinless?"

"I'm not without sin, but where there is no law there is no violation—no more concepts of good or evil, life and death, or young and old."

"And in your existence, no heaven," David said.

"Or hell. Only you, David, encased in eternal youth, and every moment of your life spent in pursuit of life's pleasures. Or, if you so choose...preserving the ones you love."

"And you can do that?"

"Yes."

"You have that power?"

"I have the power to make you into what you desire to be: exalted into a higher rank of being. I have the power to give back your youth and a life without pain. Imagine it, David: perpetual exemption from all the horrors of this world. You will still be David Anslem, maintaining all that you are now, still devoted to God, but a mighty force, free from vice or infirmity. Imagine for a moment what you could accomplish if you did not have to sleep or eat, no sickness, wants, or necessities?"

"What do you stand to gain by doing this?"

"I ask for nothing," said Fain. "I offer no terms. Besides, for me to offer you a greater power for want of something in return would be a sin in your eyes, would it not?"

"Yes. And you say that you've done this to others?"

"Yes, but there have been only a few that I have I given what I now offer you. There have been countless others that I have seized from death's door, and now safeguard their eternal essence."

"Their souls," David said.

"I saved them from death."

"Robbed them of true salvation."

"You speak of illusions, David. Heaven, offered in terms uncertain. But I offer something more, something wonderful. Through me, you could live eternally, roaming this world forever, taking it as the paradise that it was meant to be. Or would you risk yourself to the grave and the realm of spirits?"

"I can't believe I'm still even listening to this."

"Let me prove it to you. It will still be your life to do with as you choose. So think hard about your decision, because the choice you make is one of life or death."

"Eternal life..." David said in a whisper. His mind ran wild with the endless possibilities. He thought about all of the things that an immortal life would allow him to accomplish. There was a gnawing voice inside him that demanded proof of Fain's words, but at what horrible cost? Was Fain the great deceiver that Rand and Parker said he was? If Fain was lying, then to what possible sinister purpose or injury was his offer intended. If Fain had meant to do him harm, he surely would have done so by now. But nevertheless, he felt that Fain's proposition was wrong, and that there had to be more to his offer than it being a simple, kind gesture. Even though eternal life was now within his grasp, ultimately, accepting Fain's offer meant choosing against God, and that was something that David was not prepared to do.

"What is your answer, David?"

"My answer has to be no, Mr. Fain. I appreciate your offer, but what you have proposed to me is against everything I stand for."

"I am not the devil, David, or conjured by him, nor do I make this offer on his behalf."

"I believe you. And believe me, I want immortality. You were right about me. I do yearn for life without end...more than you know. But I don't want it like this and not from you."

"I'm disappointed," Fain said, stepping closer. "And I'm sorry."

"Sorry?"

"I can't let them have you. If time permitted, perhaps I would have allowed you to stay mortal, because I know that in time, you would change your mind. I've known so many like you. They all wish in the end that they had more time."

"Well I have to admit that I wondered if you would truly allow me to make the choice."

"Whether you believe it or not, you will have a choice."

"So now what happens?"

"Did you ever wonder what would happen if all the clocks stopped ticking?"

"I guess I wouldn't have to worry about being late," David said, smiling cheerlessly. "I mean that I suppose that it wouldn't matter… would it?"

Fain didn't answer.

"Is this a riddle?"

"Time is about to stand still, David." Fain reached forward with his right hand and gently clasped his fingers around David's neck.

From Fain's touch, David felt the sensation of a mild electric shock. His vision darkened and he suddenly felt that he was traveling backward through a bright tunnel, swept away at great speed. He heard static, and then everything abruptly went black. And then just as unexpectedly as it all began, he was awake and sitting on the floor in front of the church, disoriented. His fingers tingled, and he opened and closed his fist several times. He breathed in, and the air tickled his lungs. He felt more alive than he ever had.

"You're still here," he said, looking up at Fain. "I thought it was all a bad dream."

"Not a dream," Fain said. "There are no dreams in death."

"Dead?"

Fain slowly nodded. "Yes."

"And you brought me back to life?"

"Yes."

"That's ridiculous."

"It doesn't change the fact that it's true. Can you tell me what you dreamt about?"

"I don't remember."

"Come now, you know that's not true."

"I didn't dream about anything. It was all black, like the deepest and dreamless sleep."

"So you see," said Fain, "you do remember."

"Is this what normally happens?"

"Is it normal that you were a disembodied spirit, pitched into the blackest of voids? Is it normal that you are now afraid because you now know that what you glimpsed is what you would have become in death?"

"No, I—"

David stopped talking when he heard loud voices from behind him. He turned, but no one was there. The voices increased in number and loudness as if some unseen crowd had just come into the room. The voices stopped, and David turned back to Fain with a stunned expression.

"Is something wrong, David?"

"I heard voices."

"Oh, but wait," Fain said. "It won't be long now, and you will hear and see much more than you can imagine. For now I know all of your secrets, and soon you will know mine."

"You're telling me that you've read my mind."

"I know everything about you."

"Impossible."

"Would you like me to tell you something about your past?"

"Okay, yes, yes I would."

"Then ask me to tell you something that only you would know."

David thought about it for a moment, then asked, "When I was a boy, what did my father say to me on the day I learned to ride my bicycle?"

Fain closed his eyes and became lost in the images of his powerful mind. "You have such wonderful memories, David." Fain smiled as he reminisced. "Your father taught you to ride your bicycle in the driveway next to his red Corvette. He was so pleased with you when you rode the bicycle alone for the first time that he didn't say anything to you. Your father just smiled proudly." Fain opened his eyes. "And that's only one memory of yours that I now hold, and it is a pleasant one. But what of the other passions of your mind? Shall I tell you of your ambitions, vanities, anger, or love?"

"No," David said. "I've heard enough."

"As you wish. But now you understand that I have all your dreams and memories, and you have mine."

"Yours?"

"Can I trust you with my secrets?"

"I don't have your memories."

"Soon you will."

David started to speak again, but stopped when the voices in his head returned. Even more voices this time. Louder. He glanced around the room, baffled. "What is happening to me?" he said.

"My memories," Fain said. "And a host of others. It will be disorienting for a time. It can be overwhelming at first, and you will be quite vulnerable. I know a place where you can recover."

David grimaced. "I'm not going anywhere with you," he said. He held his head in his hands. "Make it stop!"

"It will, in time."

"I hear all of their voices at once. I'll go mad…" He fell to his knees, still clenching his face in his hands. The voices grew louder—deafening, like the chaos of some unimaginable and tragic battlefield. He stared around the swirling room. He tried to stand.

"I have to call Rand—" David said. He collapsed onto his back, paralyzed, staring up at the ceiling with a horror-filled expression.

Fain stepped closer. After a moment, he bent down, lifted David over his shoulder, and carried him out of the church.

15

MADISON TOWER

David regained consciousness. He sat up on a bed, confused, staring around an old, dimly lit hotel room. The large chamber was adorned with tattered turn-of-the-century antique furnishing, and everything was in a state of decay. There were holes in the walls, and the furniture and floors were covered in dust and crumbling plaster.

It doesn't make any sense, he thought. He tried to think about what had happened—how he got here and how long he had been unconscious. Other than a handful of recent jumbled memories, he had a complete loss of time. He vaguely remembered the encounter with Fain at his church and the resurrected killer's absurd offer of immortality. Even more vague were the events that followed: a private plane, a limousine, arriving at this strange building, an elevator ride several floors up, and finally arriving in this room.

He noticed that his clothes had been changed. He was now wearing a strange black bodysuit. He reached down and touched the cloth on his sleeve. The material felt like silk, but thicker, with the quality of fine mesh. There was no sign of his phone, keys, or wallet; he felt naked without them.

He stepped over to a long dresser and went through the drawers in search of anything that could help identify his location. The drawers were empty. He came next to a vaulted window that was filmed over with a thick layer of dust. He wiped the residue from one of the glass panes with his hand and stared through. It was nighttime, and he saw the backdrop of an unfamiliar cityscape. There was a large office tower directly across from him. Several stories below, he could make out the rooftops of smaller buildings; and even farther below, a city street busy with people and cars.

He stared down at the dust on his hand as he considered what to do next. He took a deep breath and felt a strange tingling sensation in his lungs. He blew the dust from his open palm. There was a tingling in his chest again, and suddenly he realized why.

"Dear God in heaven," he said, taking in another breath.

He held the air in, waiting for the usual uncomfortable, internal cue that would tell him that his blood had become starved for oxygen and that he would need to breathe again. Time passed—time enough that his lungs should have been bursting for air, but they weren't. He felt the same as he had when he first breathed in the air.

"It's true," he whispered. "I should be unconscious. Fain was telling the truth. I don't have to breathe." He stared at his own reflection in the window. *How is it possible? What have I become?* David immediately went to the front of the room, flung open the door, and entered a long hallway of numbered doors. Only a handful of the original hall lights remained active; lamps dotted the corridor, going all the way to the end of the passageway. He proceeded to the end of the hall and turned right. He passed through more winding corridors. *The building must be enormous*, he thought as he continued forward.

The final corridor opened into a massive two-story ballroom. The room's furnishings had been moved to the fringe, leaving the center of the vast chamber open. A vaulted glass ceiling revealed a star-filled night sky. To his left a grand marble staircase led up to a second-level balcony. A colossal marble fireplace dominated the far right side of the room. Two throne-style chairs bracketed the hearth. A man wearing a black suit sat in the chair on the right. The man's legs sprawled forward with his bare feet flat on the ground, and his left arm dangled over the chair's hand rest. He appeared to be sleeping.

"Hello…" David said. He set out across the room toward the man. The man in the chair didn't answer, and as David came closer, he realized why. The man was dead. David stared down at the body, horror-struck.

The man's flesh was drawn tight around his bones, and the veins glowed blue under the skin. His blond hair was wild and his eyes stared forward, vacant like that of a dead bird. His head was bent forward so that his nose cast a long shadow down past his chin, and his mouth gaped open, half-smiling. David noticed that his two incisor teeth were missing.

"His name was Galatin," a man's voice said from behind David.

Startled, David turned toward the sound of the voice. A thin elderly man in a gray business suit and black tie stood not far behind him.

"Who…who are you?" said David.

"My name is Bondurant," the man said in a low-pitched voice. His speech had a cultivated tone, and he spoke with an accent that was unrecognizable. He walked up to where David was standing and held his vein-riddled hands in a steeple toward his lips, staring down at the deceased man in the chair. "Galatin—the golden one. "

David stepped backward, stealing a glancing over his shoulder. He looked for a way out.

"What's wrong?" Bondurant said.

"Everything is wrong. I was abducted and brought to this godforsaken place by a murderer, and there's a dead man in a chair. A dead man that you knew."

"All that you have spoken is true. But you must calm yourself. You needn't fear. You are in no danger here."

"That's what Fain said at my church before he…"

"He what?" Bondurant said, smiling.

"Where is he?"

"Mr. Fain will be along shortly. He left me to look after you while you are our guest here."

"Where is 'here'?"

"This is the Madison Hotel in New York, of course. Don't you remember?"

"No, I don't remember, and I'm having a hard time remembering anything past yesterday. It's as though my mind has been erased."

"And that is precisely why I'm here to look after you. Now, I suppose the polite thing to do is to ask you if there is anything you need, but I already know the answer to that question. No. You're body no longer needs anything. Well…almost nothing."

"What do you mean?"

"I think it would be best if we waited. In time you will figure it out for yourself." He turned his gaze toward the corpse in the chair again.

"I'm leaving," David said. "Where are my clothes?"

"They were discarded, and replaced by the suit that you are currently wearing. Your new attire will help improve the time of your recovery. Not only are they functional, but very stylish, I think. Don't you?"

"Recovery? What do you mean?"

"Indeed, the cloth is made of two-ply rubber and nylon webbing, and is coated with compressed, powdered steel."

"Why do I need it?"

"You're body is changing, David. Even as we speak, your cells are advancing, strengthening, your epidermis hardening, and becoming unbreakable—a body fit for eternity. So you see, your clothing too must be resilient. That unique material will also aid in restraining you."

"Restraining?"

"Dampen your body's natural electric field. But I'm getting ahead of myself. In time you will understand all that has happened to you, on your own. Mr. Fain has seen to it. It's too complex to explain, and besides, the answers you seek are already implanted into your mind."

"That's where you're wrong," David said. He walked toward the doorway. "I'm not seeking anything. I didn't ask for any of this. I just want my life back. I want out of this nightmare." He left the room.

"It's too late for that," Bondurant said, following after him.

David felt like a trapped lab rat as he moved through a maze of crumbling hallways and rooms. The doors to some rooms were locked, while others were open. He came to a long dark hallway and moved quickly toward the end of the corridor, trying to open each side door as he went. Every door that he tried was locked.

At the end of the passage he came to a final white door. He stole a glance over his shoulder. His heart jumped as the old man Bondurant entered the corridor and shuffled toward him. *I've got to find a way out of here,* he thought, and reached for the final door. The silver handle felt cold to the touch. The door opened and David was immediately met with a rush of freezing air. He stepped inside an enormous storeroom and looked around, terror stricken.

A waist-high row of human bodies had been stacked head to toe and lined the entire length of the far wall. In many areas of the room, the wooden floor was rotted through. The plaster had crumbled from the walls, exposing old, broken bricks. An entire wall had crumbled through to an adjacent room. A large warehouse-style service elevator dominated the back wall. It suddenly all made sense to David as to why the room was so cold. The entire chamber had been converted into cold storage. *It's to keep the bodies from decomposing,* he thought.

Bondurant came up and stood in the doorway behind David. "His appetite is unquenchable. He's a harvester in the season of death, and man is always in season."

David spun toward him. "You're monsters!"

"What you see here is only part of it, David—the worst part of it. In time you will be astounded. What he gave you is priceless, and something the rest of the world would be willing to kill for."

"It's an abomination," David said, angrily. "What Fain did to me, he did against my will. I want to be normal. I want to be myself again."

"To reject what Fain gave you and deny what you've become is damning to you and would be infinitely costly."

"Is that a threat?" David said. Rage welled up inside him. He felt an urge to lash out.

"The problem with you, David, is that you are a good man. That is why Fain chose you. But look around you.... See your future."

"Enough—" Fain said, coming up behind Bondurant.

With Fain's arrival, David's mind felt as if it had suddenly short-circuited. It was as if he and Fain shared a subliminal link, and Fain's psyche was seeking dominance. David heard voices inside his mind. It was just like back at the church, but there were even more voices this time. He looked away, shaking his head, trying clear his mind. He finally stared back at Fain. "You betrayed me," said David. "You said that I was in no danger from you. You took me against my will."

"No, David, if I had left you behind, they would have killed you." Fain came through the door. "You have to let go of your past."

"Stay away from me," David said. He suddenly stopped talking. His brain felt as if it was on fire. He heard more voices, and all at once, a riotous flood of memories poured into his mind. He squeezed his eyes closed in an effort to suppress the images from his thoughts, but it served only to intensify them. It became impossible for him to distinguish reality from the terrors conjured by his subconscious. He tried to focus. He looked around the room, looking for a way out. Next to the row of dead bodies he noticed a doorway. *I'll have to move quickly*, he thought, *get out of the building and find help before my mind completely shuts down again.*

David ran toward the back of the room and lunged for a side door. He turned the handle—locked. He threw his shoulder into the door. The heavy oak frame held. He glanced down at the dead bodies stacked next to him. An old man's face stared out of the horrific pile of human flesh. The man's skin was glazed over, and his mouth gaped open and his eyes glared wide. The dreadful scene served to intensify David's delirium. He stepped backward and kicked at the door with his right foot. The door caved in, taking part of the wall with it. Bricks and splintered boards crumbled into the next room. The floor creaked under the weight of the rubble and then collapsed violently into the room beneath it. The fissure in the floor expanded outward, drawing in the old furniture and many of the dead bodies that were stacked closest to the doorway.

David stepped backward to avoid being drawn into the spreading chasm. Dust from crumbling plaster clouded the room. There was silence, followed immediately by the sound of splintering wood. An instant later, the outer wall caved inward, exposing a fire escape and a background of city buildings. David looked for a way to reach the metal stairs. He noticed that an uneven perimeter of broken boards still remained around the periphery of the room. He moved forward, following along the crumbling edge. He glanced over his shoulder and saw that Fain had moved next to the break in the floor. He wondered why he wasn't trying to stop him.

"Give in, David..." Fain said.

David continued to move across the fragmented rim. He came to a spot where the overhang ended, leaving an open fissure four feet across. He would have to try to jump to the fire escape. *It's not that far*, he thought, but he was disoriented by the voices and he felt faint. He stared down to his left. Past the twisted water pipes and fractured boards, he saw where the room below had caved through to another floor in the building. An elderly woman, wearing a pink bathrobe, stood in the corridor, staring at the cascade of rubble and dead bodies. The voices and images inside his mind intensified and he staggered forward off-balance, nearly overcome by the powerful hallucinations. With a fleeting grasp of reality, he reared back and leapt over the crevice in the floor, toward the fire escape. He landed hard on the metal platform. With his added weight, the heavy metal stairs broke away from their concrete moorings, throwing him over the edge. He felt a sudden sensation of weightlessness; and the ground, fourteen stories below, moved toward him at a great speed. "God forgive me...and take me," he said.

A young Asian man stood on the curb next to his parked yellow cab, smoking a cigarette and talking on his cell phone.

David landed hard on top of the cab. The roof of the vehicle crushed in, and all the windows simultaneously exploded outward, spewing shards of glass in every direction. David came to rest on his back toward the center of the cab's crumpled roof. His legs were crossed at his ankles, and both arms were spread wide. Several passers-by stopped and gathered around the tragic scene.

"Did he jump?" an elderly woman said. She stared down at David's mangled body with an expression of shock and pity.

A man in a black and gray wind suit pushed his way through the crowd. "He jumped," the man said. "I saw him jump. I was standing in front of my camera store and saw him come out on the fire escape and jump."

A black man in a business suit stepped closer to the wrecked cab. He held his cell phone to his ear with his left hand. With his free right hand he held David's wrist. There was a pulse. "An ambulance," he said into his phone. "Send an ambulance! I don't know what happened.... I think he fell from a building." He put his hand over the phone mouthpiece. "Does anyone know the name of that building?"

"The old Madison Hotel," a woman said.

"Madison Hotel," the man said. "I don't know from how high. I didn't see it happen. The old Madison hotel.... Okay, okay, an ambulance in three minutes.... I gotcha." He slid his phone into his pocket.

All at once David sat up on the dented roof of the cab, staring forward as if he were in a trance.

"Whoa," the man in the suit said. "Just take it easy."

David stared down at both of his hands with a confused expression.

"You are one lucky son of a bitch," the man said. He glanced up at the side of Madison Tower, then back at David. "You're lucky to be alive. Do you want me to contact someone for you?"

David looked at him with a blank expression.

"What's your name?" the man asked.

David stared back down at his hands. He flexed his fingers and slowly turned his palms in and out, examining his two limbs as if they were foreign to him.

"What is your name?" the man asked again. He spoke more loudly and slowly this time.

David looked up . "My name?" he said. "I...don't know."

16

MONSTROUS

Butler steadied the rope ladder as Thomas climbed out of the pit. "It's definitely a door," Thomas said. "I didn't notice it at first because we dug straight past it. It wasn't until I uncovered the wood floor that I noticed the timbers in the sidewall. And they appear to be interconnected at the base."

"That's interesting," Butler said. He took Thomas's hard hat and put it on, and adjusted the light on top. "It's probably the base where the colonist finished digging the well."

"So you think this hole is a well?"

"It's more than likely. Did you notice any holes or openings in the wood floor?"

"No, there were no openings. It was solid lumber on the floor. Same with the door."

"And you're sure the wood didn't go all the way around the interior of the shaft? Settlers would always reinforce the walls of their wells with timbers. I'm actually kind of surprised that we haven't found more wooden trusses higher up in the walls."

"I went all the way around the perimeter with the spike," said Thomas. "I didn't detect any resistance."

Butler nodded. "Curious…" He knelt on one knee with his back toward the pit. He held on to a guide rope and inched backward on all fours, feeling for the ladder with his feet. He secured his footing on the first ladder rung and stood up on the inside of the rim, looking over his shoulder, focusing on the light bulb at the bottom of the pit.

Thomas and the other students gathered around.

"Any guesses on what we'll find on the other side of that door?" Butler said, trying to contain his excitement. "I'll bump the student that guesses correctly an entire letter grade." He took a step down.

"We all have an A in your classes already," Thomas said.

"In your dreams," Butler said.

"I think it's a food cache. Cold storage of some kind," Sidney said.

"A very good guess, Sidney," Butler said, stepping down several more rungs. "But it's awfully deep into the ground for a meat locker." He squeezed past the first crossbeam supports that they had erected. Three feet below the buttress, a second pair of crossbeams expanded outward horizontally, pressing curved wooden plates into the earthen walls. Butler moved past them. After a moment he reached the bottom and stepped off the last rung of the ladder. The wood floor clunked under his boots as he landed.

The air was damp and considerably cooler at the bottom. Butler took the hanging light bulb and shined it around the perimeter of the pit. He located the outline of the wooden frame and made a mental note that Thomas had done a thorough job cleaning around it.

"What do you think it is?" Thomas shouted down. "A door, right?"

"I don't know yet," Butler said. He stared up the shaft of mud. At the top he could see the student's heads circling the pit, staring down at him. "Make sure you're all holding on to something up there," he said. "I don't want you falling in here and breaking your neck or mine. Thomas, what did you do with the spike?"

"On the ground behind you."

Butler retrieved the spike and pushed it into the hard clay above the wooden rectangle. He hung the yellow light bulb on the end of the spike and angled the light toward the strange structure. *The wooden outline is the right size for a colonial door,* he thought—*just under six feet high.* Four railroad-size timbers framed the wooden barrier and a rusted metal mass existed where the handle would be on a normal door. *Whatever it is, it's exciting to see,* Butler thought. He paused, contemplating how he should approach the large artifact. He dried his hands on his shirt and retrieved a camera from a zippered pocket on his pants leg. He took several angled photographs of the wooden rectangle and put the camera back in his pocket.

"You did a great job prepping it, Thomas!"

"I was taught by the best," said Thomas.

"You're such a suck-up," one of the other students teased.

Butler continued to examine the object, listening to the students as they laughed and talked high above him. The interior wood was indented slightly from the outer framework, and there was grooved border still packed with mud. Butler retrieved a small flat spade from his bag and pushed it into the slit at the top of the frame. The metal edge penetrated the mud easily, and he began to move the blade back and forth horizontally, clearing the sludge away. He continued cleaning down the left and right side of the door.

"Someone lower down a crowbar," said Butler. "Make it the five-pounder with the chisel end."

"Is it a door?" Thomas said.

"I'm inclined to believe so," Butler said. "We'll soon find out." *But there are no hinges*, he thought. He waited while the crowbar was lowered down to him on a rope. He unhooked the heavy metal rod and tugged on the end of the line, sending it back up the shaft. He felt around the groove at the top of the frame with the fingers of his left hand. The space was wide enough for him to insert the tips of his fingers. He pulled on the frame to loosen it, but the panel was too heavy. He retrieved the crowbar, wedged the chisel side under the base of the panel, and lifted the plank of wood up while simultaneously pulling it toward him. The timber door opened about six inches. It was now wide enough for him to insert his left hand. He pulled the panel forward again.

"It's open!" he shouted.

He leaned forward, peeking through the open space. There was a tunneled-out chamber on the other side. It was too dark to make out any details. He gave the students a thumbs-up sign. "Give me some slack on the light bulb cord," he told them.

The light on the end of the orange electrical cord moved slightly, and then the excess cord came down and coiled onto the floor.

"That's all of it," Thomas said. "What happened to the light on your hard hat?"

"Oh yes, of course." Butler said. He reached up and flipped the switch for the lamp on his hat, but nothing happened. "That's my luck. Oh well..." He picked up the light bulb and took up the slack in the orange extension cord, looping the long cable around his arm. "Okay," he whispered to himself.

He crouched and pushed his light forward and moved past the outer door into a vault-shaped underground chamber. The ceiling was barely high enough for him to stand. He noticed two additional tunnels branching left and right. He unclipped a small walkie-talkie from his belt and pressed the call button. "Can you hear me?" he said.

There was burst of static followed by Thomas's voice. "Loud and clear. And we're dying up here. Tell us what you've found in there."

"A subterranean cave of fairly good size, hewn out of solid rock."

"Oh, that's awesome, Dr. Butler. Is that all?"

"I'll give you an update as I go." Butler moved further in. Ten feet ahead, the tunnel forked. The light cord was out of slack. He put the bulb on the ground and switched to a flashlight. He aimed the beam down the left passageway. The tunnel was unremarkable; it ran twenty feet before ending at a rock wall.

He moved down the tunnel to his right. The passage led into a much larger chamber with several connecting tunnels that branched in all directions. Directly ahead was a large wooden door. The door seemed incomplete; it had been constructed haphazardly with bulky, uneven boards and had wide gaps between each plank. There was no handle or keyhole. The planks were fastened to the door with long, jagged nails that stabbed through the frame from the opposite side as if it had been closed off in a hurry.

Butler stepped closer and tried to open the door, but the frame was locked solidly into place. He removed his hard hat and tossed it on the floor. He positioned the end of the flashlight flush with a break between two boards and then peeked through the crack. He saw only a rock wall directly ahead of him and could see nothing peripherally. He took out his camera, attached a ten-inch-long wire probe to the front lens, and activated the small light on the end. He threaded the thin cable between the slats in the door and watched the color display on his camera. He counted three more doors. There was a massive tunnel entrance with an iron gate. On the other side of the gate, was a mound of large boulders piled to the ceiling.

Butler moved the camera lens around the right side of the room. Something shinny flashed across the viewfinder. He panned back and then zoomed toward the wall. At first he thought he saw a painting, but as the image enlarged and became clearer, he realized he was looking at a decorative mosaic. It was encrusted with seashells, coins, and rocks. The montage was artfully worked into the shape of a man's face. He snapped four photographs and then retrieved his radio and pushed the call button.

"I found some artwork down here," he said. "It's amazing."

"Sa—again," Thomas's voice scratched "Y—r breaking up."

"So are you," said Butler "I'm coming out. I'm going to need some help down here."

"Dr. B—lr?"

Butler clipped his radio to his belt and retraced his steps back to the well. He found the light bulb on the ground where he had left it. He picked up the orange electrical cord and wound it as he moved toward the cave entrance.

Something thudded in the dark behind him.

"Hello?" he said. He turned and shined the light around in the dark. Nothing. The room was empty.

"English," a voice said from somewhere in the shadows.

"Oh my God!" Butler said. "Who is in here?" He aimed the light bulb down the tunnel. The passageway was deserted. "Is someone there?" He walked back into the caverns. The light cord ran out of slack, jerking the light bulb out of his hand. The bulb fell and exploded on the stone floor, plunging the cavern into total darkness. Butler snapped on his flashlight and aimed it around in the dark. He froze when he heard the thumping sound again.

"Hope was lost that any would finde theere way thither," the strange voice said.

"What did you say?" Butler said, moving deeper into the cave. He came back to the wall where he had discovered the door with the shuttered window. He sensed that there was someone on the other side. He put the flashlight against the crack in the door, pressed his face against the thin opening, and looked through. No one was there. He heard a shuffling sound from behind him and turned with his light aimed outward.

Out of the dark he saw a man's gaunt face and wild blue eyes.

"Dear God in heaven," Butler whispered.

The man wore no clothing, and his bare skin was so darkened by dirt and mud that his body blended in with the blackness of the cavern. His head seemed to dangle in the dark like a floating skull.

"Just take it easy," said Butler. "I'll get you out of here. Are you injured?"

"Come closer that I mae toych you," the man said. "In by your spirit I mae depart this dismal place."

"Good lord," said Butler, "what happened to you? How did you get in here?"

"Thayd fleed to him for shelter, but he bay damned, and all that live in him will parish, and to what purpose is the multitude sacrificed?"

"What is your name?" said Butler.

The man didn't answer. He came closer, his face looming down, and his curious eyes pouring over Butler as if he had never seen another human being.

Butler picked up his radio. "Thomas…Thomas, can you hear me?"

He heard a burst of static followed by Thomas's broken voice. "Dr. Butler?"

"I found someone down here. I think he's in shock."

Thomas stepped closer to the rim of the pit. "Could you repeat that last message, Dr. Butler? Say again, Dr Butler."

The radio made a clicking sound, followed by Butler's distorted voice. "Dear God…no!" Butler shouted. He screamed, and the radio turned to static.

Thomas held the radio to his mouth. "Dr. Butler?" He looked at the FBI agent who was standing near a floodlight.

"Is there a problem?" the agent said.

"It's Dr. Butler. He said that there is someone in the cave."

"What?" said the agent. "What exactly did Dr. Butler say?"

"Dr. Butler screamed," Thomas said. "It was garbled, but I think he said that he found someone. That's everything we could understand. We haven't been able to raise him on the radio. Shouldn't you go down there?"

The agent thought for a moment. "No," he said. "Let's try him on the radio again. May I?"

Thomas handed the agent his walkie-talkie. The agent held it up to his mouth. "Dr. Butler, this FBI Agent Charles Taft. Come in please." His coat opened as he talked, and the students saw the gun in the leather holster under his arm.

Taft looked at Thomas. "Does Dr. Butler have any health conditions?"

"None that we're aware of, and I do know that he's an avid runner."

Taft pressed the side call button again. "Calling Dr. Alan Butler— do you read me? This is FBI Agent Charles Taft. If you are unable to speak, please press your radio call button."

"That can't be good," Sidney said. "This is really starting to scare me."

"Someone needs to go down there and find him," another student said.

"Everybody calm down," Taft said. "You're letting your imaginations run wild here. It's possible that you misunderstood him. He's pretty far underground. It's hard to get a signal out at that depth, and I'm surprised you could hear him at all."

"So you think he's okay?" said Sidney.

"I don't know. We're going to find out."

"By going down there?"

"If necessary, yes."

"Let me borrow your Glock and I'll go down there," Thomas said, gesturing at the service pistol under the agent's arm. "I know how to use one of those."

Agent Taft rolled his eyes. "Listen to me. No one is going down there yet, and certainly not half-cocked."

Sidney screamed. She covered her mouth with both hands and backed away from the edge of the pit.

Agent Taft stepped up to the edge of the hole. "Just stay calm, everyone."

"It's probably the doc," Thomas said. He leaned past Agent Taft with his flashlight out. "Dr. Butler?" He moved the beam of light around in the dark.

"There, behind the door," Taft said. "There is someone in the cave."

Thomas focused the light on the open area behind the door. He saw an unfamiliar face peering up at him. An instant later, a naked man came out from behind the door and stood at the base of the pit, staring up at them.

"What the hell?" Taft said. "Keep your flashlight on him."

"Eww—he's naked," one of the girls said. She shielded her eyes.

"That's sick," Thomas said. "I bet he did something to Dr. Butler."

Taft removed his sidearm and pointed it at the ground. "Let's not speculate."

"Speculate?" Thomas said, shaking his head. "Take a look at him. He's a freak. He had to have done something to him."

The man reached for the ladder, and everyone screamed.

"Shoot him!" Sidney shouted.

"Calm down," Taft said. "He's not armed. Everyone just stay back."

Thomas ran over to a tool chest and retrieved a small hatchet. He moved past agent Taft and knelt next to the pit. "Let that bastard just try to come out of there," he said. Thomas raised the hatchet but froze when he noticed the man's hideous face staring at him over the edge of the hole in the ground.

"Get back!" Taft shouted.

It was too late. The man was already out of the pit and had Thomas by the arm. Thomas screamed. The man reached for Thomas's throat.

"Let him go!" Taft shouted. He fired a warning shot over the man's head.

The man released his grip. Thomas's limp body slumped to the ground and slid headfirst into the hole.

Taft moved backward toward the students, who were huddled together behind him. He leveled his gun in the man's direction, took aim and fired off three rounds. All three bullets struck the man on his bare chest. The tips of the bullets flattened out and fell to the ground.

"What in God's name?" said Taft.

Before he could fire again, the man moved forward with blinding speed and clutched Taft's right wrist. He forced the gun from the agent's hand, seized him by the head, and twisted sideways, breaking Taft's neck with a loud crunch.

"Run!" Sidney shouted. The students dashed into the woods. They stayed together, moving up and down several ravines, trampling over saplings, feeling their way in the dark. Moments later they emerged into an open field, coughing and panting, trying to catch their breath. A few were sobbing. Ahead of them they saw the outline of a barbed wire fence and the silhouettes of several cows that were grazing in a pasture. The students helped each other over the fence, moved past the animals, and stopped just inside the wire.

"Oh God!" Sidney hissed. "Behind us!"

The man from the well stood on the opposite side of the field, behind the fence. He was wearing Agent Taft's white shirt and pants. He stood motionless with his hands on the barbed wire, watching them.

"It's him," Sidney said. "He's going to kill us all." She broke down crying.

"Shut up! Keep moving," one of the girls said.

"Watch out!" a guy's voice shouted in the dark. "The cows…"

The herd of spooked animals was moving in their direction.

"Run!" Sidney said. She reached for the top wire. She screamed and slumped to the ground. Panic set in, and they all reached for the fence.

"Wait!" someone said. "I think it's electrified!" The warning came too late; they were all climbing the wire. The hum of electricity filled the air. A moment later the entire herd of cows crashed into the fence, pinning the flailing students against the wire.

17

ANNIVERSARY

"**W**ill this table be sufficient? the maître d' asked in a heavy Spanish accent.

Rand looked at his wife Renee. "Hmm?"

"Perfect!" Renee said. She brushed her red hair back, sat down, and settled into her chair.

The maître d' unfolded Renee's napkin and placed it carefully across her lap.

Rand sat down and unfolded his napkin, but caught himself when the waiter arrived to handle it for him. The waiter plucked the napkin from Rand's hands and draped it across his knees. He gave Rand a long look and then glanced around the table, taking a quick inventory of the number of glasses and utensils. He handed Rand the wine list. Rand peeked over the top of the menu and raised his eyebrows at his wife. Renee smiled playfully and winked back at him. It was inside joke they shared. She knew how he abhorred extravagant restaurants.

The waiter nodded and left, winding his way back toward the bar, stopping at each of his tables along the way.

Renee laughed and pouted at her husband. "You don't like my choice of restaurants?"

"It's nice."

"And the food?"

"Well, it's overpriced and I'm usually underwhelmed," said Rand.

"You know I was going to pick Tolliver's for you, but they're closed for a remodel."

"That was thoughtful of you," Rand said. "And one of Tolliver's thick steaks with a no-nonsense baked potato on the side sounds great."

"You could have that here."

"You know that I'm kidding. I'll find something." He put the wine list down, picked up the dinner menu, and looked at the food choices. The restaurant was known for it progressive trans-global cuisine, with a menu that changed daily and offered anything from wild Texas boar to Hong Kong-style seared scuttle fish.

"Well, for the record," Renee said, "I think this place is much more intriguing and romantic."

Rand looked around the restaurant. He agreed that the faux finished walls painted in mustard, the modern, backlit wall sconces, and the soft city lights twinkling in the window provided romantic atmosphere, but he was not about to admit it. He looked across the table at his beautiful wife, whose seductive smile and expression-filled eyes told him that she felt like they were the only two people in the room.

"Happy anniversary," Renee said.

Rand smiled. "You too." He looked down at his menu and back at Renee. She was still looking at him, smiling. He pursed his lips into a playful smooch.

"What do you have a taste for?" Renee said.

"Well, that depends." Rand winked and softly nudged her leg under the table.

"On the menu, Detective."

Rand smiled and looked back down at the menu. He shook his head as he read the names of the elaborate dishes. "I'll definitely be following my rule tonight," he said.

"Which rule is that, sweetheart?"

"I'm not ordering anything that I can't pronounce, and I'm not about to let you talk me into anything."

"Not feeling adventurous tonight, darling?"

"Absolutely not! The last time we were here you talked me into that...what was it?"

"I'm trying to think of the last time we were here?"

"Lunch," Rand said, frowning.

"Oh, that's right. The scrambled tofu and smoked salmon sandwich. It was wonderful!"

"I had to take a half a day of vacation because of that sandwich, and that horrible soup."

"The Portuguese chowder?"

"The clogged sink bisque is more accurate."

"This, coming from a man who judges quality food by how quickly he gets indigestion?"

"I don't mind indigestion," said Rand. "It's the having my stomach pumped that I could do without. But not tonight. There will be no miniature marinated squid, no sea snails, or sea weed, for that matter."

"You have to try a little sushi or freshwater eel," Renee mused.

"I don't think so. I don't see how you eat it."

"I love it, and it's healthy."

"Maybe that's why you still look so good."

"Really?"

"Yes," I think you're more beautiful now than when we first met."

Renee smiled. "You're such a liar."

"It's the truth."

"Well I know what you're up to, but you can just stop right now, because you're going to get lucky tonight."

"Oh, am I?"

"Oh yes."

"Then I'm certain that I should stay away from the exotic dishes on this menu. I'm not about to let anything get in the way of the plans I have for you tonight."

"Promises, promises."

"You won't be disappointed."

"I never am."

Rand smiled. "Well then. Now that we got that settled, if you will excuse me, I have to wash up. If the waiter comes before I get back, I'll have the filet, medium rare."

Renee looked skeptical. "This isn't a business-related bathroom trip is it?"

"No."

"Honey?"

"I promise." Rand took out his cell phone and placed it on the table. "I'll leave it with you." He stood and pushed his chair under the table. He was halfway across the room when the sound of his cell phone ringing stopped him in his tracks.

Renee reached for his phone. "Hello?"

"Renee?"

"Yes, how are you, Mark?"

"I'm great," said the voice on the other end of the line. "I hope you are. It's been a while. I need to borrow your husband for a moment."

"Is it important? It's our anniversary."

"I know, and I'm sorry I had to interrupt your evening, but he will need to know about this. It will only take a minute."

"I'm going to hold you to it."

"Thanks," Shullman said. "And congratulations. How many years does this make again?"

"This is our tenth."

"Wow. You deserve a medal."

"I agree. Well here he is, Mark."

Rand walked up, looking inquisitive. "Who is it?"

"It's Detective Shullman, and you better remind him that it's our anniversary."

Rand took the phone and eased into his chair. He gave Renee an apologetic look. "Mark what's going on? Good news, I hope."

"Hello chief. I'm afraid not."

"I'm listening."

"We've identified more bodies…. A lot of them with the same neck wounds."

"How many?"

"I don't have a count yet, but it's major."

"Where?"

"Madison Tower Hotel."

The converted tenant house," Rand said. "I'm not far from there. Take control of the scene, and wait for me?"

"Tino's men have already secured the area, and I'm en route."

"I'll be there in ten minutes," Rand said.

"Hey…" Renee said. "Can't Mark handle it?"

Rand switched off his phone. "I'll make it up to you. It won't take long I promise."

18

DELIRIUM

David was lying on his back, staring up at the ceiling. He tried to concentrate. *Get up, move,* he told himself, but it was as if an unseen force held him down, trapping him in his own body. Peripherally he could see railings on the side of his bed, and two women—doctors in white lab coats—standing on the right side of the bed. One of the doctors read from a metal clipboard. David remembered the ambulance, and arriving at the hospital emergency room. His mind felt blocked. He focused on the fluorescent lights on the ceiling above him. He tried to remember what had happened to him and why he was here; but mostly, he tried to remember who he was.

The attending emergency physician looked at David and looked down at her metal clipboard. She shook her head as she thumbed through the medical data. "It's really quite remarkable," she said.

"You're saying that there wasn't a scratch on him?" the consulting neurologist asked. She reached down and touched David's shirtsleeve. "And what is he wearing?"

"Not so much as a bruise on the outside of his body. And as far as his clothes go, it's some kind of jogging or biking suit. We weren't able to remove them. They're tightly fitted and it's almost as if they're glued to his body. We contemplated cutting his clothes off, but I no longer see the necessity in that since there are no external injuries. There doesn't seem to be anything physically wrong with him. Outside of some elevated concentrations of oxygen in his body tissue, he's in superb physical shape—which, quite frankly, I find to be astounding considering the height from which he fell or jumped, whichever the case may be."

"You said elevated oxygen. Hyperoxia?"

"Borderline, but no oxidative damage to his cell membranes. We took him off O_2 as a precaution."

"So what is wrong with him?" the neurologist said. "And why do you want us to take him?"

"There's nothing more we can do for him in here. A loss of consciousness was noted at the scene for an unknown duration, but when emergency medical services arrived, he had stable vital signs. He scored eleven out of fifteen on a Glasgow coma scale. He's barely coherent but certainly not comatose. His pupils are reactive, he feels pain and sees things around him, but doesn't respond to simple commands. A person falling from fourteen stories should be dead and, at a minimum, have broken bones and some brain damage. Eyewitnesses stated that he landed horizontally on his back and totaled a Yellow Cab upon impact with it. Somehow there's not a scratch on him."

"His brain should be mush."

"I agree. He shows no evidence of brain injury, but there are anomalies within his brain. That's why we wanted you to have a look, and make a recommendation."

Anomalies?"

"Yes, and I'm no expert in neurobiology by any stretch of the imagination, but I've seen enough brain scans to know when one is very unusual. You're the expert; you tell me what you think." She handed her colleague the clipboard. The top page showed four separate scans of a brain.

The neurologist glanced over the report. "Remarkable," she said. "The lack of water signal resembles an image of a newborn's brain."

"Definitely an image of a developing brain. Now look at this image." She reached over and flipped to the next page. "Sorry, the images are out of sequence; this image is the first one we took when he arrived."

"Well, this can't be accurate."

"It's correct, and I've already checked the equipment. It's working fine."

"Taken first?"

"Yes, about an hour apart."

"There's higher water content, lower macromolecular concentration, and reduced synaptic density. This resembles a brain of someone who is post mortem."

"Amazing, huh? How long would they have been dead?"

"By the look of this brain, I would guess that death occurred twenty-four to thirty-six hours ago. But I know that our John Doe here isn't dead."

"But don't you find it unusual?"

"It's astonishing! The difference, I mean. There appear to be age-related changes in the brain. The original image can be explained. In some instances it's difficult to tell the difference between a postmortem brain and that of a brain suffering from severe refractory post-traumatic cerebral edema. But in this instance, there's nothing to explain the correlation between the two abnormalities, or the drastic changes in the diffusion characteristics in such a short period of time. I agree with you that this should be looked into, but not here in the Neuro-ICU. I'll sign to have him transferred to the emergency psychiatric ward." She looked down at David. "Let's see if they can piece together his story."

19

DEATH ASPECT

Rand pulled his black Suburban in front of the Madison Tower and parallel-parked next to a long line of police cruisers. The hotel entrance was active with emergency workers and police officers attending to the frightened residents. The entire base of the massive building was marked off with a long ribbon of yellow police tape.

Rand stepped out of the vehicle and hung his FBI badge around his neck. He studied the old hotel for moment, taking note of the building's ruined state.

"The building should be condemned," Tino said, coming down to meet Rand. "It should have been shut down years ago."

"It looks like something out of a Edgar Allan Poe story," Rand said.

Tino nodded and shook Rand's hand. "I agree, and what we found inside this godawful place makes *The Fall of the House of Usher* seem like a story for kindergarteners."

"Shullman reported over fifty bodies."

"The count is over a hundred now," Tino said somberly. "Just when you think you've seen the worst this city could throw at you, this happens."

"Is Shullman still on the fourteenth floor?"

"Yes, with your other partner, Parker." Tino gestured toward the front entrance.

Both men crossed the sidewalk and ascended a broad set of concrete stairs. They ducked under the yellow police tape and entered the building through a pair of vaulted doors that were propped open with two red leather lounge chairs. They continued into a crowded foyer and emerged at the main lobby, which resembled a Middle Eastern bazaar. Soiled Persian rugs and minaret columns lined each side of the atrium, separating the abandoned retail shops from the clerk's offices.

The lobby was crowded with frightened residents, all moving toward the front entrance with shocked and bewildered expressions like terrified passengers trying to escape a sinking ship.

"It must have been some hotel in its day," Rand said.

Tino nodded. "Yes, fifty years ago. Now it's a rat-infested dump. The building has been so altered by neglect and decay that it has lost any architectural significance it might have had. Is this your first time in here?"

"Yeah. I've driven past it on more than one occasion, but haven't ever had a reason to come inside. I pulled up a few files on the way over here. A decade ago, this building made our top ten list of New York's most dangerous places."

"Not much has changed," Tino said. "It keeps the precinct fairly busy. Some of the worst crimes in the city emanate from these premises."

"Jesus, what a shit hole," Rand said.

"I thought they were mannequins," an elderly woman in a pink bathrobe said. She stood near the front desk addressing a young detective. "How many times do I have to tell this story to you people?"

Rand and Tino walked over and listened in.

The agent nodded at them and continued with his questions. "Did you know the tenant who lived above you"—he looked at the woman's ID—"Ms. Zabinski?"

"I didn't know that anyone lived above me. The elevator only goes up to the twelfth floor. I always asked Mr. Bondurant why the elevator showed fourteen floors but never went past twelve?"

"And what was the property manager's response to your inquires about the upper levels of the building?"

"Am I under arrest?" Ms. Zabinski asked.

"No, you're not." The agent handed back her driver's license. "We just have a few more questions and you'll be free to go."

"Go where?" she said. "They told me that we had to leave the building—that it's not safe. And what about all my stuff?"

The agent gave her an exasperated look. "You'll be relocated and the city will help you with a new dwelling while the building's structure is evaluated. Now back to my questions. What did the building manager, Mr. Bondurant, tell you when you asked him about the upper levels?"

"Mr. Bondurant said it was storage. Stuff from the days when the building was a hotel."

Rand turned toward Tino. "Where is this Mr. Bondurant now?"

"We've isolated him in his office. I wanted to wait for you to get here before we interviewed him."

The agent continued with his questions. "And you never met anyone from thirteenth and fourteenth floors?"

"No," said Ms. Zabinski.

"Do you know everyone in the building?"

"Not everyone. They come and go so quickly."

"How long have you lived here?"

"Six months."

"Alone?"

"Yes."

The agent studied his notes. "Ms. Zabinski, you told the arriving officers that you felt your apartment shake, and when you came out into the hallway you saw the bodies where they had crumbled through from the floor above yours. Is that accurate?"

"Yes."

"Is that when you saw the man?"

"Yes I did, but I didn't see him very well."

"Can you describe him?"

"He was a white man, wearing dark clothes, and he was moving along the wall, staring down at me. He looked as stunned and terrified as I was."

Rand and Tino stepped away. "What do we know about the thirteenth and fourteenth floors?" Rand asked.

"From what we've gathered so far, the two top floors were rented out under an automatically renewable fifteen-year lease that was paid in advance by some European jetsetter named Theios Galatin. It's no surprise that none of the other tenants have ever seen him, and we have thus far been unsuccessful at verifying his existence."

"So you're telling me that one man owned two full stories of this building."

In essence, but he didn't actually own them. He acquired the upper floors through a long-term lease—a kind of unmanaged charter."

"I think it's time to talk to this building manager."

"He's this way."

Rand followed Tino down a short hallway past the clerk's desk. The walls contained hundreds of small tarnished brass mailboxes. The hallway ended at large wooden door, where a young police officer stood guard.

"We'll take it from here," Tino said.

The officer nodded and stepped away from the door.

They found Bondurant inside the darkened room. He stood behind a large oak desk, staring forward as if he were awaiting a firing squad. Beside him was a large, worn-out, brown leather office chair. Rand noticed that the chair and desk were covered in a thick layer of dust from disuse. The room was packed with an eclectic mix of dust-covered antiques. In the far right corner, a band of seven-foot-high stone gargoyles stared down with disapproving glares. Several more statues of all shapes and sizes were scattered around the room with their eyes facing toward the door.

"Holy terrors," Bondurant said, breaking the silence.

"I beg your pardon?" Rand said.

"The grotesques that you see inside this room. They keep me company and remind me that I'm never alone, and that nothing goes unobserved while I'm away. The limestone demons still adorn many of the higher balconies of this building, perched too high for thieves to reach."

"Are you a collector of these things?" Rand said.

Bondurant nodded. "Salvaged them from the tower's lower elevations."

"Why did you call them holy terrors, Mr.—"

"Bondurant, William Bondurant,"

"Property manager," Rand said, retrieving a small notepad and pen from his back pocket.

Bondurant nodded. "Holy terrors, you asked? The building was originally a hotel designed by a Catholic architect. Like many churches of the late nineteenth and early twentieth centuries, they adorned their buildings, as they did their houses of worship, with gargoyles. It was believed that the church overcomes and converts to good even the most monstrous forms of evil."

Rand and Tino exchanged peculiar glances.

"Well, enough about the damn statues," Tino said. "I'm interested in things that can talk. People. Witnesses. Someone has collected over a hundred bodies upstairs. You stated earlier that you knew nothing about it. There has been a massacre here, and we need you to tell us everything you know about the tenants living above the twelfth floor."

"Most certainly, Detective," Bondurant said with a mocking recognition in his tone. "I'll do what ever I can to help."

Tino appeared agitated. "About the tenants on the thirteenth and fourteenth floors?"

"Tenant," Bondurant corrected. "His name is Theios Galatin, and he rents out both floors, but he dwells in the old Corum room above them both. It's the largest in the building."

"Didn't it seem strange to you that someone was interested in so many rooms, yet lives in only one?"

"No. Mr. Galatin was gold," Bondurant said. "He paid cash, fifteen years in advance."

"Didn't that seem odd?"

"It was cash, and it didn't seem that unusual, considering that he wanted to buy the whole building."

"Why didn't he?"

"The consortium of developers who owns the building turned him down."

"You would think someone would be eager to dump this place," Rand said.

Tino shook his head. "They're slumlords. They know this building would never pass an inspection. They can't sell it because they can't control the bank inspectors like they do the city health guys."

"I spoke to the owners of the building earlier today," Bondurant said. "Their intentions are to restore the building and donate it to the city for the museum project."

"Was that before or after you told them about the collapsed floor?" said Rand. "It would take millions to restore this building, but risking prosecution, I imagine that they would say just about anything. Slumlords are all the same. None of them are interested in maintaining their buildings, just collecting their profits."

"Regardless of your opinion of me, Detective, the building is inspected on a regular basis. When repairs are necessary, a list is compiled and submitted for review. Beyond that, it is out of my control."

"Let's forget about the building and talk about your tenant Mr. Galatin. Did you ever ask him why he rented out the floor below him, but didn't use it?"

"Yes. It was due to the noise from the heating registers between the twelfth and thirteenth floors, all of which permit sounds emanating from the lower levels to be easily heard."

"He wasn't trying to keep sounds out, but keep noises from his chamber of horrors in."

Bondurant nodded.

"What was he like?" Tino asked.

"I couldn't tell you. He was a private man, and I rarely dealt with him face-to-face."

"When was the last time you or any of your staff were on his floors?"

"Not since he moved in, about four years ago. He wanted his own heating and air conditioning. He upgraded the roof units out of his own pocket. I had to let the contractors in to rework some of the vents."

"You're telling me that you haven't been in his apartment in four years?"

"Not once."

"What about spraying for bugs?" Rand said.

"Look around, Detective."

"I'm inclined to believe him," Tino said. "He probably couldn't get in even if he wanted to. All of the access routes to those floors are locked tight. The only way in is through a dedicated, industrial service elevator. The lift bypasses all the other floors and goes straight down to a furnace room."

"Convenient," Rand said.

"Even the fire escape stairs have been soldered off above the eleventh floor."

Rand shook his head. His phone beeped. He looked down at the display and pressed the side call button. "Go ahead, Mark."

"What's your ETA?"

"I'm here in the building now, just finishing up with the building manager. Where are you?"

"I'm on the fourteenth floor, right off the service elevator. You can't miss us."

"I'm on my way up."

Tino placed a folded sheet of paper on Bondurant's desk.

"What is that?" Bondurant said.

"It's an action form, in case we need to contact you. We'll need a copy of your driver's license, social security card, address, and phone number. It's voluntary. Do you mind?"

Bondurant stared down at the paper. "I don't mind at all, Detective."

"We're also putting in a warrant for Mr. Galatin's lease agreement. We'll need to review the contract he signed with you. I assume you require some form of identification from your tenants?"

"Of course,"

"And references?"

"Yes, but you can forgo the warrant. I'll get you what ever information you need."

"Thanks," Tino said. He opened the office door and waved the officer over. "Once Mr. Bondurant gives us his contact information, he's free to leave."

Rand stepped closer to the desk and handed Bondurant a business card. "If you remember anything, don't hesitate to give me a call."

Bondurant took the card and glanced at it. "You'll be the first to hear from me, Agent Rand."

Rand and Tino exited Bondurant's office and made their way to the front of the hotel. The main lobby was mostly deserted. A small group of police officers huddled by the front door, sipping coffee, joking, and laughing. Tino and Rand crossed the lobby, ascended a flight of stairs, and entered into a large kitchen. They exited into a long service tunnel and finally came to an open freight elevator. A police officer standing guard moved to one side as Rand and Tino entered the lift.

"You have to hold the red button in to go up," the officer said. "The black button is down."

"I know, I know," Tino said. "I've been on this thing already—unfortunately." He located the two control buttons at the bottom of the numbered panel and pushed the red button all the way in with his thumb. There was a loud metal scraping noise as the heavy steel doors closed with a jarring clang. The sound of machinery could be heard under the floor, and then the elevator shuddered and slowly reeled upward.

20

NIGHT SHIFT

Dr. Jane Carol entered the hospital's emergency psychiatric ward through the first of two security doors. The twenty-nine year old psychiatrist waited in a holding area that was divided by a four-inch-thick barrier of Plexiglas. She covered a yawn and checked her watch, dreading the long night ahead. After several moments, the lock on the secondary door sounded with a ping, and a guard inside a locked control room waved her through.

"Sorry about the delay, Dr. Carol," the guard said, leaning out of his office door. "There seems to be a short in the signal box."

"That's okay, Timmy. Give maintenance a call." Jane continued through to the main lobby. A pair of L-shaped black leather benches lined the back wall. A thin middle-aged woman in a tan raincoat sat on one end of the couch with her head down. She looked up drowsily as Jane walked past her.

"Hello, Dr. Carol," the woman said.

Jane recognized her. "Hi Betty. What are you here for?"

"Just a refill. Will you get it for me?"

"I'll find Dr. Bentson and see what the delay is."

The woman frowned and leaned her head back against the wall.

Jane continued down the hall and emerged in the psychiatric center's core: a large room filled with comfortable couches and chairs. A dozen clinicians were scattered around the room sipping coffee and filling out reports, waiting for the shift to change. The day crew and night shift mirrored each other; all together, there were two attending psychiatrists, two therapeutic patient workers, two social workers, and six psych nurses.

"Hi, Dr. Carol," said one of the day shift nurses.

"Good evening everyone," Jane said. She waved at Dr. Bentson and pointed back toward the lobby. "You have a visitor."

"Betty," Bentson said, rolling his eyes. "I know." He held up a prescription pad. "I'll see her on my way out."

Rita, a day shift therapist, started passing around report sheets that listed all the patients on the docket for the day.

"How many new ones?" Jane said.

"Only three new so far," Rita said.

Jane smiled. "Wow only three new ones? It's our lucky night."

"But the night is still young," Rita said. She knocked on the side of the wood table. "Remember what happened Friday? It started slow and we ended up with eight within a two-hour period."

"So lay it on us," Jane said. "Who are the three new crazies?"

Rita read from the first file. "Jack P. He's a self-referred thirty-nine-year old divorced white male seeking detox from alcohol. Mr. P's blood alcohol count was 0.10. His blood pressure was up when he came in, so we gave him one milligram of Ativan. He has been calm and cooperative. He's snoozing it off over in Room 4."

Rita opened a second file. "Our next little lovely is Suzuki C., a seventeen-year-old Asian female cheerfully delivered to us at 5:41 p.m. by New York's finest. A friend of Ms. C called police after she stated that she was going to kill herself, because her boyfriend broke up with her for a cheerleader. She tried to overdose with painkillers and alcohol. She ingested her mother's leftover Codeine prescription—roughly five pills—and then washed it down with a bottle of vodka. The police found her in her backyard threatening the neighbor's dog with a steak knife. We have her in four-point restraints, and she has calmed down somewhat, but keeps urinating on herself—three times in two hours." Rita smirked. "Good luck with that one. Oh, and for our third new contestant, Dr. Henderson over in the emergency ICU wanted us to give some special attention." She held out the final file in Jane's direction. "He's an attempted suicide and a John Doe."

Jane turned toward Bentsen. "Have you seen the John Doe?"

"No, they just brought him up from ICU."

"How did our mystery man try to kill himself?"

"He's a flyer," Rita said. "Jumped off a building. He was screened for any potentially harmful, self-inflicting objects and placed under suicide watch over in Room 6." She paused, skipping through the report. "Our Mr. Nobody here jumped off a fourteen-story building, and get this: not a scratch on him. Not on the outside, anyway." She pointed to her head and swirled her fingers around. "He came in through the acute care side, medical emergency room. He was medically cleared and sent here for a psych eval. We have him scheduled for an MRI."

"Why? Wasn't his brain scanned in the ER?"

"Yes. CT scan, followed by a secondary MRI."

"And now a third scan?"

"Evidently there were some irregular findings."

Jane nodded. "Okay, but I want to talk to him first."

"He's all yours, Doc," Rita said. She handed Jane the file and gave her a teasing smile. "I saw him when they brought him in. He's wearing a black body suit that doesn't leave a whole lot to the imagination, and he's good looking. I'm talking movie star good looks." She slung her bag over her shoulder and winked at Jane. "If he can be fixed, I might just have to give him a spin on the Von-Rita express."

Jane laughed. "Go home, Rita, before you get yourself into trouble—again."

"Good night, people," Rita said. She walked out the room with the rest of the day shift following behind her.

Jane opened David's file and stared down at the notes. "Okay," she said. "Another crazy night."

21

BODY COUNT

Tino and Rand stepped out of the elevator and were immediately stunned by the frigid air. Shullman and Parker stood in the middle of the room talking with a group of agents. They saw Rand and Tino and came over.

"Can you believe this?" Parker said, blowing warm air into her hands as she walked up.

"It's insanity," Shullman said. "This entire room has been converted into a freezer. It was nineteen degrees in here earlier. We found two thirteen-ton freezer exhaust units on the roof. I suppose he kept the room frozen so he could dispose of the bodies at his leisure. We cut the power to the roof and discovered that each freezer had its own backup generator. We shut everything down. The bodies are already starting to defrost. We're going to have to hurry; the room is warming a lot faster than we anticipated." He looked down at a small digital thermometer. "It's forty-nine degrees in here now."

Rand stared around the room, surveying the carnage. To his immediate left a row of stacked bodies ran the entire length of one wall, ending by a collapsed opening in the floor. Several more toppled bodies, stiff with frost and rigor, lay scattered around the hole.

"People from all walks of life," Shullman said. "No pattern so far, and at first glance the scene has the appearance of a mass suicide."

"Those bodies didn't stack themselves," Rand said. He stared around at the loss of life. He was disgusted and angry.

Shullman nodded. "And take a look at this." He guided Rand and Tino over to a large round wooden table that was scattered with a collection of the victims' belongings. There were several women's handbags, men's wallets, and coins and jewelry.

"There's still money in the wallets," Parker said. She pulled on a pair of rubber gloves and picked up a random handbag and looked inside. "Interesting that he never tried to pawn any of this stuff."

"I don't think money was an issue for this guy," Rand said.

Parker examined the contents of the purse. She found a key chain, a package of tissues, and a checkbook with a driver's license. "Shallice Warrington, born 1983, New York, and a movie ticket to *Juno* from way back in 2008."

Tino said, "The bodies that fell through to the twelfth-floor hallway have already been moved off site. They were nearly thawed when they were relocated to the morgue. I requested that the autopsies be expedited. There were ten bodies in all, and of those, we have positive IDs on five. We've begun cross-checking them for missing persons, arrest records, or any other links. The rest of these bodies will take more time. There are no visible wounds on the remains we've evaluated so far."

"Mostly suffocations," an older agent said, walking up next to them. He held a green Sprite soda bottle in one hand and pair of old boots in the other. He took a sip from the green bottle and plopped the boots on the table.

"What are you doing in here, Frank?" Tino said.

"John said you needed someone old and knowledgeable."

"Well, he was half right. You're old, and usually drunk, and should still be on suspension."

"I returned to full duty on Wednesday. You need to read your e-mails."

Tino shook his head. "Frank Jaycasltle I would like you to meet FBI Special Agent Jason Rand?

"I've seen you around," Jaycastle said, holding out his hand, "but never had the pleasure."

"These are Detective Rand's partners, Mark Shullman and Dana Parker. Everyone, this is Detective Frank Jaycastle, one of my best detectives—that is, when he's not drunk or passed out in his office."

"I beg your pardon," Jaycastle said. "I've never passed out from drinking in my life. I'm a Navy man for Christ's sake."

"Whatever you say, Frank."

"Do you need me here or not?"

"What do you think, Agent Rand?" Tino said. "Frank here is a walking forensic encyclopedia, and has a shockingly detailed knowledge of just about every major pending case in the precinct. And he knows about every agent on every case, down to how long they take on their lunch, or who doesn't wash his hands after taking a leak."

Rand smiled. "We could always use an extra pair of eyes."

"Good," Jaycastle said. He sat his Sprite bottle on the table and walked toward the row of stacked bodies.

Tino picked up the green bottle and smelled it. He detected the scent of lemon and alcohol. "That drunk bastard."

"It is awfully cold in here," Rand said. "And alcohol makes great antifreeze. You can't blame a guy for keeping his soda from going frozen on him, now can you? So what did Jaycastle do to get himself suspended?"

"A couple weeks back he was promoted to captain and we had a little after-work party. Jaycastle got crushed drinking shots of Jaeger and had an accident on his way home from the party. He drove his cruiser through a mile of orange construction cones before running into the back of a garbage truck. No one was hurt, but sanitation made a federal issue out of it. He is brilliant though, but I would never tell him that."

Jaycastle walked over to the middle of the row of stacked bodies. He looked down, glancing right and then left at the bodies nearest the service elevator.

"Do you want me stop him?" Tino said. "It's your crime scene— your investigation."

"That's okay," said Rand. "Let him do his thing."

"Some of these corpses have been here for a while," Jaycastle said. He pulled on a pair of rubber gloves. "I like to start with the most recent victim."

"Save it for the medical examiner," Shullman said. "We'll be here all day."

Jaycastle shot Shullman a stern look over his shoulder, and continued with his observation. He turned left and made his way to the end of the row of waist-high bodies. The top corpse at the end was that of a shirtless, elderly white man, wearing a black belt and a pair of weathered black trousers. "Male, Caucasian, appearing to be late fifties, early sixties. Rigidity is incomplete."

"A fresh one," Tino said.

"That was fast," Rand said.

"I told you he was good."

They all walked over and watched Jaycastle as he began his examination of the first body.

Jaycastle said, "Lightning-bolt tattoo over the right bicep, and a red star on his chest just below his right shoulder." He manipulated the man's frozen arm. "No needle or needle track marks. Decedent has a well-healed linear surgical scar, from radius to elbow. Wardrobe consists of a pair of black pants with a black belt, and a distinctive silver eagle belt buckle."

Tino and Rand exchanged glances. "Another trapdoor belt," Rand said.

"Check that buckle, Jay," Tino said.

Jaycastle glanced at Tino and Rand over his shoulder and turned his attention back to the corpse. He adjusted his rubber gloves and fumbled with the silver belt buckle. After a moment the buckle opened, revealing a tiny white pill. "Interesting," said Jaycastle. "I take it you've seen this before?" He produced a pair of tweezers and retrieved the tablet and held it out for everyone to see. "Is this that what I think it is?"

"It is," Tino said. "Cyanide."

An agent stepped forward, holding out a plastic evidence sleeve. Tino placed the pill in the bag and waited as the agent handed it to Tino.

Jaycastle continued his examination. He swiped his right thumb over both of the deceased man's cheekbones and checked his eyelids and the rest of his facial skin. "The victim's face is marked with scattered blood-dot hemorrhages. There's blood in his ears and contusions on the victim's neck. We should start our investigation with him. From what I can tell, he appears to be the last victim placed on the pile. I suspect that he was the last to die. Okay, it's Miller time. Who's buying?"

"Not so fast," Tino said. "You have about seventy more bodies to go."

Another agent came up to Tino. "We found a large safe in one of the main living quarters."

"I'll get a crew up there to cut it open," Tino said.

"It wasn't locked."

"Anything out of the ordinary?" Rand said.

"I don't know—maybe." He handed the list of contents to Tino.

Tino glanced over the report. "Various cosmetics," he said. "Nylon stockings, hair dyes—many of these items are used to change or conceal a person's identity. The tools of the trade for someone on the run."

"We also discovered ten semiautomatic rifles, two shotguns, an anti-tank type weapon, brass knuckles, a thousand rounds of ammunition, and around ten thousand dollars in cash. The brass knuckles and some of the ammunition have been modified through the insertion of some kind of blue material."

"That's a lot of firepower," Tino said. "And I'll bet that the blue material inserted in the ammunition is the same as the electrical rounds we found in Gelder's Marston handgun. It's getting more interesting by the minute."

"Where do you want this one?" a strained voice asked from across the room. They all turned and saw two agents wearing large white masks and mirrored goggles struggling to balance a dead man in a black suit on a narrow stretcher.

"Over here with the rest of them," Tino said.

The agents brought the corpse over and sat him on the ground next to the other bodies.

Rand stared down at the cadaver, noting the dead man's unusual appearance. The body lay stiffly on the ground in a slight sitting position. He wore a black formal suit jacket and pants. The man's stark white hands and bare feet contrasted harshly with his dark clothing. He had the face of a scarecrow, with wild blond hair and weathered skin that was drawn tightly, and his mouth by some curse of nature was set into a permanent grin.

"Where did you find him?" Rand said.

Shullman said, "In the ballroom, sitting in a chair next to one of the largest fireplaces that I've ever seen. The area was cleared and photographed, and I asked Tino's men to bring him in here to be inventoried with the rest of the bodies. With the temperature rising, we need to start moving these corpses out of here. This one brings our total body count to one hundred one." He looked down at a notepad. "Seventy-four bodies in here, seventeen that collapsed through to the floor below, and another ten that tumbled through to the twelfth-floor hallway."

"Looks like it's going to be a late one, Frank," Tino said.

Frank smiled. "I'm going to need more Sprite."

Rand's phone rang. "He looked down and saw his wife Renee's name flashing on the display. He held the phone to his ear. "Hi honey," he said.

"Are you ready for me?" Renee said. "Tonight is your night."

"Our night…" Rand said.

"You won't think that when you see what I'm wearing."

"Damn! What are you wearing?"

"Well I don't want to ruin the surprise, but it's red and slinky."

Rand smiled. "I'm wrapping things up here. I won't be much longer."

"You'd better hurry."

"I'll be there in about an hour."

"Really?"

"I promise."

"Then I'll see you in an hour, Detective."

"Is that Renee?" Shullman asked.

"Yeah," Rand said. He slid the phone into his coat pocket.

"Is she pissed?"

"Not yet. The wine from dinner hasn't worn off."

"Why don't you take off and I'll handle all the paperwork on our end."

Rand checked his watch. He surveyed the room. *The tower is secure,* he thought, *and there are more than enough able-bodied agents on the scene.*

"We've got it under control," Shullman said.

"Okay then," Rand said, "Call me if anything changes."

"I'll walk you out," Tino said.

The two men turned and entered the service elevator. Rand pushed in the black button and waited for the metal gate to lower. Parker ducked under the door at the last second.

"Calling it a night, Dana?" Rand said.

"Yeah. I'll meet you back in the morning. Remind me to bring a heavier coat."

"Amen!" Tino said. He rubbed his hands together and thrust them into his coat pockets in an exaggerated fashion.

The door clanged closed and the elevator shuddered loudly as it descended.

22

MR. NOBODY

Dr. Jane Carol and a nurse stood in the hallway outside David's room, observing him through a small window in the door.

"Amanda, what did the ER guys say when they brought him over?" Jane said.

Amanda shrugged. "The usual. That he wasn't their problem and that he doesn't appear to be a threat to anyone or himself. 'He's all yours,' they said. In other words, the usual dump-and-run."

"What's he been doing since we've had him?"

"He's just been lying in his bed, staring off into space."

"So you agree that he's not dangerous?"

Amanda shrugged. "He doesn't appear to be."

Jane opened the door and made a mental note that the patient didn't react when she entered the room. She closed the door behind her. There was still no reaction. She looked down at his chart and read over the file notes: Male, Caucasian, early twenties, six feet, one hundred eighty-five pounds, blue eyes, and brown hair. Toxicology is negative for drugs. No identifying data, and his legal status is unknown. The subject jumped from the roof of Madison Tower. *Not a lot to go on,* she thought.

"Can you help me?" David said groggily.

"Well, hello," Jane said, looking up from her file. "My name is Jane Carol. Doctor Jane Carol."

Several moments passed without a word.

"A doctor?" David said, finally. He sat up and swung his legs over the side of the bed.

"Yes, I'm a psychiatrist." She rolled a chair over. "How do you feel?"

"Where am I, I…" David trailed off, his face an expression of horror. He stared around the room slowly as if he were watching series of terrifying scenes.

"What's wrong?" Jane said. She stepped sideways and studied David's reaction. She noticed that he didn't respond to her question, nor did his eyes focus on or track her movements. His behavior resembled those of patients she had treated in the past who suffered from dementia, hallucinations, or drug intoxication. Although she stood directly in front of him, it appeared as if he couldn't see her. She took out a pen and clicked the end. She glanced him over again and wrote a note in her log: *There is a substantial measure of phasing and flanging effect of hearing and vision.* She looked up from her file and noticed that he was now watching her. She sat down in the chair across from him. His eyes now followed her actions.

"It's rhythmic," David said.

"Rhythmic?"

Several moments passed.

"Yes."

Jane looked down at the medical file. *The patient's reaction time is improving,* she thought. According to the file notes, when he was brought into the emergency room and admitted to the psych ward for evaluation, he wasn't able to process sensory input at all. It appeared now that he was at least seeing and hearing the real world, but with a delay. She noted the time in the log and was eager to see if the frequency of lucidity would increase.

"Can you tell me your name?" she asked.

More time passed.

"I don't know," David said finally.

Jane noticed that it took less time for him to answer her question. "You're reaction time is improving."

"Reaction time?"

Jane nodded. "Very good. You responded immediately to my statement."

"You have to help me," David said.

"I'm going to try."

"Make the nightmares stop."

"I'll try, but you will have to work with me. Are you having nightmares now?"

"Yes. I can't turn them off."

"Can you tell me what the bad dreams are about?"

"Mortality, death, killing over and over, and a multitude of agonizing voices.

There are so many. It's terrifying."

"Tell me what you see?"

David stared blankly.

"You said that the images that you see are rhythmic."

"Yes the intensity is, but the images are always there, like a kaleidoscope of all kinds of horrific events."

"Are the images always bad?"

"Yes."

"What makes them so terrible?"

"Because the dreams are of people dying. Because they feel like memories, but not my own."

"How do you know they're not your memories?"

"Dear God in heaven, they can't be."

"Are you seeing them now?"

"Yes."

"Why don't you close your eyes and tell me what you see?"

"I dare not close my eyes."

"Why not?"

"The images…" he trailed off. His eyes showed dramatic activity, and his body jerked uncontrollably like someone suffering a mild epileptic seizure.

Jane leaned closer and shined a light into his eyes and noted that his pupils had a strong reaction to light. His facial expression was restricted, and his eyes strained to see her even though she was directly in front of him. She turned off the light and withdrew her hand.

David immediately recoiled from her movement.

Jane wrote in the chart: *Patient is positive for visual hallucination and movements as aggressive.*

"The voices…" David said. He reached both hands toward Jane as if he were feeling for something solid to touch. He touched her knee and brought his head up quickly, focusing his eyes on her.

"Can you see me?"

"Are you real?"

"Yes, I'm real. Why don't you describe to me what you can see? Keep looking at me. Focus here, on my face. Tell me what you see?"

"Okay…I'll try to focus." He stared at Jane for several moments. "I see your face. I see your red lips, your blue eyes and brown hair…" He smiled. "You're beautiful." His face turned serious. "But everything else I see is deformed, ugly, and frightening—and the voices." He stopped talking and looked away, looking around the room with a bewildered expression.

"Fugue state," Jane whispered. "Try to focus on my face again. Do the voices you hear always start out with one voice and then develop contrapuntally, or is it all at once?"

David continued to look around the room with a frightened and dazed expression, "So many souls," he said. "I…" His thoughts became derailed again.

Jane leaned forward. "Focus on me."

"When I get close to the surface…"

"What happens?"

"It's like some mysterious force washes over me, possessing my body, draining my life away. Do you believe me?"

"I do believe you."

"So many voices," he said. "I can't think straight."

"What are the voices saying?"

David fought off a tic. "They urge me to do bad things."

"What are they telling you to do?"

"Things I fear that I soon won't be able to control. And…"

"And what?"

"He'll be coming for me."

"Whom are you talking about?" Jane said.

David didn't answer. He slumped forward, exhausted with the confusion of the inner madness showing on his face.

Jane waved her right hand in front of his face. He didn't seem to notice. "Well, you're in there somewhere," she said.

23

INFERNO

RAZE THE TOWER appeared on Bondurant's phone. A second communication followed: ZURICH 0003872-23890.

"Fain," Bondurant mouthed as he considered the message. *Fain is done with me,* he thought. *And I will finally be unbound from the dismal tower.* He smiled and became lost in thought as he considered the Zurich bank account. The money would mean a new beginning and a new life, with more wealth than he ever dreamed of.

He made his way toward the back of the room and squeezed past the assembly of stone gargoyles. A bookcase built into the wall concealed a hidden door. He entered into a bunker and turned right, feeling along the wall in the dark. He exited through a rear door. A single bulb hung down from a thin cable in the ceiling. He reached up and felt around for the light cord. He pulled a string and the low-wattage bulb flashed on, illuminating a narrow staircase. He descended the stairs two stories down to the building's basement. Garbage and old hotel storage lay scattered about the cluttered chamber.

Bondurant disabled the freight elevator by tripping the main breaker. He made his way to the incinerator. Fist-sized metal bolts circled the furnace door, and a long asbestos-covered handle resembling a crowbar angled out from door's center. He reached out, pushed the handle all the way down, and pulled the door open. An intense blast of heat scorched his cheeks and hands, forcing him backward.

He turned and made his way over to a small utility closet where he retrieved a large kerosene canister. He unscrewed the lid and kicked the cylinder over on its side, sending a long stream of flammable liquid gushing across the floor. He took a second canister and poured fuel over the bags of trash, and then walked the perimeter of the room, dousing the walls. He retrieved a chair leg and wrapped the end with the fabric from an old seat cushion.

He returned to the stairwell. Once he was inside the passageway he ignited the end of the makeshift torch and heaved it into the middle of the room. Fire exploded upward and expanded across the floor in every direction. Bondurant slammed the door closed just as the flames reached him.

24

THE PLAN

Jane sat at her desk dangling a tea bag into a mug of hot water. She glanced over David's file, picked up a handheld recorder, and spoke into the microphone.

"The patient's thought process is confused, paranoid, and delusional. He thinks he's going to die and that someone is going to find him here. He presents with extreme impaired memory—no immediate recall. The patient is internalizing an enormous amount of painful effect, which has contributed substantially to throwing him into considerable overload. Patient remains quite emotionally distressed, related to transfunctional feelings which he seems to be quite unclear about. The patient continues to struggle with feelings that something happened, or that a lot has happened long ago, and he can't remember and doesn't want to remember. As a result, he has become emotionally overloaded. He has shown a very limited tolerance for stress confusion, processing information, and reality testing. Patient John Doe's underlying turmoil is so extensive and intense that some sort of explosion in the form of comprehensive, regression, and decompensation seems likely."

She took a sip of tea. "His controls now are at best tenuous, and he seems poised in a manner of constantly anticipating disaster. He's a time bomb, and the amnesia is going to be the challenge. I'm going to recommend a multiphasic personality inventory, thematic apperception testing, secondary clinical interview, sentence completion blank, Rorschach, and finally—if and when he has recovered adequately—a

Shapley-Hartford intelligence scale with a treatment team follow-up. The key now is to get him to understand and trust my motives."

"Doctor Carol?" a woman's voice said through a phone intercom on Jane's desk.

Jane pressed a button on the phone keypad. "This is Doctor Carol."

"Our Mr. Nobody's MRI is complete. We moved him into the sleep study room for his EEG."

"Okay," Jane said. "I'm on my way over there."

25

LAUGHING CORPSE

Frank Jaycastle turned his attention away from the row of dead bodies, staring now at the single smiling corpse that lay on the ground. He held his phone to his ear with his left shoulder as he made notes on a metal clipboard.

"Right here," he said, pointing the crime scene photographer toward the body. "And get a good one of his mouth. It appears that someone has removed his lateral incisors—probably gold teeth."

"His mouth looks like a carved pumpkin," Mike Mendez said. The veteran crime scene photographer stepped forward, laid down a yellow numbered marker, and took several photographs of the deceased man's head and neck.

Nearby, Jaycastle was talking on his phone. "Yes, I'm here," he said. "Where the hell is everybody? I need more hands up here to help move these bodies. It's the biggest New York crime scene since 9-11, and we've got nobody up here to handle the bodies. The service elevator? What's wrong with it? What? Well you better get it running before these bodies start melting all over the place. And send up Tino and those FBI guys. They asked to be here when we started removing the victims." He put his phone on his belt and rubbed his neck.

"What's the problem?" Mendez said. He took another photograph and checked the image on the back of the camera.

"The elevator's out."

"You mean were stuck in here with this crap?"

"Apparently."

"Did you see this?" Mendez said, pointing toward the smiling corpse's chest. "Thawed blood." He traced the flow of blood up the strata of jumbled bodies. Midway up the pile, blood pooled toward the back of an old man's head and streamed down a woman's arm, onto the grinning corpse on the floor.

"That's a problem," Jaycastle said. "If they don't get the lift running we're going to have a mess in here. I told them that it was a mistake to turn off the freezer units before we moved the bodies, but do you think anyone listens to me?"

26

FLIGHT

Bondurant stumbled through his office door, panting. His old heart throbbed painfully in his chest. He took a moment to regain his composure.

There was a knock and a police officer leaned through the doorway. "You have to leave," he said.

"Is something wrong?" said Bondurant.

"The building is on fire."

"What?"

"You need to leave the premises."

Bondurant nodded. "I understand. I'll just need to gather a few of my personal effects."

"There's no time for any of that" said the officer. "You've got to go now."

"How bad is it?"

"The fire started in the basement and it's burning fast, so follow me."

Bondurant followed the officer to the front of the hotel. Two officers waved them over to the front door. The lobby was deserted. Across the atrium, smoke poured out of the twin elevator shafts and collected in the ceiling.

Bondurant exited the building, relieved to see that the fire department had not yet arrived. He joined the crowd of police and evacuees. He turned back, watching and waiting for the building to burn.

27

SLEEPER AWAKENS

"**S**till nothing," Jaycastle said, standing in the fourteenth-floor elevator with his thumb on the down button. His phone rang. He recognized the number.

"Tino," he said into the phone, "any luck down there figuring out what's wrong with this lift? I have power here. The problem has to be on your end."

"Don't worry about it, Frank," Tino said. "We have a fire down here."

"A fire? How bad?"

"It's more than likely that we'll lose the building,"

"What?"

"Who's with you up there?"

"Just me and Mendez."

"Are you still on the fourteenth?"

"Yes."

"Think you can get over to that fire escape?"

"I think so."

"Good. Make your way down to the eleventh floor where the stairs are welded off. We'll get a ladder to you."

"Those telescoping truck ladders only extend a hundred feet," said Jaycastle. "At best, that places it between the ninth and tenth stories."

"That should be close enough. Just hang tight for now, and I'll let you know what the fire guys say. They just arrived."

"Ten-four," Jaycastle said. He clipped his phone to his belt and stepped out of the elevator. "Mendez, you're not going to believe it. Mendez?"

Mendez lay motionless on the floor with the upper half of his body in a pool of blood. The strange smiling corpse that he had been photographing was nowhere to be seen. Jaycastle started to move toward his downed colleague but stopped when he noticed across the room a blond-haired man wearing a black suit. The man was grooming himself in front of an old mirrored dresser. The man leaned close to the mirror and cocked his head to the side, checking his face and hair. He stepped back and brushed his hands down each coat sleeve. He looked at his hands briefly and then watched Jaycastle through the reflection in the mirror.

28

HOME IS WHERE THE HEART IS

Rand completed the twelve-mile drive to his home in Montclair, New Jersey, in record time: twenty-seven minutes. It was his personal best. Barney, his black Labrador retriever, greeted him eagerly as he came through the front door.

"What's up, big boy?" Rand said. He dropped his keys on a mirrored credenza and hung his coat on the stair railing. Barney left the room and returned holding a stuffed-rabbit chew toy in his mouth. He nosed the toy into Rand's leg and backed up and waited.

"Sorry, big boy," Rand said. "Not tonight." He knelt in front of Barney and held the dog's head between his hands. "We'll play tomorrow." He gave the dog a robust pat on his shoulder and then started up the stairs. He made his way to the bedroom and eased the door open. The room's only light came from a reading lamp on a side table and the silent television. Renee reclined in bed with her legs snuggled under the thick comforter. She wore a red nightgown. The right shoulder strap had fallen down. She tinkered with her phone and didn't notice Rand.

"Hello," Rand said.

Renee looked up. "Well, hello."

"I think that has to be the sexiest thing that I've ever seen."

"Oh please," Renee said. She looked down, checking herself. "Oops," she said, pulling the loose strap back over her shoulder. She held a small gift-wrapped box on her lap.

"What's that?" said Rand.

"Just a little something."

"Don't move," Rand said. He walked toward the closet.

Renee held out a second box. "Are you looking for this?"

"Why you little sneak! Found my hiding place, did you?"

Renee smiled and reached for the bottle of champagne that sat on the side table. She poured two glasses and held one toward Rand. "Should we open them now or later?" she said.

Rand came over and took the glass. "As if you could wait." He bent down, gave her a kiss, and took a sip of champagne. "That's good," he said. He took another sip, picked up the remote from the nightstand, and aimed it toward the television. The picture on the screen showed an image of a blazing building surrounded by fire trucks.

Rand stared at the screen for a moment. Something about the image struck him strangely. He switched off the TV and placed the remote on the table along with his phone. He unbuckled his shoulder holster and hung his service revolver on the back of a small desk chair. He turned toward Renee with a puzzled expression.

"What's wrong?" Renee said.

Rand didn't answer. He turned the television back on. The screen was now showing a tasteless advertisement for a local used car dealer.

"What are you doing?" she said.

"That burning building…"

"What about it?"

"It was a scene of a crime, it—" Rand stopped talking as the news programming resumed. The station was now showing sports highlights. He quickly changed channels, clicking through several local stations until he found the burning building story again. "Damn it." He turned the volume up and listened as a frenzied reporter described the building disaster.

"What is it?" Renee said.

"I was there earlier," Rand said soberly. "When I left that building, it was secure. I have men in there."

"If you have to go, I understand."

"You always do," Rand said. "You're too good to me. You know, before I got into law enforcement I used to see scenes on cop shows where an agent is rustled out of bed in the middle of the night by an important phone call, and the agent's girlfriend or wife goes ballistic. I used to shake my head and wonder if it really happened that way or that often. And now I live through it on a nightly basis."

"It hasn't really been all that bad," Renee said. "It does make it worse, though, on a special occasion."

As if on cue, Rand's phone rang.

Renee frowned. "Let me guess—that will be Mark."

Rand put the phone to his hear. "What the hell happened, Mark?"

"You heard?"

"I'm watching the news."

"It went up like a powder keg."

"Tell me all of our guys are out of there."

"Yeah, but two of Tino's men are unaccounted for: one officer named Mendez and Agent Jaycastle. They were still on the fourteenth floor when the place went up. And we lost the entire crime scene. It's all gone."

"Jaycastle," Rand said. "I was just starting to like him. I want to know how it happened. This was no accident. I want to know how and by whom. Where is that Bondurant character?"

"I don't know where Bondurant is now, but the police officer that was assigned to watch him states that the old man never left his office."

"What a disaster," Rand said, looking at his wife with a cheerless expression. "Mark, I'll meet you in Tino's office in an hour."

29

GOLDEN

Bondurant exited the convenience store, sipping from a water bottle. Down the street smoke poured out of the fire, and the air around him was filmy and gray. Two blocks in the distance, Madison Tower was burning. Black plumes of smoke and orange flames licked upward, high above the building's roofline, illuminating the slow passing clouds with a strange amber glow.

Bondurant smiled and took a final sip of water. He threw the empty container into an alley. He grabbed his car keys and walked across the street to a private parking deck and into a stairwell.

"You have betrayed me," a cryptic voice said from the shadows.

Bondurant froze. He recognized the odd accent. His heart pounded in his chest as he looked around in the dark. Underneath the stairs he glimpsed golden hair and a flash of razor-sharp teeth. After a moment, Galatin emerged and faced him. He still wore the tattered black tuxedo, but his body had reconstituted itself; his youth had been fully restored.

"Impossible..." Bondurant said, staggering backward.

Galatin stepped closer, staring at Bondurant with a menacing smile. "Come, and talk with me. Tell me where I may find the one you now serve?"

"Please..." Bondurant whimpered.

"Viro Andronicus?" Galatin snarled. He stepped closer. His lips parted, flashing his pointed teeth. "I am aware that he goes by the name Harold Fain now."

"Harold Fain?" Bondurant swallowed hard. "Yes."

"Continue."

"What do you want to know?"

"Where?"

"I don't know where. Fain released me from his service."

"When is your next rendezvous?"

"There isn't one."

"You should know better than to deceive me."

"I swear it."

"Then tell me more. Tell me something that will save your life."

Thoughts raced wildly through Bondurant's mind. "I don't know anything," he said.

"What about the man you spoke to in the tower? You called him David."

"You saw?"

"Yes."

"David is Fain's new Realtor."

"I see. And does this new slayer have a last name?"

Bondurant didn't answer.

"Shall I rend the information from your lifeless body?"

Bondurant shook his head. "Anslem, his name is David Anslem. Fain took him last night. He brought him here to your tower. But before his conversion was complete, Anslem lashed out and, as you are probably aware, your old lair didn't survive the discord."

"But I survived," Galatin said. He folded his hands behind his back, and leaned toward Bondurant with his callous eyes looming. "Now tell me why Anslem was chosen?"

"I don't know."

"Where is he?"

"No one knows. Not even Fain."

"How strong did Fain make him?"

"Only Fain knows the answer to that."

"And now to the matter of your disloyalty," said Galatin.

"I thought you had perished!"

"Death?" said Galatin. "How amusing."

"How could I have known?"

"Of course you couldn't have. But once you thought I was departed from this world, how fast your allegiance changed."

"Fain spared me if I agreed to continue to manage the tower."

"And now the tower is gone."

"Yes, and Fain no longer has need of my services."

"And neither do I."

"Please…"

Galatin turned away, lost in his thoughts. "Anslem rebelled. Interesting."

"I've told you all that I know," Bondurant said. He backed away and turned and lunged for the open door.

In an instant, Galatin appeared in front of him, cutting off his escape. Galatin dragged Bondurant into the darkness of the stairwell and drove the long index finger of his right hand like a dagger into the back of Bondurant's skull, killing him instantly, and siphoning away a lifetime of memories.

30

BRAIN SCANS

Jane sat in the radiology imaging lab, staring at four large flat-panel computer monitors that showed various 3-D images of David's brain. She retrieved a sheet of X-ray film of the same brain that had been taken upon his admission into the ER earlier that day. She angled the image toward the florescent ceiling lights and read from the ER notes, speaking into the end of a small recorder.

"Noted from Dr. Michael Henderson's records. Small areas of increased signals on T-1 weighted data sets are noted in the white matter. The scattered areas of increased white matter signals are compatible with MS plaques."

Jane stopped recording. "Multiple Sclerosis?" she said softly. "What the hell is going on with this guy's brain?"

She stepped over to the wall and placed the film on a lighted panel. She studied the image briefly and returned to the desk and studied the more recent computer brain images. She spoke into the recorder again.

"None of the earlier lesions are now seen on the T-2 data sets, and there appear to be no surrounding edemas. Unfortunately we don't have older studies to use for correlation. The rest of the brain is well preserved. The midline structures are undisplaced. There is no intra- or extra-axial effect. The repeat MRI of John Doe's brain reveals no significant cerebral atrophy. Dr. Michael Henderson and Dr. Van Jacobs noted that there were small caudate nuclei bilaterally, and both physicians concurred that these findings can be compatible with a diagnosis of traumatic brain injury. Since there is evidence of sclerae, the pathogenesis of the plaques would need to be explored, and a demyelinating disease would have to be considered. Based on the current MRI data, there is no evidence of brain trauma or disease. There's nothing wrong with John Doe's brain."

A nurse entered the lab, pushing a metal supply cart.

Jane paused the recorder. "Hi, Linda."

"I didn't mean to interrupt your notes, Dr. Carol."

"No worries. I'm pretty much done here."

"So there's nothing wrong with him?"

"Oh there's definitely something wrong with him."

"I thought I heard you say—"

"His brain seems physically fine." Jane placed the recorder on the table and looked at the computer monitors. "But there is definitely something wrong here."

"What do you mean?"

Jane gestured at the negative on the lighted wall. "That's a snapshot of his brain imaged this morning. It shows evidence of some unknown disease and physical damage, but now there's nothing."

"Are you're sure that they're the same brain?" said Linda.

"According to the chart notes, it was verified."

"How do you explain it?"

"I currently don't have an explanation for the drastic change. It's possible, I suppose, that the occurrence was episodic and that could account for the MS, but the recovered brain damage is very peculiar. The intracranial injury was quite severe. A lot has changed since this morning. There appears to be a change in cortical thickness as well—which, quite frankly, is impossible. That and the absence of the earlier surface abnormalities make me wonder if it's even the same brain. We have contradictory pieces of information here."

"Well, if it *is* the same brain, this guy has a great immune system. I didn't think people recovered from brain damage that quickly."

"Your right. They don't. None of it makes sense, and since ana-lyzing volumetric data is not my field of expertise, I'm not going to worry about it. Dr. Henderson should have spent more time on this one before shipping him over here, but since he didn't, and since our John Doe seems now to have a physically healthy brain, it's time to concentrate on his psychological trauma."

31

MISSING

Rand entered Tino's office.

"Ah, good, you're here," Shullman said. He sat on a short leather couch next to Tino's desk with his feet propped on an old office chair.

"Where are Parker and Tino?" Rand said.

"Tino's somewhere in the building, and Parker hasn't checked in." Shullman took a deep breath and blew it out. "Brace yourself."

"What is it?"

"David Anslem is missing."

"Damn it!" Rand said. "What do we know about it?"

"It doesn't look good. When the agent that was dispatched to watch Anslem's church didn't check in, the branch office sent a car over. They found the agent murdered—shot in the back of the head. Anslem's vehicle was still on the premises, and his keys, cell phone, and wallet were discovered inside."

"I gave Anslem my word that I would keep him safe," Rand said. "Why would they want him?"

Tino came through the door.

"I'm sorry to hear about your men," Rand said.

"Yeah," Tino said. "Me too."

"What happened up there tonight?"

Tino shook his head. "It doesn't make any sense," He walked over to a shelf on the wall and glanced at a collection of department memorabilia. He picked up a framed photograph of himself and Jaycastle at department Christmas party. "This was last year," he said, flashing a cheerless smile. "And officer Mendez had only been married for two years. His wife just had a baby…a girl. And Jaycastle…well, he was Jaycastle, a good friend and colleague. It should have been easy to get them out of there tonight. I had just spoken to him when the fire crews arrived. We had a plan, and they both had plenty of time to get out. But they didn't make the rendezvous point, and the building had become too unstable for the fire teams to go in."

"What about radio contact?"

"Initially we did, but we lost contact." Tino put the photograph back on the shelf and walked behind his desk.

"Damn peculiar," Rand said

"I lost two good men tonight," said Tino, "and I want to know why. It's my opinion that the fire was started deliberately."

Shullman said, "But the crime scene was secure. The entire build-ing was locked down tight."

Tino slid into his chair. "I don't know."

"That crime scene was deliberately destroyed," Rand said.

Tino glanced at his watch. "It will take days to dig through it all. But rest assured that we're going to sort this all out."

"Any more information from your Madison Tower teams?" Rand said.

"Statements are still coming in. Several of the Madison Tower ten-ant interviews are ready for review."

"The sooner my men start their analysis, the better," said Rand.

"When the scanning department finishes digitizing the briefs, I'll give you the code to access our statement logs and agent reports."

Rand took a deep breath. "It's going to be a late one."

"Well…" Shullman said. "Tell Renee that I tried."

Rand pulled out his phone and dialed his wife. "Hey," he said, "it's me. Yeah, don't wait up. I'll have to make it up to you."

32

TESTS

A nurse raised David's bed so that he was half-reclining. She placed several dozen electrodes around his skull and then attached two individual electrodes on long wires to each side of his face, at the corners of his eyes. Jane stood at the foot of the bed overseeing the procedure.

"What are you doing to me?" David said, staring up at the nurse.

The nurse adjusted David's pillow. "Just running a few tests," she said. She moved to a stainless steel medical cart and began unwrapping supplies.

"EEG," Jane said. She made a note on a clipboard and came over to the left side of the bed. "Electroencephalograph. We're going to study your brainwaves. Do you remember us discussing the procedure earlier?"

"Yes."

"Well, it's a good sign that you remember. Is anything coming back to you yet?"

"Sorry, but no," said David.

"Is there anything that you can tell me? Anything at all that would be helpful. Maybe you can remember a name, or perhaps some symbol of your past? Anything?"

"No, I'm sorry, but there's nothing."

A technician reclined the bed so that David was lying flat on his back. "How's that?" said the technician.

David nodded.

The nurse returned to the right side of the bed, holding a tray of syringes and vials of medications. She looked down at David's arm and noted his peculiar clothing. "Why isn't he in a hospital gown?" she asked.

"We've had trouble removing his clothes," Jane said.

The nurse shrugged, reached down, and touched the fabric of David's shirtsleeve. The cloth was tight against his skin, and she found it difficult to get her finger under the cuff. With some effort, she rolled the material back, revealing his wrist. She tried rolling the sleeve some more, but the strange fabric was too strong. She retrieved a syringe and began looking for a suitable vein on top of David's hand.

"What are you giving me?" David said.

"A mild sedative to help you relax," said the nurse. "It's a very low dosage. Anything stronger would upset the results of the test."

David nodded uneasily.

"Well, you appear much more alert and oriented," Jane said. "Tell me what you're thinking?"

"I'm trying not to think."

"I see…. And what about the flashback and intrusive imagery that you were having?"

"Are you interested in the answer to that question, or are you trying to distract me?"

"Both."

"I seem to suddenly remember that I don't like needles."

Jane smiled. "Maggie here is very good with a needle—so fast you'll barely know you've been stuck."

Maggie held David's arm and swabbed the back of his hand with antiseptic. "This might sting a little," she said. She carefully lined up the syringe on a vein on top of David's hand, and stabbed the needle downward at a slight angle. The needle glanced off the skin. She tried the injection again, but this time she lessened the angle and the needle caught on the skin. She applied steady pressure until needle penetrated David's hand. "Sorry," she said, looking up at David. "Is that uncomfortable?"

"No," he said. "I can barely feel anything."

Maggie pulled the needle out and placed a sterile cotton ball on the back of David's hand. She looked at the syringe with an odd expression. The end of the needle was slightly bent. She placed the damaged syringe into a hazardous waste pail and rolled the medical tray out of the way.

"You should start to feel a bit dopey," Jane said. "This will help you fall asleep."

"Sleep?" David said. "No!"

"Its okay," Jane said.

"But it's *not* okay."

"For us to get an active response, we will need you to be unconscious."

"I told you that I'm not able to sleep."

"You shouldn't worry about your—"

"I'm not worried for myself."

"What do you mean?"

"I'm not going to sleep."

"We're going to leave you now," said Jane, "but we will be monitoring you from a control room down the hall." She pointed at a video bubble in the ceiling. "Please try not to resist sleeping. The rest you get will do your mind some good. It will also enhance our results." She reached over and made a final adjustment on David's electrode helmet, and then turned and left the room.

33

RECALL

Jane watched David on a video monitor as he lay motionless in bed. A small blue screen on the bottom right corner of the monitor displayed a series of flat white lines produced by his brainwaves. She took a pen from her white lab coat and made a notation in his file: *4:30 a.m. and patient is resting quietly, without any complaints.*

"Maybe he's an insomniac," a technician said.

"He should have been out cold hours ago," Jane said. "He hasn't closed his eyes in nearly four hours, and the scan indicates that he hasn't even blinked in that time. Something's not right here."

"How is he not able to blink?" said the technician. "His eyes would dry out of their sockets."

"It's very odd."

"What's his malfunction anyway?"

"Still to be determined," Jane said. "But think of him as a prisoner of his own mind. He's a prisoner of the lower strata of his subconscious, to be exact. The way he processes information is all backward. His powerful subconscious thoughts break into awareness in the form of illusions, and the boundaries between what is real and unreal are lost. He's caught in the wash and is completely unable to respond to the environment around him."

"Wow, that sucks."

"Yes, it does. Now, cut the lights. I think we've been more than patient. Let's go to pitch-black inside his room. Switch the monitoring cameras to infrared."

The technician took a sip of coffee and typed in a code in the control panel. "There go the lights," he said. "Now let me just switch cameras." The monitor displayed a green-hued image of David's room.

There was a ping on the EEG monitor.

"Now were getting somewhere," Jane said. She examined the line-tracing stage on the monitor readout, noting the changes in David's brainwaves. The image showed a sudden burst of single-complex k-waves. Heavy spindling appeared across the background like a small tremor on a Richter scale.

"He's out, just like that," the technician said.

Jane leaned in closer to the video monitor. "That wasn't a sleep burst," she said. "He's not asleep. He's still wide awake." She watched David on the monitor as he sat up in the bed and stared around the room.

"Oh my God," the technician said, pointing to the EEG monitor. "What do you make of that?"

"Busy little neurons," Jane said. The monitor showed several tight zigzag lines with jagged spikes up and down the screen. "It appears to be a massive photo paroxysmal response," said Jane, "and it happened as soon as we cut the lights. No wonder he doesn't like to close his eyes. It's like a grand mal epileptic seizure." She picked up David's chart and made a note in his file: *Abnormalities presented at 4:45 a.m. The irregular patient response was elicited by elimination of central vision fixation. Patient appears to be scotosensitive. Specific precipitating stimulus was a zero-potential lighted room that induced a high-amplitude occipital or generalized paroxysmal discharge.*

"Umm...Doctor Carol, you might want to see this?"

Jane looked up from her chart notes. The technician was staring at David's vital sign monitor. The heart monitor alarm sounded with a steady ping and showed a flat line.

David could be seen on the video monitor standing next to his bed. He had removed the electrodes from his head and was now removing the heart monitor from his chest. The respiratory alarm now beeped alternately with the heart monitor.

"Lavsrister," said David.

"What's he talking about?" the technician said.

Jane shook her head. "His speech is confused, like someone talking in his sleep."

"Lavsrister!" David repeated, but louder this time and his speech changed. He sounded angry.

"Was that in German?" Jane said.

"Komm Lavsrister," David said.

"It sounds like he's losing it," the technician said.

"We are invincible," David said.

Jane continued to stare at the monitor. She watched as David reached for the side of the bed, broke the metal handrail away from the mattress frame, and threw it against the wall. He spoke in a rambling manner. Jane could only make out a few words in English. His words ran together and his dialect changed several times from German to Chinese to Spanish. He walked to the front of the room. kicked at the reinforced metal door, and flew into a rage, overturning his bed and smashing medical equipment.

Jane picked up the phone and dialed security. "This is Doctor Carol. We have a situation in the Sleep Study Room 4. I need guards with a four-point restraint to meet me in front of that room ASAP." She put the phone down and pushed a button on the console that reactivated the lights in David's room. With the lights now on, David calmly walked over and sat in a chair next to the bed.

"How bizarre," Jane said.

34

SUPERIOR RANGE

Jane returned to David's room, accompanied by four large security guards. The room's heavy metal door was slightly open and had a large dent in its center. Jane peeked through the shattered window. David sat calmly in a chair next to his bed with his hands on his lap. He appeared for the moment to be in control of his thoughts and actions. She tried the door handle. The door felt stuck and scraped slightly as it opened.

"Come in, Dr. Carol," David said.

Jane walked to the center of the room. She left the door open, with the four-man restraint team waiting behind her.

"The ordeal seems to be behind you," she said.

"I'm okay now," David said.

Jane waved off the security guards. She turned and surveyed the damaged room. There were several holes in the walls, and the damaged door had broken away from its reinforced concrete frame. The EEG equipment had somehow remained intact; a red light chirped quietly on the front monitor. David sat calmly, watching her.

"I have to admit," Jane said, "I've never seen anything like this before."

"My apologies, Doctor Carol, but I did warn you."

"About sleeping?"

"Yes."

"But you never fell asleep."

"You drugged me."

"I'm aware of that. The medication we gave you seemed to have no effect. When we cut the lights to your room, however, you became hyper-adrenalized. Do you recall what went through your mind? What caused you to lash out and destroy your room like this?"

"I remember."

"Do you want to talk about it?"

"I remember everything, Doctor Carol."

"Tell me what you mean by that?"

"I feel better now and wish to leave this place."

"I see…" Jane said. "That's good to hear, and it is my goal as well. I want to help you." She walked to the EEG counter, retrieved a four-wheeled stool, and rolled it over to where David was sitting. "Quite a mess in here," she said. "Just before you lashed out, you shouted something." She referred to her notes. "Livsri—"

"Lavsrister," David interrupted.

"Yes, that's right. I've never heard that word before. It doesn't sound English."

"It's a Norwegian word."

"What does it mean?"

"It means 'life shaker.'"

"That's very interesting. Do you speak Norwegian?"

"Yes."

"What does 'life shaker' mean?"

"Its not important."

"Then why did you say it?"

"I said a lot of things."

"Yes you did, and you spoke in several different languages. Do you remember?"

"Yes."

"How many languages are you fluent in?"

"A few."

"You obviously come from some education, then. When I entered the room earlier, you said that you remember everything. Do you re-member your name?"

"My name is David Anslem."

Jane sat down and wrote David's name in the file. "What else can you tell me about yourself, Mr. Anslem?"

"What would you like to know?"

"Everything. Where are you from? What do you do for a living? Your favorite color. All of your likes and dislikes." She made a note in her log. *Patient is focused. Seems now vividly aware of his surroundings.*

"Is this a test?" David said.

Jane looked up. "It's the beginning of one. Is that all right?"

"Yes."

"Can you tell me now if you have, or ever have had, any desire to do harm to yourself?"

"I did not try to kill myself, if that's what you think."

"And Madison Tower? How did you—"

"I fell."

"Do you want to elaborate?"

"No."

"Why not?"

"I would prefer not to talk about it."

"Well it's obvious that the incident is still causing you some anxiety. I would like to help you. I want to know what happened to you."

"You could never understand what has happened to me."

"Why don't you try me? You were in pretty rough shape emotionally when they brought you in here, and now this violent display you—"

"I needed time," David said.

"Time?"

"To recover."

"Do you believe that you are now recovered?"

"Yes."

"Well, I'm glad you feel that way. And now that you have shown signs of regained memory, I would like to evaluate you. Why don't we move to a more comfortable setting?" She walked to the open door and waved the guards over. "We're coming out." She turned back toward David. "Mr. Anslem, would you mind following me?"

Jane turned toward the guards as she came through the doorway. "Could one of you track down Kim Sing and have him meet me in the conference room?"

One of the guards nodded and left the group.

David and Jane continued down the hallway with the three remaining guards trailing slowly behind them. They heard a man's muffled voice shouting obscenities from one of the rooms farther down the corridor. After a moment they came to a room with bookshelves and a long wooden conference table.

Jane closed the door and gestured at a row of black leather chairs. "Have a seat," she told David. She retrieved a book and several file folders from a cabinet and placed them on her side of the table. "Let's start with this." She placed a blank piece of paper on the table and sat facing David. "Do you recognize it?" she said. She slid the page closer to him.

"It's just a blank piece of copier paper." David said.

Jane took the page, wrote the name ANDREA, and turned it toward David. "Can you read this?"

"It says 'Andrea.' Is this necessary?"

"I'm trying to help you, Mr. Anslem."

"I told you that I'm recovered."

"No offense, but I hear that all the time," said Jane. "If you are going to be released, I'll have to determine that you are ready." She drew a small star on the paper. Can you tell me what that is?"

"It's a star."

Next to the star Jane drew a circle, a square, a triangle, and an octagon. She turned the page over.

"Don't you want me to tell you what they are?"

Jane shook her head and looked up at the clock. "Not yet. This is a simplistic, short-term memory recall measure. We'll give it a few minutes. Try not to think about anything for a moment." She glanced over the file and wrote a few notes in the margins. Several minutes passed without a word. She noticed now how David's behavior had changed. He was well-poised and alert, and he made strong eye contact.

"Okay," said Jane. "can you tell me what I wrote down a few moments ago?"

"In order?" said David.

Jane nodded.

"Initially you drew a star, followed by a circle, square, triangle, and an octagon."

"Perfect. Now, if I asked you to, can your recite your ABC's?"

"That's ridiculous," said David.

"Humor me." She took out a red cloth bag and dumped out several children's wooden blocks on the table. She sorted through the toys until she found the block with the letter A on it, and placed it in front of David.

"What is it?" she said.

"It's the letter A."

"I know this all seems simplistic and—"

"The letter A," David said. "is the first letter in the English alphabet, it's also a blood type. In school, the letter is a grade to indicate excellence, and in music it represents the sixth tone in the scale of C major. Shall I continue?"

"No," Jane said, trying to hide her amazement.

"May I leave now?"

"No. I have to be frank, Mr. Anslem. I'm impressed with your recovered memory. Having it back all at once is very rare. Earlier your memory loss and delayed recall had all but incapacitated you, but now—"

"I'm fully recovered."

Jane retrieved a book from under her files. "You certainly seem much improved." She held the book out for David to see it. "Do you like trivia?" she said. "I often use it as a basic intelligence-measuring rod. Let's see how you do." She opened the book to a random page and read a question. "British chemists William Ramsey and Morris Travers named this element in 1898 shortly after discovering Krypton."

"Neon," David said. "Neon's atomic number is 10. Neon is a noble gas, and its name is derived from the Greek word for 'new.'"

"Very impressive."

"May I go now?"

"You seem to be in an big hurry to leave, Mr. Anslem."

There was a soft knock on the conference room door.

"Come in," Jane said.

The door opened and an elderly Asian man stepped through. He wore a pair of gray overalls and black boots.

"Hello, Mr. Sing," Jane said. "Please come in."

"I heard you wanted to see me," said Mr. Sing.

"Yes. I would like you to meet someone. Mr. Anslem, this is Kim Sing. He and his wife own Sing & Clean. They have contracted with the hospital for all of our janitorial needs—and do fabulous job, I might add."

Sing smiled and gave a little bow in David's direction.

"Mr. Sing, this is one of our patients, David Anslem. Mr. Anslem speaks Chinese. I was wondering if you wouldn't mind asking him something in Chinese for me."

"What would you like me to ask him?"

Jane took out a piece of paper and concealed it from David. She wrote down a question and handed it to Sing.

Sing glanced at the note and shrugged his shoulders. He looked up and said in Chinese, "Where are you currently located?"

"Mr. Anslem, did you understand what Mr. Sing asked you?"

"Yes."

"Answer Mr. Sing's question, but in English for my benefit."

David nodded. "I'm on the sixth floor, of Mercy Hospital, in New York City, in New York state, in the United States...the planet Earth, Milky Way galaxy, et cetera, et cetera."

"Thank you Mr. Sing," said Jane. "That will be all."

"You didn't believe me?" David said. "Did you just think that I was just rambling in the dark earlier?"

"I believe you, but I'm a doctor, and everything that I see and hear must be verified. Can you tell me if you are still having the visions and the violent ideation? Are the voices still urging you to hurt people?"

"I don't want to harm anyone," David said.

"You didn't answer my question, Mr. Anslem."

"I still hear the voices, but now I'm in control.

"What do you mean by that?"

"I like you, Dr. Carol. You're intelligent, beautiful, and you have your whole life ahead of you. I don't wish to see you harmed because you helped me."

"Harmed?"

"I need to leave here before…" he trailed off.

"Before what?"

"Anything that I say now will only encourage you to keep me longer, to try to help me when help is no longer needed. And now you are in danger."

Jane started to make a note, but stopped when she noticed the peculiar way in which David's eyes seemed to mirror the light.

"Please stop writing, Dr. Carol. It's no longer necessary."

Jane started to speak, but she stopped when she heard the patient emergency alarm sound through the room's overhead speaker. She walked to the intercom and pushed the button.

"Timmy, what's going on out there?" she said.

There was no answer. She turned back to David. "Let's get you back to your room, Mr. Anslem." She opened the door and stepped into the hallway. The guards were gone. She looked down both sides of the corridor. There was no sign of any other staff, and she heard raised voices coming from around the corner. The commotion seemed to be coming from the patient common area.

Jane and David turned right and walked a short distance down the hallway. Just ahead of them, a female patient wandered in their direction. Jane recognized her.

"What's wrong, Vicky?"

Vicky didn't answer. She cupped her hands to her eyes and moved past them toward the end of the hall.

"Will she be all right?" David said.

"There's nowhere for her to go," said Jane. "The corridor is closed off. I'm more concerned about what provoked her, and why there's no staff accompanying her."

They rounded the corner to discover the patient activity center in turmoil. Couches were overturned and two orderlies lay unconscious on the floor. There were frightened patients huddled in small groups around the edges of the room. The main door was locked, jammed through the handles with a broken mop head. Several guards could be seen through the reinforced glass window, struggling unsuccessfully to break through the blocked entrance. In the far left corner of the room, a large bald patient threatened two terrified nurses with the jagged end of the broken mop handle.

"What seems to be the problem, John?" Jane said calmly.

The large man turned toward her. His eyes were crazed, and uncontrollable rage showed on his face. The tip of the broken mop handle was soaked in blood, and one of the nurses sobbed and held her hands over her stomach. Blood stained the front of her white uniform.

"There's no need for any of this, John," Jane said. She edged sideways toward the barred entrance. "Why don't you put the stick down and we'll talk about it?"

The large patient snorted and charged toward her.

David stepped in front of Jane.

"John...don't do it!" Jane shouted.

John paused briefly, towering over David. The large man bellowed something inaudible and stabbed at David with the mop handle. David easily sidestepped the clumsy assault and gripped the demented patient by the wrist, neutralizing his makeshift weapon. John swung down hard with his free right hand. David caught the fist in his open palm. He now held both of the man's arms. David slowly began to squeeze, applying constant pressure. John screamed and fell to his knees. David squeezed harder, crushing the bones in both of the man's wrists.

"*Kill him,*" a voice urged inside David's mind. The sight of the helpless man filled David with a feeling of euphoria. A single thought resonated inside his mind like a second voice: "*Destroy him.*"

"Stop!" David shouted. "I have to stop..." He released his grip, and John slumped, whimpering, to the floor, cradling his injured hands.

Jane hurried over to the main door and removed the makeshift wooden bolt from the handles. She stepped aside as the four-man security team came through. She followed the guards back to where David was standing. "Thank you for intervening, Mr. Anslem," she said. "That was quite an impressive display."

"I understand it all now," David said. "What I've become."

"You mean *whom* you've become, don't you?"

"Yes, I suppose." David watched as the four guards secured John in a restraint jacket. A nurse injected John with a tranquilizer, and an instant later the large man stared up at the lights with an enormous smile on his face.

"I'm afraid this little incident is going to require a lot of paperwork," Jane said. "But I would like to continue the conversation that we were having earlier."

David shook his head. "I don't want to cause you more trouble than I already have, Dr. Carol. I have to leave here."

"You said that once before, and you said that I was in some kind of danger because of you."

"Yes, that is true."

"Do you want to tell me why?"

"No."

"Why not?"

"The less you know, the better. And the sooner I leave, the better."

35

VISITOR

Timmy Halverson sat in the psych ward guard station, lazily thumbing through a *Car and Driver* magazine that he had read at least a dozen times over the past two weeks. He glanced at his watch, stifled a yawn, and wondered how he was going to make it through the final thirty minutes of his shift. He looked back down at the magazine and then glanced over a long row of surveillance monitors. The screen on the far right showed a grainy image of a tall man dressed in black. He was standing by the front entrance. The man reached for the door. There was a soft buzz and a green light flashed on Timmy's control panel. He pressed the intercom button. "What can I do for you?" he said.

"I'm here to pick up a patient," the man said.

"I wasn't informed," Timmy said. "What is the patient's name?"

"David Anslem."

"The name doesn't sound familiar," Timmy said, turning toward a computer monitor. He pulled up the patient records and studied them. "No, no, David Anslem's under our care—sorry."

"I'm aware that he was admitted as a John Doe last night."

"Oh yeah," Timmy nodded. "I'll let Dr. Carol know you're here. You can wait in the lobby." He pressed the buzzer and unlocked the outer door. "I didn't get your name."

"My name is Harold Fain."

36

THE APPEAL

"You can't just leave the psych ward, Mr. Anslem," Jane said. "Why not?"

"It's still too early, and I would like a team to review your case."

"Dr. Carol," a man's voice said from across the room.

Jane saw an orderly standing next to a wall, holding a yellow phone.

"It's Timmy at the front desk," said the orderly. "He said that he needs to talk to you."

Jane sighed. "Wait right here, Mr. Anslem." She walked over and picked up the phone. "What's up, Timmy?"

"There is a gentleman here who would like to speak to you about one of our patients."

"I'm in the middle of something," she said. She glanced at her watch. "Tell him to make an appointment."

"He was rather insistent."

"Which patient is he asking about?"

"It's regarding the John Doe that came in last night. The man says he knows him. He says the patient's name is David Anslem."

Jane looked over at David. "The John Doe who was admitted last night? I just found out that his name is David Anslem," she said.

"What do you want me to tell Mr. Fain?"

"What is the gentleman's name?"

"He says his name is Harold Fain."

"Tell Mr. Fain that I'll be out there in a moment." Jane hung the phone on the wall and came back over to where David was standing. "Mr. Anslem, do you know someone named Harold Fain?"

"Yes," David said without emotion. "Why?"

"He's out in our main lobby. Who is he?"

David didn't answer.

"Wait here in the patient common area, Mr. Anslem. I'll be back in a moment." She turned to leave, but David grabbed her gently by the arm.

"Wait," David said. "I would like to go with you."

"I'm sorry," Jane said. "No visitations for seventy-two hours." She looked down at David hand.

David released her arm and watched as she left the room.

37

REVELATION

Rand stood in Tino's office. It was 7:55 a.m., and he was exhausted from working through the night. Tino was asleep on the couch beside his desk.

Shullman came into the office in a hurry. He held his cell phone to his ear and covered the receiver with his left hand. "I have Sheriff Cole on the line."

"Cole?" Rand asked.

"Carter's Grove, Virginia—the dig!" Shullman said.

"What does he have for us?"

Tino sat up on the couch and looked around the room groggily. "Doesn't the FBI give you guys an office of your own?" he said. He stood up and put on his suit coat and moved behind his desk.

Shullman pushed the speaker button on his phone and placed it the corner of Tinos's desk. "Sheriff Cole, I have you on loudspeaker. I have with me Special Agent Jason Rand and Chief Detective Ralph Tino of New York homicide."

Rand leaned in. "Jason Rand here. What's going on down there?"

"It's a disaster down here!" Cole said. "That's what's going on. What the hell do you have us involved in?"

"What happened?"

"It's better if I show you. I know you guys don't like these kinds of images sent over the airwaves, but you've got to see this." The display on Shullman's phone beeped. Shullman tapped the screen and waited for the image to materialize. The image showed a mass of dead cows piled up next to a tangled barbed-wire fence. Mixed with the deceased animals were several human bodies.

"What the hell are we looking at here?" Rand said.

"What you're seeing is an area of Carter's Grove," Cole said. "Do you remember Dr. Alan Butler? Well, you're looking at a bunch of his student archeologists deceased in a pasture less than a quarter mile from that pit your team discovered. Butler was found inside an underground cave that bordered the dig. His neck was broken."

"What happened to the cows and those people?"

"A dozen or more dead cows and half a dozen deceased college students. They all apparently died of electric shock. And get this: there is no electricity around the area. We had no storms last night, which rules out lightning, and the barbed wire fence wasn't electrified. And even if it was electrified, livestock wire isn't strong enough to kill."

"What about our agent?"

"Dead too, I'm sorry to say. There was a live camera over the excavation. I know it's FBI property, but with what had happened we took the liberty of reviewing the footage. Most of the recording is insignificant. Has your watch station monitor contacted you regarding what's on that camera?"

"Not yet."

"Do you have access to the recording?"

"We do," Rand said. "I'm not sure why the off-site monitor hasn't notified us? That camera had live feed."

"The time sequence you will be interested is 10:45 p.m. You will need to see what happens after that time."

Rand nodded at Shullman.

"Give me just a minute here," Shullman said. "Hang on the line, Sheriff." He retrieved his phone and entered a series of codes and passwords. "Here it comes," he said. After a moment, the edge of the Carter's Grove pit came into view. They could see the time and date sequence in the upper left corner. Shullman skipped forward to 10:44 p.m. A minute later they heard the sounds of frantic people screaming in the background. It was too garbled to hear what the people were saying. A young man came up to the side of the hole and raised a hatchet over his head. The small phone display made it difficult to see much detail. The next series of frames showed a bizarre man's face emerge from the darkness. He came out of the hole and seized the young man by the hand.

"What the hell is this?" Rand said.

"He's not wearing any clothes," Shullman said.

The video image continued. The young student's limp body went headfirst into the hole, and the naked man stepped out of view. Gunfire could be heard, followed by screams, and then the recording ended.

"We need to upload the rest of that video," Rand said.

Shullman reached down and pressed a button on his phone. "Sheriff Cole, are you still with us?"

"Yes," Cole said. "What the hell do you have us involved in down here?"

"Were there any survivors?" Rand said.

"We don't know yet. We don't know how many archaeologists were on site."

"Seven, not including Butler," Shullman said. "That's how many we approved, but it was late and I'm not sure how many came and went. Our agent there should have a kept a log. I'll look into it."

"And you say that you've not heard from our branch office?" Rand asked.

"No, I haven't. I was about to call them, but thought that I should call you first. And I need to know what we're up against here. Who the hell was in that hole in the ground? I can't exactly put out an APB on a naked maniac."

"I understand. And trust me, we're as surprised about this event as you are. Why don't you bring me up to date on what you have so far, starting with what you found at the bottom of that hole?"

"I don't have enough information to fill the back of a bar napkin right now, but we did find a door at the base of the excavation and a network of old tunnels. That's where Butler bought it. One of the passageways led to the museum basement. We found an old door that had been sealed over with bricks and mortar. The door appears to have been sealed for some time, however. We really don't know anything else at this time."

"Well, that's something," Rand said, shaking his head. "I'll notify our branch office. Thanks for your help, and let's stay in touch."

Shullman ended the call.

"Can you rewind that video?" Rand asked.

Shullman nodded. "I'll have to start it over." He pressed a button on his phone and fast-forwarded the video to the time when the man came out of the hole.

"Stop the image," Rand said.

Shullman paused the screen. The image froze on the naked man as he was just about to walk out of view. He was looking up slightly, and the camera caught a clear image of his face.

"Zoom in right there," Rand said. "Lets get a close-up of that face. Can we get a hard copy of that somewhere around here?"

"Yeah," Tino said. "I'll have one of our guys get you a print."

"Well, this is a new twist for certain," Rand said. "Every time I think we're close to getting a grip on this case, the answers just seem to wiggle from our fingers."

A plainclothes detective knocked on Tino's open office door. He held out a legal-sized case folder. "The Chan file you asked for."

"Chan?" Tino said.

"The Chinese floater. The report is still in draft. We're waiting on the autopsy."

"Oh yes," Tino said. "That's okay. I still need to see it."

Rand took the file and passed it to Tino. Tino glanced it over and placed it on the bottom of the stack of papers on his desk. There was another knock on the door and Tino's secretary came through, holding a stack of letters under her arm. She was an attractive, slender, older woman with blonde hair.

"Ms. H, I know you've met Detective Rand. This is his partner, Mark Shullman."

"Canary Grey, it's a pleasure," she said. She held the mail under her left arm and extended her right hand. She turned back to Tino. "The high school forwarded your daughter's grades. They're on top."

"Thanks, but I saw them at the house yesterday."

"Oh, so she did have them?"

"Once I told her that I had contacted the school, she decided to come clean. Her grades weren't as bad as I thought they would be." He turned to Rand and Shullman. "She's a smart kid, just not in the books."

Ms. H. handed Tino a second inter-office envelope. He looked at the department that the packet hailed from, and placed the packet on top of his pile.

"Can I get you gentlemen anything? Coffee?" Ms. H. said.

"Coffee would be great," Rand said. "Thank you."

She looked at Shullman.

Shullman nodded. "Yes, black, thank you."

Ms. H smiled and left Tino's office.

"I'm curious," Shullman said. "Your secretary's name is Canary Grey, so why do you call her Miss H?"

"The H is for Hawaii," Tino said. "As in Miss Hawaii. Canary was in the Miss America pageant a few years back."

"I see," Shullman said, nodding thoughtfully.

"How close are we on concluding the Madison tenant interviews?" Rand said.

"Close," Shullman said.

Tino said. "What are your thoughts on the preliminary coroner's report?"

Rand looked disappointed. "Of the twelve bodies moved before the fire, seven had identification and were confirmed residents of the hotel, and of those only two had lived there more than a month. Most are locals, elderly; and surprisingly none were connected to any missing persons files. Autopsies are pending, but at a glance, we're able to determine that the majority of the deaths occurred from asphyxiation. What's strange, though, is that we ran prints on the other five and had no luck with state or national databases thus far. A bunch of nobodies."

Tino's secretary came to the door again. "There's a kid here asking about a reward."

"Reward?"

"Officer Timms sent him up here. He was about to kick him out, but the young man referenced the Madison Tower incident."

"Where is he now?"

"He's waiting over in robbery, and I've got to warn you that he's a toxic dump."

Tino sighed. "Have Timms get a statement."

"He has, and that's why he wanted you to talk to him. Timms said the young man states that he saw, or thinks he saw, a man jump from the Madison Tower fire escape at the time of the collapse."

"That puts someone on the fourteenth floor," Rand said.

Tino nodded. "Send him over, and make sure he has an escort. Have Timms look into why I'm just now finding out about this jumper. That attempted suicide report is sitting on someone's desk, and I want to know who the hell is asleep at the wheel."

Rand said, "How many tips have you received since you ran it?"

Tino looked at his watch. "It's been less than twelve hours now, and we've had twenty calls. Only a handful of those could be considered genuine leads. Some were pranks, but most of the callers were only interested in cashing in on the reward."

Tino's phone rang. He pushed the speaker button. "I have a call for you," the operator said.

"Put it through," Tino said.

"I've tried sending it through, but the caller keeps calling back stating that they're getting a fax signal."

"Hold on," Tino said. He put the call on hold and dialed his secretary. "Ms. H, is there a problem with homicide's phone line?"

"I'll check," she said. He heard a click and then a lounge piano version of John Denver's "Calypso" song could be heard. A moment later, Ms. H came back on the line. "There does seem to be a problem with that line."

"Great. No wonder it's been so quiet in here. Have the watch commander look into it, and all of our calls should be patched through to vice, extension 8036, for the time being."

"I'll take care of it."

A police officer showed up outside Tino's door with a skinny, long-haired young white man wearing green rubber flip-flops, blue jeans, and a dirty white long-sleeve button-down shirt. The man's hands, feet, and face were smudged with dirt like that of a homeless person. His soiled hands trembled as he played with the buttons on his shirt. His head twitched, and his eyes darted around the room in a constant orbit.

"Who do we have here?" Tino asked.

The officer stepped through the doorway and looked at the name on the edge of a file. "His name is Mark Deforno." He passed Tino the file. "He has a fairly clean background. He's had only one prior possession-related arrest, nothing major."

"Come in, Mr. Deforno," Tino said.

"That's okay," Deforno said. "I'm a little claustrophobic."

"You're not in any trouble, Mr. Deforno," the officer said. He gave Deforno a pat on the shoulder and left the room.

"We just want to talk to you," Tino said.

"About the reward..." Deforno said, edging just inside the open doorway.

Tino nodded. "That depends on what you know."

"Can I talk to you from here?"

"That's fine," Tino said. He looked at Deforno's file.

Shullman whispered to Rand, "Where is our resident FBI behavior expert when you need her?"

Rand nodded.

Tino looked up from the file. "Are you currently taking any medications?"

"Yes. Methadone, Ativan, and Zofran."

"What are you taking the Methadone for?"

"For my stomach pain. Crohn's disease."

"How many did you have in the past twenty-four hours?"

"Seven, and three Ativan."

"What dose?"

"Two milligrams, I think."

"Is it safe to mix the two medications?"

Deforno shrugged.

Tino glanced over the file. "You were on the street when you saw the man jump off the roof of the building? Not a lot of details in your statement here, just that you saw a man jump from Madison Tower."

"Yes, but he didn't go off the roof. He jumped off the fire escape."

"The fourteenth story?"

"I don't know what floor. He was near the top of the building."

"Are you certain?"

"Yes, and I wasn't the only one who saw him. There was a whole crowd of people there, but only a few of us saw him on the fire escape."

"Was it the opinion of the onlookers and yourself that he was pushed, fell, or jumped?"

"I think he jumped. I remember thinking something was wrong with the building when I noticed that part of the outer wall had disappeared. *Whoosh* and it was gone, and then the man came out and went over the rail."

"With the building in peril," said Tino, "the man could have conceivably been trying to escape, and just fell."

"It's possible, I suppose," Deforno said.

"It must have been some scene when the man landed."

"I'll say it was. He landed on top of a Yellow Cab; the roof caved in and glass was everywhere."

"And it's your opinion that it was a suicide."

"I didn't say that. How would I know what that guy was thinking? If you want to know if it's a suicide, why don't you ask the man who jumped?"

"Right," Tino said, frowning. "How about we show a little respect?"

Deforno shrugged. "I'm just saying—"

Rand stood up. "What *are* you saying?"

"I'm saying that you should ask the man who jumped because he didn't die. In fact, he didn't have a mark on him. Do you know what they call those guys that survive plane crashes and everyone else dies?"

"I give up, Tino said.

Deforno shook his head. "No, I'm asking."

"Lucky?" Tino blurted out sarcastically.

"'Long Shot Paradox' or something like that, I think?" Shullman said.

Rand shook his head. "Are you telling us that man fell nearly fifteen stories without a scratch on him?"

"Yep," said Deforno. "He sat right up on the car like nothing happened. He might have been hurt on the inside though, because he wasn't talking, and they took him away in an ambulance."

"Do you remember what name was on the side of the ambulance?"

"Sorry," Deforno said. "Can I have my money now?"

"You'll be taken care of," Tino said

Deforno held out his hand.

"What do I look like, a bank?" Tino said. He pulled out a small pad of paper and signed his name on the bottom. He tore off the sheet and handed it to Deforno. "Go down the hall and hand this to my secretary, Ms. H—Canary Grey. You can't miss her. She's on the right-hand side, just inside the two main doors. Big poster of the Hawaiian islands behind her desk."

Deforno looked at the sheet of paper. "Five hundred dollars," he said under his breath. "Easy money," he said, and turned and hurried out of Tino's office.

"I think I made his day," Tino said.

Rand nodded. "I think he just made ours."

An agent wearing a thick red sweater and black pants came to Tino's office door. He knocked on the door and leaned through.

"Torres, what can I do for you?" Tino asked. "And what the hell are you wearing?

"The sweater?" Torres asked, staring down the front of his chest. "The wife made it. She's taking up crocheting."

"What the hell did she knit it with, two telephone poles? I can see your nipples, for Christ sake."

Torres frowned. "Here, I heard you were looking for this," he said, holding out a file folder. "It's an attempted suicide. Some nut jumped off the roof of Madison Tower. It's that building over—"

"Have you been living in a vacuum?" Tino said. He came around the desk and took the file. "Madison Tower chatter has been all over the department. Haven't you been watching the news?"

"This isn't my case," Torres said. "It's Agent Swartz's."

"Margaret's case? Well, where the hell is she?"

"She's off this week."

"Are you her backup?"

"Yes."

"Well, there you have it," Tino said.

"Jesus," Torres said.

"You may go now," Tino said. He opened the file and started reading the notes. He turned the file around and handed it to Rand. "It appears they took him to Mercy Medical Center."

Rand took the file and looked it over. The right side of the folder contained a two-page vehicle collision report, along with witness statements. Rand flipped several more pages until he came to the EMS report. "It's amazing that he survived the fall," he said, reading over the notes. He noticed an inverted photograph paper-clipped to the inside cover of the file. Rand took the picture and turned it around. "Damn!" he said, showing the photograph to Tino and Shullman.

Tino shrugged.

"You got to be kidding me!" Shullman said. "The preacher?"

"David Anslem," Rand said.

"You know him?" Tino said.

"He was Harold Fain's prison minister in Florida. He helped us with the case."

"What was he doing here?"

"I don't know," Rand said thoughtfully. He looked at Shullman. "Get a call off to Mercy Medical. Make sure Anslem's still there. Then lets get a team over there. Tell our guys not to do anything until we arrive. Fire off a scan of Anslem's photograph, and make sure that he doesn't leave. I want a secure perimeter around the hospital."

38

PURSUIT

Jane came into the lobby. A tall man stood by the front door with his back to her. He had long black hair and wore a long, tailored black coat.

"Mr. Fain," Jane said, walking over to greet him. Fain turned toward her and she paused, momentarily stunned by his strange appearance. After a moment, she continued toward him with her hand out. "I'm Dr. Carol."

Fain didn't speak. He stared down at Jane's outreached hand for a moment before taking it. There was a slight snap of static when their hands touched, and his skin felt cool to the touch. She glanced him over. His face was smooth like porcelain, and he was extraordinarily handsome. Everything about him exuded human perfection, bordering on angelic, except for the radiant blue eyes that stared down at her harshly.

"What can I do for you, Mr. Fain?"

"I'm here seeking information about your patient, David Anslem."

Jane folded her arms across her chest. "I see. And may I ask what your relationship is to Mr. Anslem?"

"We are friends."

"How did you know he was here?"

"I was on my way to visit him and I heard that there was a horrible accident. How is he?"

"Do you know what happened to him?"

"They said he fell."

Jane nodded. "Yes, he fell fourteen stories. It's a miracle that he's even alive."

"Indeed," Fain said. "May I ask why he is here? I would think he would be in the medical wing."

"He was medically cleared. There wasn't anything wrong with him physically, just…"

"Yes?"

"Well, I've already said too much, Mr. Fain. Your friend's health is confidential. I can let you know that he is here and under our care, and that he is improving."

"Improving?"

"If you would like to leave your information, I will pass it along to Mr. Anslem. After his seventy-two-hour mandatory observation period is up, he will be evaluated and a determination regarding his capacity will be made. At that time he will be able to receive visitors and make phone calls."

"Has David been admitted to this ward?"

Jane didn't answer.

"Why has he not been formally admitted?"

"Why would you assume that?"

"Is it because he has had a return of full capacity and there is no longer a need for your services?"

"Another assumption."

"An educated guess. Your reaction proves that my suspicions are correct."

"What do you want, Mr. Fain?"

"I'm seeking the release of David Anslem by the officer in charge. Is that person you, Dr. Carol?"

"It is, but I'm not about to release him to you."

"Are you planning to involuntarily admit him?"

Jane shook her head. "With all due respect, Mr. Fain, that is none of your business."

"Dr. Carol, I'm not going to argue with you about whether or not he needs continued treatment or what treatment has been delivered. Ask yourself whether you believe that he needs to be hospitalized."

"Okay, is this where you quote the Mental Health Act and the extra-legal deprivation of liberty mumbo jumbo? Save your breath, because

Mr. Anslem will remain with us for a minimum of forty-eight hours, and if I believe that he is a danger to himself at the end of the period, I'll hold him longer—and involuntarily—if necessary."

"Has he asked to leave?"

"Of course, as most patients do."

"Then you will hold him against his will?"

"It's my belief that I'll be able to convince Mr. Anslem to be a voluntary patient."

"Why don't we ask him now," Fain said, looking past Jane.

"Admitting and retaining me here is no longer necessary," David said from behind her.

Jane turned around. "Mr. Anslem? How did you get out of the patient activity center?"

"Don't worry, Dr. Carol, I left without incident."

"How are you feeling, David?" Fain said.

"Illuminated."

Jane glanced uneasily in the direction of the guard station.

"May you and I speak a moment in private, Dr. Carol?" David said.

They walked a short distance. Jane glanced over her shoulder at Fain. She turned her attention back to David, speaking to him low voice.

"What are you mixed up in, Mr. Anslem?"

"Do you remember what I told you earlier, about someone eventually coming to look for me?"

"Yes, and as I recall, you were terrified that they would find you." She glanced back at Fain again. "Does he mean you harm?"

"I told you that people around me would be in danger. Fain means me no harm, and he's not the only one seeking me out. There are others who will come, and they will not be so polite."

"He wants you to leave with him."

David nodded. "And he won't take no for an answer."

"Well, we'll just have to see what security has to say about that."

"Doctor Carol, you don't want to do that. You have to believe that I am recovered. You have to discharge me or…"

"Or what?"

"Do you remember what I did to your patient John?"

"Yes."

"Fain will do that to anyone who tries to stop us from leaving, and I won't be able to stop him."

"I'm calling hospital security."

"Please, listen to me for just a moment. I know none of this makes any sense, but I want to propose something, and make you a promise."

"What kind of proposal?"

"I'll come back."

"Yeah, right."

"I give you my word that I'll come back. And I'll give you a name, an FBI name. After we're gone I want you to call the FBI branch office and ask for Detective Jason Rand. But for now, I want you to open that door so that we may leave without incident. And then you can go about your normal business. Go back to your office and fill out a discharge summary for me. Make it by the book. I wouldn't want you to get in trouble."

"What should I tell the FBI?" Jane asked.

"Give Detective Rand my name and tell him that I will be in touch soon."

"Okay, I don't know what's going on here, but I don't want anyone hurt."

Jane walked over to Fain and stood in front of him with her hands on her hips. "I'm releasing Mr. Anslem," she said, "AMA—against medical advice. Patients with severe isolated memory loss have an increased risk of developing dementia, Mr. Fain. Your friend should be closely followed up. I would like to see Mr. Anslem again, to check on his progress."

"That sounds reasonable to me," David said.

Jane went into the security booth, and returned a moment later with a pair of scissors. She cut off David's medical wristband. "Timmy," she said, "would you buzz the outer door?"

Timmy peeked out of the office door, and a moment later the main door buzzed. Fain and David departed into the main holding area, and waited for the secondary door to open.

Jane came into the security office. "Hold on, Timmy," she said. She studied Fain and David through the window.

"Is there a problem, Doctor Carol?" Timmy said.

"No, no problem, Timmy." She reached down and buzzed the outer door and watched as David and Fain walked down the corridor. Once the two men rounded the corner, Jane picked up the phone, dialed information, and waited for an operator.

"Yes, New York, New York," said Jane. "I need the number for the FBI branch office. The Federal Bureau of Investigation, that's correct. Yes, the Manhattan office is okay. I'll hold, thank you."

She waited on the line, listening to elevator music. After a moment she was linked to the FBI branch office. Once inside the FBI phone server she listened to several menu options. She grew impatient and pressed zero and hoped for a human voice. She listened to more music, and then a man's voice came on the line.

"Jennings," he said.

"Hello this is Jane Carol. I'm trying to reach a Detective Jason Rand."

"Hold please," he said.

"The FBI?" Timmy said. "What's going on?"

"It's complicated," Jane said. She noticed that Timmy was staring past her at the front entrance. On the other side of the door were a half a dozen men in black business suits. One of them held up badge of some sort. Jane laid the phone down and studied the video surveillance monitor. On the badge she saw an FBI insignia and the name JASON RAND.

"Timmy, buzz the door," said Jane.

Jane came around to the front entrance and waited as two agents came through. The other men waited in the hallway outside.

Rand flashed his credentials again. "I'm Agent Rand, and this is my partner, Agent Mark Shullman. Were looking for a patient named David Anslem."

"Detective Rand, I was just trying to call you," Jane said.

"What did you just say?"

"I said that I was trying to call you. David Anslem requested that I call you."

"Where are you holding him?"

"I'm sorry, but he's gone."

"Gone?"

"That's right. You just missed him."

"Damn it!" Rand said.

Shullman said, "The exits are all covered."

"Then he should still be on the premises," said Rand. "It's time to get hospital security involved. I want this entire hospital closed off."

Shullman nodded and went into the guard station.

Rand put his radio to his ear. "David Anslem has left the psych ward. See what you can do out there. Shullman and I will handle things in here. Do not engage him. I want to know as soon as he's found." He turned his attention back to Jane. "So David Anslem is admitted to an emergency psychiatric ward, tells you to call the FBI, and then you let him leave?"

"I did," said Jane, "and I had my reasons. Is he dangerous?"

"No. He's *in* danger. And he was supposed to be under our protection. Did he say where he was going?"

"No, he didn't. But he did say that he would be in contact with you. They left in a hurry."

"They?"

"Someone came for him. The man said that they were friends, but I have doubts about their relationship. He was a rather odd fellow."

"Did Mr. Anslem's friend have a name?"

"Yes, he said his name was Harold Fain."

Rand looked shocked. "Fain?"

Jane nodded. "Harold Fain."

"That's impossible," Rand said. "Harold Fain is dead."

"That's the name he gave me."

Rand retrieved his cell phone. He thumbed through several photos and held out an image of Fain on the display. "Is that who you saw David Anslem leave with?"

"That's him."

"Unbelievable."

"Whether you believe me or not, it is true."

"And you say Anslem left willingly with this man?" Rand said.

"Yes. Mr. Fain insisted."

"Did Mr. Anslem seem concerned?"

"He didn't. Not for himself, anyway. Mr. Anslem was more worried about my safety and that of the staff if I refused Mr. Fain's request to let Anslem leave."

"Is that why you let him go?"

"Well…in the record it will be documented as an administrative decision to discharge Mr. Anslem. I discharged him AMA. Technically he appeared to have recovered, but obviously that wasn't my main motivating factor for releasing him. My safety and the safety of the staff were most important. Mr. Anslem seemed to believe that Mr. Fain would not take no for an answer, and that he was quite capable of causing us great harm. I'll admit that I thought Mr. Anslem's characterization of Fain's abilities were quite exaggerated, but—"

"Trust me," Rand said, "if that was truly Harold Fain, Mr. Anslem wasn't exaggerating."

"I contemplated calling security."

Rand shook his head. "Be glad that you didn't." He looked at his phone and forwarded the photo of Fain to the rest of his men. He put the phone on his belt and picked up his radio. "All units, be advised that we are now looking for two—I repeat, two—persons of interest. Check your phone display for the image I just sent you. This man should be considered armed and dangerous. If he is encountered, do not attempt to apprehend. I repeat, do not arrest. Your orders are to terminate." He put his radio away and turned back to Jane. "Would you mind answering a few questions?"

"That all depends on whether or not I'm in any trouble," said Jane. "Do you think I need a lawyer?"

"No, I don't, and you're not in any trouble. You made the right decision."

"What do you want to know?"

"I want you to tell me about David Anslem."

"There is a certain thing called patient confidentiality, Detective."

"I understand that, and I could take the time to get a court order, but the time it takes to get one could cost your patient his life."

"Okay," Jane said. She walked over to the security station and picked up the phone. "Hello Amanda, it's Dr. Carol. Could you go into my office and bring me David Anslem's file? I'm in the lobby. It's on my desk. It should be on top of the pile. Thank you." She came back over to Rand. "I'm bringing up Mr. Anslem's file."

"Thank you," Rand said. He pulled out a pen and paper. "At any time did David Anslem tell you how he arrived in New York or ended up at Madison Tower?

"I don't have any of that information. Our dialogue was medically directed. We did, however, talk about his fall."

"Did you establish that he fell?"

"Yes, and initially we thought he had attempted suicide. But when he regained his memory, he denied any suicide ideation."

"Memory?" Rand said.

Amanda came into the lobby holding David's file. She stared at the agents with a confused look on her face.

"I'll explain later," Jane said, taking the file.

"Do you need anything else?" Amanda asked.

"No, and keep this between us for now. I don't want the staff getting all worked up."

Amanda nodded and left the room.

Jane handed David's chart to Rand. "That's everything we've done since he came into the facility."

Rand took the file and looked it over. "He fell fourteen stories and was medically cleared?"

"That's how we got him here. Anslem's case is unique, to say the least. He was nearly comatose when he came into the ER, and his MRI showed some abnormalities within his brain. We assumed that the effect was due to the fall. His brain scan results were consistent with someone suffering a concussion, which is understandable considering what happened. Hours later, however, a secondary MRI of Mr.

Anslem's skull showed normal brain function. His mental state was a whole different scenario."

"What do you mean?"

"To begin with, he had long-term memory loss."

"Amnesia?" Rand said thoughtfully.

"Yes, and he had overpowering hallucinations that manifested into day terrors. He had flashbacks evincing some kind of post-traumatic stress. He had internal fear like I've never seen in a patient before. And since the time that he has been in our care he has shown great evidence of aggressive ideation."

"That's all very interesting," Rand said. "And this aggressive ideation—did you determine if the thoughts of violence were directed?"

"I said aggressive, not violent. And it was never made clear. Initially, sensory examination was difficult to assess because of a lack of verbal output. When he had recovered his memory, I didn't have the time to inquire systematically about the full range of the aggressive thoughts."

Rand's radio beeped. He pressed the side call button. "Rand here."

"This is Leeds. Hospital security states that they had a ping on a fire door—unauthorized access."

"Where?"

"The twelfth floor. It looks like they're heading toward the roof."

Another voice broke in on the radio. "Nicholson here. I'm out front and have a confirmed visual of helicopter on point to land on the rooftop."

"Is it a Bell Life Flight?" Rand said. "Any markings?"

"Negative. Aircraft is a Sikorsky S-76, no markings, all black, and very slick."

"Damn, they're out of here," Rand said. "Resourceful and well-funded, whoever this Fain impersonator is. Let's get some eyes in the sky. If that bird gets off the roof, I want to know where and when it lands. Leeds, English and Perez to the roof. I'll have Shullman round up hospital surveillance camera footage."

Rand went into the security office and studied the wall of security monitors that showed various locations around the psychiatric ward.

He turned to the guard. "Can these patch into the rest of the hospital surveillance network?"

Timmy nodded. "They're all tied in together, through the computers. I'm only authorized for the psych ward. I'll have to get permission." He picked up the phone and dialed his supervisor.

"I like this guy," Rand said. He walked over to Jane. "Is your cell phone the best number where you can be reached?"

Jane handed Rand her business card.

"This is Leeds," a voice said over Rand's radio. "Bird's away. We missed them."

"Can you confirm whether or not Anslem was aboard?" Rand said.

"That's a negative. No visual on either man. There's no one on the roof. The aircraft had a southeast heading."

Shullman poked his head out of the guard station. "Surveillance is up."

"Good," Rand said, coming over to join him.

Timmy typed in a number, and the computer showed two dozen thumbnail images at various locations throughout the hospital. "Every camera in the building," he said.

"Are they all live feeds?" Rand asked.

"No. What you're seeing are stills from earlier in the day. They're all numbered and time sequenced. Just touch an icon and that image will convert to live footage on one of the overhead monitors."

"Show me the roof," said Rand.

"I don't think the roof view will help you." Timmy said. He touched the screen. A down view of the parking deck displayed on one of the larger monitors. The screen split into six additional roof views of the street twelve stories below.

"None of those cameras actually show the roof," said Timmy, "and there are no cameras up there that do. Your best bet would be the twelfth-floor elevator monitor. That camera shows the stairwell and the hallway leading to the roof."

"Let's see it," Shullman said

Timmy searched through the collection of tiny images. He touched the screen again. After a moment, a grainy black and white image of a deserted elevator and hallway came into view. Several medical staff passed by, and an orderly with a cart full of bed linens came to the elevator and waited.

"Is that a live feed?" Rand asked.

Timmy nodded. "Hold on and I'll take it back a few minutes." He typed in a code, and they all watched as the video rolled backward. Patients and hospital staff came in and out of the shot, moving backward for several moments, until Rand recognized David's face.

"That's Anslem," Rand said. "Stop the image right there."

Timmy returned the video to regular speed. After a moment David and Fain came into view on the monitor and slowly walked the length of the corridor.

"Harold Fain," Rand said under his breath.

"Or someone that looks an awful lot like him," Shullman said. "And Mr. Anslem isn't putting up much of a fight."

"It's damn odd," Rand said. "We're going to need copies of all of this footage." He walked over to Jane. "Tell me again what Mr. Anslem's degree of impairment was when you released him?"

Jane thought for a moment. "Off the record, still?"

"Yes."

She nodded slowly. "As I already said, when Mr. Anslem came into the facility through the ER, he was nearly comatose. When we received him, he was incapacitated; he could barely speak. He had no memory of who he was, and he was delusional. Whatever was inside his mind was causing him great distress."

"And when you released him?"

"His mental status had greatly improved. He was functional."

"You're certain?"

"Yes, I personally ran him through several cognitive tests, and he functioned within the superior range."

"You sound impressed."

"Awed is more accurate. I suspect his IQ is off the scales."

"Suspect? You didn't examine his intelligence fully?"

"No, I was hoping to run more tests on him, but then his friend showed up and we never completed his cognitive status exams. I still needed to assess his long-term memory, and I was very curious about his history. You said that he was helping you with an investigation?"

"He was," Rand said. "Did he tell you that he was a priest?"

"No, and that's interesting, especially when considering some of his memories."

"What about them?"

"He appeared to have a rather vicious past. I suspect a form of post-traumatic recall, and his flashbacks were horrific."

"But you said he had recovered."

"He had shown great improvement. His speech was logical and goal-directed with normal rate and rhythm. His mood had become euthymic, his effect was full, and he had lost his feelings of hopelessness. All of his psychotic features appeared to have abated."

"And his memory?"

"Returned in full, and then some. I suspect even genius level."

"Did Anslem and Fain ever talk alone?"

"No. Fain asked Mr. Anslem how he was feeling when he first saw him, but they had no other exchanges before leaving together. It seemed to be a forgone conclusion that Mr. Anslem was going to leave with him, and he did go with Fain willingly, but I didn't have the impression that it was preplanned."

"He told you he was going to be in touch with me. Did he say when?"

"No, he simply said that he would be in touch."

"We can't wait for that to happen," Rand said. He turned to Shullman. "Let's start by bolstering our surveillance on his church and house on Marco Island. And let's make some calls to friends and family."

"I'll get on it," said Shullman.

"I just remembered something," Jane said. "Something Mr. Anslem said before he left. I don't know if it's important to you or not, but he told me that he was going to come back here."

"Did he say why?"

"He was worried about me getting in trouble for letting him leave. I'm not sure, but I think in some way he wanted to prove to me that he was normal."

"Would you be opposed to me assigning one of my men to keep an eye on you?"

"No," Jane said. "I would be grateful if you did."

Rand handed Jane his card. "Thanks for your help Doctor. If you remember anything else, please call me."

Rand regrouped with Shullman and the rest of his men in front of the hospital.

"Every time we get close…" he said, shaking his head.

"What about Fain and Anslem?" Shullman said. "What in the hell is going on? This is getting downright spooky."

"Has Parker checked in?" said Rand.

"I've left her two messages."

"It's not like her to miss all the action."

"Wait till she hears the latest twist," said Shullman.

A black Suburban pulled up next to the curb. Shullman walked over, opened the back door, slid into the seat, and rolled his window down.

Rand opened the front passenger door, propped his foot on the floorboard, and waited for the rest of their team's vehicles to gather.

"Anslem's alive," Shullman said. "And he appears to be, or has become, a bigger piece of the puzzle. He tried to contact you. It appears that he tried to help us."

"Yeah," Rand said. "It appears that way, but since Fain's execution, we've been on the defensive or playing catch-up. Nothing has added up, and we've just been dealt the biggest curveball yet." A phone rang inside his coat pocket. He retrieved two phones, checked them both, and answered one before it rang again.

"It took you long enough," said Rand. Yeah, I know where that is. I owe you big on this one." Rand switched off the phone. He took out the battery, slid it into his pocket, and threw the phone into a city trash can nearby.

"You want to tell me what that's all about?" Shullman said.

"Lithium batteries are terrible for the environment," said Rand.

"Funny. Now, seriously?"

Rand smiled triumphantly. "I just called in the biggest marker of my life at the State Department. Actually, I did it yesterday after our little call from Simons."

"What did they get you?"

"A location on Simons. He's working out of a counter-terrorism 'vaults' right here in New York. It's time to go on the offensive." Rand climbed into the front seat and picked up his radio. "This is Rand. All vehicles fall in behind us."

39

CONTROL

Rand's SUV pulled up in front of an unmarked four-story Brooklyn warehouse. The building's front door was covered in graffiti and all of its lower windows were smashed out. A long alleyway concealed an inconspicuous vehicle entrance. A few midmorning pedestrians strolled along the sidewalk.

"Leeds?" Rand said over his radio.

"Leeds here. We're in place on the back side of the building. I see one industrial door and a fire escape in the alley."

"Remember that these guys are on the same team," Rand said. "Everyone sit tight. Mark and I are just going to have quick chat, and bust a few balls." He put the radio on his belt and opened the car door.

"And then we all get fired," Shullman said, stepping out of the vehicle.

Rand joined him on the sidewalk. "Simons can't be that powerful. And if my hunch is correct, he'll be the one with the explaining to do."

They walked to the front entrance. Rand tried the handle; the door was locked. They heard a buzz, and Shullman tried the handle again. The door opened this time, and they proceeded into an old foyer that had a gated-off stairwell and secondary door. A vent in the ceiling concealed a bubble security camera. They heard a burst of static through an overhead speaker that was followed by a man's voice.

"Good afternoon gentlemen. Mr. Simons will see you now."

Rand looked at Shullman. "So much for our surprise visit."

The door opened and an agent wearing sunglasses came through.

"Gentlemen," the agent said. "If you would, please?"

He stepped aside and allowed them to come through. On the other side of the door, a second agent guided them down a narrow, dimly lit corridor. They came to a high-tech situation room, a long chamber with rows of computer monitors that gave off an eerie blue glow. Agents wearing headphones sat in the dark behind the monitors, watching and listening.

"Manned around the clock," a voice said from across the room. "Always alert and ever watching." A man with short black hair, wearing a black suit and a red tie, came out of the shadows. "Counter-terrorism," he added. "I'm Jack Simons. Who do I have the privilege of thanking for blowing our location?"

"Sorry," Rand said sarcastically. "I guess our little motorcade got some heads turning out there."

"It doesn't really matter," Simons said. "Our work here is done. Besides, it's no secret that we're here, and our interests are slightly broader in scope than the drug dealers and armed robbers that infest this part of the city. I believe that's your department's specialty."

Rand nodded, "As are serial murderers, Agent Simons, and they're not your department's specialty."

"What can I do for you, Agent Rand?"

"You told me to keep you advised."

"I said that I would be in touch."

"Well, I saved you a phone call. Now I would like to know what the hell is going on."

"That is precisely what I would like to know," said Simons, "starting with why you felt that it was necessary to find me, to come barging in here like this?"

"And I'll explain, just as soon as you show me your security clearance."

"That's rich. A junior bureau captain vetting a CIA station chief in his own office." Simons reached inside his coat pocket and pulled out his CIA credentials and handed them to Rand. Rand glanced them over. They appeared to be in order, and Rand handed them back to Simons. Rand reached into his coat pocket to retrieve his FBI badge, but Simons stopped him.

"I know who you are, Mr. Rand," Simons said. "I've been following you and your investigation for some time now."

"Why?"

"National security," he gestured at a row of surveillance monitors. "We're in a dangerous, quirky, and ever-changing world, Mr. Rand. There is an element of humanity that has pledged itself to our country's destruction, and I report to those powers charged with the life and death decisions in protecting our great nation."

"Maybe you can explain to me the correlation between a serial killer and strategic decision making?"

"I'm not following your meaning, Detective."

"Harold Fain was just seen leaving a hospital with someone who was supposed to be under Bureau protection."

"And how is your men's incompetence my problem?"

"You don't seem surprised that a murderer who was sentenced to death, and executed, appears to have risen from the dead."

Simons smiled. "Is that what you believe?"

"No."

"Yes, I suppose zombies would be hard to explain in a report."

"But it won't be hard for me to describe how the CIA was reluctant to assist in our investigation, or how your inaction resulted in the death of several innocent people. You won't be very popular up the chain on either side."

"The powers that I report to aren't concerned with collateral damage," said Simons. "They demand results, and it's my duty to deliver them. The source and method used to obtain those desired outcomes are not my concern."

"What about Gelder?"

"Gelder?"

"The Jane Doe that Fain murdered in the subway. You told me that she was retired CIA."

"So I did."

"You didn't have to tell me that."

"I didn't have to tell you anything."

"But you did. You threw us a bone. I made a few calls, and now we're here. It wasn't hard finding you."

"You wouldn't be here unless I wanted you to be."

"Then tell me why I'm here?"

Simons didn't answer.

"Gelder wasn't retired, was she?" Rand said.

Simons thought for a moment. "No she wasn't."

"It makes sense now, why we couldn't identify her. Sad too. She was buried as a nobody, in a potter's grave. Doesn't it bother you that one of your agents was unclaimed and buried in a mass grave with a bunch of homeless people?"

"You have no idea what you're even talking about, Agent Rand."

"Well, then why don't you bring me up to speed on things, starting with Fain? Who was he?"

"Who *is* he?" said Simons.

"Is? No. Fain was executed. Harold Fain is dead."

"Didn't you just say that you saw him leaving a hospital with a man charged with your agency's protection?"

"I have my doubts about whom I saw with David Anslem."

Simons smirked. "Don't believe your own eyes?"

"Just tell me who Fain is, or was, or whatever. Just tell me his story."

"Harold Fain is a criminal—an enemy and a threat to our national security."

"So Gelder—"

"Gelder disobeyed orders and confronted Fain alone. Her reckless and irresponsible act turned the tide. It gave Fain the upper hand."

Rand was puzzled. "Fain was caught and incarcerated because of her murder. You know that. Why didn't you have him transferred into your custody?"

"You can't just take someone like Fain into custody."

"We did."

"Yes, because he let you. And what happened while he was in your charge? What did he do? He devastated your friend Tino's intake team, and then dictated new rules to suit his needs." Simons turned his head to the side. Rand saw a radio receiver in Simons' right ear.

"Who's talking to you?" said Rand.

"It's your lucky day," Simons said, smirking. "Why don't you come up to my office, and we'll talk more?" He gestured at an open door.

Rand and Shullman followed Simons down a narrow hallway that opened into a carpeted lobby, where they entered a service elevator and ascended to the top floor. Two men in black moved aside as they entered a long room that resembled an airplane hangar. Built into each wall were tall windows that stretched from floor to ceiling; the glass panes were painted with gray primer so that no light could penetrate. There were a half a dozen computer stations at the center of the room and at the far end of the chamber. A single row of drafting tables faced a long wall of TV monitors. The sound was off, and most of the televisions were broadcasting news feeds from various locations around the world. The concrete floor was bare, and several piles of scrap wood and sawdust lay scattered about. There was a hollow echoing sound as they walked. Several half-packed wooden shipping crates lay scattered around, and the room had a feeling of impermanence.

"You're here in time for our last hurrah," a woman said from behind them.

Rand recognized the voice. "Dana?"

"Sorry," Parker said. "I know how you hate surprises."

Rand's shock gave way to anger. "My God! How long?"

"She has been with us from the start," Simons said.

"You've been feeding Simons information regarding our investigation all along."

"It was necessary," she said.

"Your interference—your inaction—cost lives, lady!"

"Regrettably yes, but now it's over. Or rather, your part in it is over. Our partnership and investigation into the serial killer Harold Fain is concluded. It ended with his execution."

"Not even close," Rand said. "Because here's where it stands: David Anslem has been abducted, there is a Harold Fain doppelganger running around, and bodies are still piling up."

Parker folded her arms across her chest. "That's not Fain's double."

"Come again?"

Simons came over, holding a red classified folder. "Agent Rand, we're prepared to make an exception."

"I'm listening."

"I'm going to brief you on intel that only a handful of people at the Justice Department are privy to." He flashed Rand a photograph of Rory Gelder. "Recognize her?"

"Of course. Your agent. Fain's victim from the subway."

Simons looked at the photograph thoughtfully. "Agent Gelder was a career government scientist—one of our youngest and brightest. She was the youngest agent ever to be promoted to overseeing all of our current science, technology, and weapons analysts. Within a year of that promotion, she was promoted again to information warfare and emerging technologies, and finally to the department that I currently oversee. I handpicked her for a special project. Gelder ran a shell company called Strategic Labs, a private research foundation, that was funded by the government."

"The Legion Project," Rand said.

"That was its last iteration. The program was previously known as Speed Cell. The scientists working under Gelder made some rather astonishing genetic breakthroughs. Their research led to a new breed of human. Agent Gelder's masterpiece was Harold Fain. Within Fain she was able to trigger a spontaneous, human, metabolic, immortal event. So now you can see why he didn't want you to obtain his DNA."

"Immortality?" Rand said.

"That's correct. Every modern government on earth since early in the twentieth century has pursued a super-soldier agenda. Legion is one such program. Harold Fain is a weapon—an invincible weapon. This is a brief," he said, handing the red folder to Rand.

Rand opened the file and read through the notes. The first few pages were outlines of complex genetic research and longevity studies. A header on one page read "Self Repairing Organisms."

"Abalone," Rand read aloud.

He laughed nervously. *It all seems so bizarre,* he thought, *like some strange fantasy story or the substance of science fiction.* There was no reference to human subject or mention of Harold Fain. A lot seemed to be missing. *Perhaps it's incomplete because it isn't a real file,* he thought.

"Abalone...synithisia...total recall... enhanced memory?" he muttered. "This is all interesting research, but hardly groundbreaking. Gene splicing and rodent merging, for instance, is old news. Any sixth-grade middle school student could tell you that."

Simons shook his head. "I can assure you Gelder was far beyond transgenic mice and merging pigs with human blood, Agent Rand. She was leaps and bounds beyond. Gelder's team consisted of a group of the world's leading neurogeneticists—her 'genetic tribe,' she used to call them. With Harold Fain they made an astonishing breakthrough. The world's first advanced human—a super-human, if you will. With his creation, aging and death were eliminated. For the first time, a living organism had become a force greater than natural selection. Gelder delivered eleven additional units, all males, and each of them was engineered differently. To some she gave brains, to others she gave brawn. But Fain had it all, and he showed amazing potential for the arena he was commissioned for: bioweapons. And there was an additional outcome that Gelder had not anticipated: Fain's ability to read minds."

"Telepathy," Parker said. "He isn't able to stand next to you and read your thoughts, but he has the ability to render you unconscious, taking you to the brink of death. In that moment before you die, he can capture a snapshot of your entire life. Can you imagine the value in this from an intelligence perspective? An agent like no other—an invincible spy who is able to read our enemies' thoughts, who is empowered in the field to act as a judge, jury, and executioner."

Simons said, "But Fain's most unique ability—which truly sets him apart from the others—is his capacity to convert or remake people in his own image. The others can't do that, and we don't know why. Gelder suspected that it was viral, but she never had a chance to study or prove it."

"Why?" said Rand.

"Because Fain killed her."

"What went wrong?"

"Gelder's notes revealed that Fain began to develop a form of schizophrenia and a rather nasty egomaniacal personality," said Simons. "He believed himself to be omnipotent. And believe me, he is invincible. Imagine for a moment what would happen in a world with a race of such beings? Gelder had time to ponder her discovery, and over time she began distancing herself from her team. She became disillusioned with our ultimate objective. It became apparent that she had her own ambitions. She viewed herself as a genetic vanguard for the future of the human race. It's our belief, too, that she was motivated by profit. And who could blame her? After all, she is only human, and what she had discovered would impact the human race like nothing else known to mankind: aging and death eliminated, forever. Her private journals later confirmed this. In the end she went rogue, and unfortunately Fain found her before we did."

"If what you are saying is true," said Rand—"and I'm not saying that I even believe all of this craziness—then you have a rather nasty rogue agent on your hands. And you're saying you can't stop him?"

"You witnessed how he went through Tino's intake team at his arrest," said Simons. "How many men was it?"

"Around ten men. I'll admit what he did was impressive, but I know a few special forces operatives that can do that kind of damage."

"Could any of them pass through a death chamber? Survive an electric chair?"

"No, no one can."

"I see," Simons said. "I can understand why you're still having doubts." He walked over to one of the packing crates and retrieved a crowbar that was on the ground. He handed it to Rand.

Rand examined both ends of the metal bar. The iron felt heavy and cold to the touch.

Simons turned and motioned for the two agents by the elevator to come over. "I want to introduce you to agent Abrix and Mantilla."

Rand could see them more clearly now. Their skin was pale and their eyes glinted in the light, just like Fain.

Simons took the crowbar from Rand and handed it to one of the agents. "Abrix, if you would, please. Twist that into something interesting for us."

Abrix gripped the steel bar on each end and effortlessly bent it into a horseshoe.

Simons nodded, and Abrix dropped the twisted metal to the ground.

Shullman stared down at the bent crowbar. He looked at Rand and shook his head.

"So why tell me all this now?" Rand asked.

"The game has changed." Simons said. "We've spent the last few months tracking Fain, but avoiding direct contact with him."

"What about fighting fire with fire?" Rand said, gesturing at Abrix and Mantilla.

"We've tried that before," said Simons. "Of the eleven, Fain destroyed all but two: Abrix and Mantilla, here. They're no match for Fain, and too valuable to lose."

"So you're going to wait until Fain hunts you down one by one?"

Simons shook his head. "I said Abrix and Mantilla are no match for Fain, but together they should be able to retrieve David Anslem."

"Anslem?"

"Anslem is our new target."

"Why?"

"We have reason to believe that Anslem has been transformed by Fain. Fain brought him here to New York alive, and despite a fourteen-story fall, Anslem still lives. No human being could survive a fall like that."

Rand's phone rang. It was an unfamiliar number. The name on the display read NORVRON HEALTH. He put the phone to his ear and stepped away from the group. "This is Rand."

"Agent Rand, this is Dr. Jane Carol."

Rand lowered his voice. "What can I do for you, Dr. Carol?"

"I just thought you should know that two agents from the Justice Department came to see me."

"What did they want?"

"Well after they got into a rather heated shouting match with the agent you left behind regarding jurisdiction, they proceeded to interrogate me regarding you and Mr. Anslem. They were quite rude, and I have a mind to file a formal complaint. They presented a warrant and cleaned out all of my records regarding Mr. Anslem. I told them the same thing I told you. They acted like they didn't believe me, and if your man hadn't intervened, I think they were going to take me in for questioning. Their behavior was outrageous."

"You were wise to call me," said Rand. "I'll be in touch." He slid the phone into his pocket and walked over to Simons.

"Well, we've taken up enough of your time," Rand said.

"We came clean," Parker said. "And we didn't have to."

"You've divulged some facts out of necessity. I can appreciate that, but let's be clear on why you did. It's only because you found out that I had the final part of the puzzle. And before you ask, the answer is no—Anslem has not contacted me."

"We'll expect to be informed when he does," said Parker.

"If," Rand said. "If he contacts me."

"You don't know where Anslem is?"

"No. And when I eventually do hear from him, you'll have to forgive me for savoring the moment. I know it has to be frustrating for you both, knowing that I'll soon know where to find him."

"And I'll know where to find *you*," Simons said.

"That sounds an awful lot like a threat," said Rand.

Simons frowned. "You're very good at what you do, Mr. Rand. No one can deny that. But your part in this investigation is complete. We'll handle it from here on out. I'll need you and your men out of the way. You can start by pulling your surveillance teams away from Anslem's home and the church property."

"I'm not going to do that."

"We don't want anyone caught in the crossfire."

"I agree."

"As I said earlier, the case, as far as you are concerned, is closed. You will end your inquiries. Under the definition of classified information, your case is to be terminated and the information that is in your investigation will be closed. Do you understand?"

"You're going to classify my investigation?"

"That's right: open source intel. Your investigation involves national security and therefore the entire case product will need to be classified, vaulted, and known only in sensitive channels. If you speak of this case again in person, by phone, text, or e-mail, you will be prosecuted."

Rand shrugged. "Well, I can tell you this: I will see my investigation to its conclusion and file my report."

Simons put his hand on his hips. "Time to take a long vacation, Agent Rand. Mr. Abrix, escort these men out."

Abrix stepped inside the elevator and waited for Rand and Shullman to join him. Everyone was quiet as they descended to the main level. When they reached the bottom floor, Abrix passed them off to a waiting agent who escorted them to the front entrance. The front door closed behind them.

"What the hell was that?" said Shullman. "What have we gotten ourselves mixed up in here?"

Rand looked up at the side of the building. He wondered if Simons was watching. "It's too convenient, Mark. We've spent months investigating these murders. Now the answers are hand-delivered to us—boxed and gift-wrapped with a neat little bow on top."

Shullman shrugged. "Now what?"

"Finish what we started."

"Listen, I don't think I would play chicken with Simons on this. If he thinks that you're going to expose his highly classified program along with his protected sources and methods, there's no telling what he's willing to do."

"Not a damn thing," Rand said. "I've got him right where I want him. Now I know what my silence is worth to him. He's not about to charge me. Everything I know would become discoverable. I don't think he wants the Department of Justice to know about his little debacle. If he can clean it up, he'll be a hero. If not, he'll be finished. And besides, until we hear from Anslem, we're untouchable."

40

INVINCIBLE

David stood by the penthouse window of the Royal Zmoda Hotel, staring out at over Miami's Biscayne Bay. Fain owned the entire top floor of the building, and the dwelling was one of many secure residences that he held around the world.

David had removed the black bodysuit and changed into clothes that Fain had provided. He now wore black pants and a black silk long-sleeve shirt. The pants fit comfortably. The shirt had a tailored fit but the sleeves were too long. David rolled the sleeves up to his elbows and smoothed his hands down the front of the shirt.

Fain came into the room, wearing the same black shirt and pants. "Are you more comfortable now?" he said.

"The clothes?" David said. "Yes, but with all that has happened to me, I'm not so at ease."

"Not yet perhaps, but you will be," said Fain. He came over to the window next to David. " It will take time. You and I are bound together now. You have my memories."

"And those of the multitude of souls that you have taken. And I've acquired your appetite for death and destruction."

"The tremendous desire to destroy, lash out, and kill is a small price to pay for the benefit of time without end. I know that you will prove strong enough to resist."

"How do I control it?"

"You must concentrate on the good souls that I have imparted to you. Are you disappointed in what you have become?"

"I wouldn't have believed it possible. And now…"

"Yes, go on."

"With a simple touch of your hand you changed me—granted me eternal life. You've given me great power that I've barely begun to understand. You've given me knowledge—knowledge and experiences taken from other people's lives. I'm now immortal. I thought that perhaps with this immortality I would have all the answers to life's questions."

"But you don't, and neither do I," said Fain. "No one does. Mortals and immortals are equal in that. Not knowing, I mean. No one knows the secrets of the universe. But what you do have now are choices. And, for the first time in your life, control over them."

David nodded as he thought about Fain's words. His mind ran wild with Fain's memories and the memories of the multitude of souls he had collected over the years. The chaos that had fueled his earlier madness was now gone, replaced by a harmonious and collective voice. He knew what every person knew, and he could feel what they all felt before they were taken. But what amazed him the most was how all of the spirits continued inside him as if they were somehow still alive. He now understood how incredibly important each human being's soul is, and he understood the pain experienced by a lost soul. He saw how Fain on countless occasions had taken a life only to fail to reap the family member or loved one. This was Fain's ultimate weakness. The pain of losing a soul, and the permanence of a lost soul, were what he feared most.

It is the precious nature of a human soul that fuels his insatiable hunger and drives his distrust for the others who are like him. David could see too from Fain's memories the conflict that existed between him and his creator Pan. Their war was over souls. He saw Fain's creation at Pan's hands, the Relaters that came before him, and the others—Pan's vanquished destroyers. They were the men he made immortal and sent against Fain. Fain defeated them all. Some he destroyed. Others he allowed to live, buried in hidden tombs around the world, and in crypts like the one at Carter's Grove.

David looked back at Fain. "And now, having your memories, I know that it was Oerell who was in the ground in Virginia. Has he risen?"

"Yes."

"What has releasing him achieved?"

"Oerell served Pan. He has already begun a campaign of killing—killing his way back to his creator. Simons will have difficulty compensating for this new variable. His resources are nearing exhaustion, and now that Oerell is above ground, I anticipate that Pan will have no choice but to become involved directly. And I'll be waiting. But first I will deal with Simons. The information that he and Gelder obtained from Pan is forbidden knowledge that must be reclaimed, along with those man-made abominations that his scientist produced. Now only two remain, and they must be recovered. All evidence of their creation, human or otherwise, will be destroyed. With his power dwindling, Simons has become overly guarded; his moves are less bold, and he has shown a great deal of restraint of late."

"But he won't be able to resist me," David said. "Will he? Isn't that why you changed me?"

"I mean to keep my word, David. You may live your life as you wish."

"But Simons will come for me, won't he?"

"Yes he will. I expect that he'll commit all the resources he has left. It won't be enough. I've made you invincible. But in truth, you needn't worry about Simons. You have access to my vast resources. If it is your wish, you are welcome to take respite in any one of my many havens until I've dealt with him."

"No," David said. "I'm not going to hide. I'm going to return to my home, my church, and I'm going to make sure Simons knows where I am. I want an end to it."

"Are you certain that the church is the place you want it to end?"

"It is."

"Very well," Fain said. "I've instructed the pilot on the roof to take you wherever you wish to go." He crossed the room and departed through the front door.

David walked over to a small desk and retrieved a cell phone from a drawer. He dialed Rand's phone number from memory and held the receiver to his ear. The phone connected and rang twice before a man's voice picked up on the other end.

"Thank you for calling the office of—"

"I have a message for Special Agent Jason Rand," David said.

There was a pause on the other end. "Agent Rand is unavailable."

"My name is David Anslem. I would like to leave Agent Rand a message."

"What's the message?" the man said.

"Tell Agent Rand that I will be returning to my church tonight."

"When?"

"Just give him the message."

"He will want to confirm that you are who you say you are."

"I understand. Agent Rand and I share a security word."

"What's the word?"

"Tree."

"If you'll hold, I'll contact Agent Rand. I can patch you through to his mobile."

"That won't be necessary," David said. "Relay the message." He deactivated his phone and placed it on top of the desk. He held his hand toward a desk lamp. He could feel the electricity draw into his fingertips. The bulb flickered and went dark. A faint blue electrical corona enveloped his fingers. He clenched his fist and went back to the window, shut his eyes, and waited for the night to fall.

41

RENDEZVOUS

The helicopter flew south, low over the ocean, following the Florida coastline. Rand reclined in a chair behind the pilot, wearing a pair of oversized headphones, staring out of the left side window. The ocean was a teal color, dotted with blue patches where the sea deepened and the late afternoon sun shimmered across the surface toward the horizon. The helicopter passed over many large cruise liners and several long rows of massive cargo vessels that sat anchored at Port Canaveral. Rand heard the pilot say something about air speed, times of arrival, and a series of codes that only an air traffic controller would understand. The aircraft rocked slightly, then banked right and headed inland.

"Still no sign of Anslem," Shullman's said. He sat across from Rand with a pair of headphones around his neck. He showed Rand his cell phone.

Rand nodded, pulled off his headset, and laid it on the empty seat next to him. *The rotors are surprisingly quiet,* he thought. *I really don't need the earphones.*

Shullman said, "McCoy's team states that no one has approached Anslem's church. He had a mail delivery at thirteen-thirty-one hours, and had a few drive-bys—curious parishioners and the church custodian. Why do you think Anslem didn't call you direct to let you know he was returning to his church?"

"I don't know."

"Well, since he called our office main line, it's a good bet Simons now knows what we know."

Rand scowled. "Yeah, I'm sure he does."

"The odd thing is that we haven't been able to pinpoint any of his field surveillance teams."

Rand pointed up. "They use satellites. I'm sure they'll be somewhere within striking distance."

"Have you spoken to Renee?"

"I'll call her when we land to refuel again in St. Cloud. She gets irritated—says she can't hear me when I call from inside these things."

"Well, you don't want to add fuel to that fire."

"No, I don't." He checked his watch and looked back out the window. "When this is over, I'm going to have a lot of making up to do."

42

THE MONSTERS AND THE MEN

The front door to David's church was slightly open. A torn section of yellow police tape lay on the ground. David pushed through the unlocked door and paused briefly, staring over his shoulder at the tree line. It was a moonless night and the agents in the woods concealed themselves well, undetectable in the dark to mortal eyes. To David they appeared out of the shadows like human fireflies.

He entered the building and made his way into the main worship hall. He came to the pulpit and faced the main aisle, watching, waiting, and wondering who would reach him first. He heard the sound of vehicles approaching. Through the vaulted ceiling he heard the sound of a helicopter circling. The aircraft's powerful searchlight caught the stained-glass windows, casting a colorful kaleidoscope of light around the large room.

A moment later Rand plowed through the sanctuary's double doors and looked around in the dark. Shullman followed behind him. Shullman reached for the wall switch and turned on the lights. They saw David and proceeded down the main aisle.

"What the hell is going on here, Mr. Anslem?" Rand said. "Is it true that Fain is still alive?"

"You needn't worry about Fain," said David.

"Is Harold Fain still alive?"

"Yes."

Rand looked David over. He saw how his complexion had changed. His skin was pale and his eyes seemed to shimmer in the faint light. "What has happened to you?"

David didn't answer.

"Where's Fain?"

"I told you not to worry about Fain."

"Do you remember back in the prison when Fain asked you about Jack Simons?"

"I know all about Mr. Simons."

"Then you know that you shouldn't have come back here. Simons' men have your church surrounded. I need you to leave with me now, or I won't be able to guarantee your safety."

"There are things at play here that you can't possibly comprehend, Agent Rand."

"The Legion Project? I've heard all about—" Rand heard the sound of several automatic weapons discharging outside. Both he and Shullman pulled out their handguns.

"What the hell is going on out there?" Shullman said, chambering a bullet.

Rand unclipped his radio. "Leeds, come in." The radio crackled with static. They heard an increased exchange of gunfire, and then silence.

Dr. Parker entered the sanctuary. "You know, there was no reason for any of this, Jason."

"Are you insane?" Rand said. "Those are federal agents out there."

"I'm unarmed," Parker said, holding her hands out. "I know you don't believe me, Jason, but this is bigger than any of us. It's more important than any of our own lives."

"Where is Simons?"

"He's here." She looked up toward the ceiling. The sound of a helicopter could be heard, moving in a circle above the church. "Simons is waiting for me to bring David out. You and Mark can live through this. We would like to avoid any further bloodshed. We're pretty far out here in the country, but I suspect that it won't be long before the local police arrive on the scene. Do you want their deaths on your conscience?"

"It won't be on my conscience," Rand said.

"Anslem must come with me."

"I don't think so."

She edged forward. "With Anslem, we'll be one step closer—"

"You move one step closer and you'll be dripping off the end of my gun."

Shullman came around behind Parker with his gun forward, keeping a watchful eye over his shoulder.

"Why not tell the truth, Doctor?" David said, coming past Rand. "Tell them who you and Simons really work for. Tell them how you seek information beyond your control. Knowledge beyond your comprehension."

"That's no doubt what Fain told you, Mr. Anslem. They're implanted thoughts."

"Enough, Doctor," David said calmly. "This charade is over."

Parker shook her head. "You're delusional, Mr. Anslem. But not to worry. It's a normal part of the transformation. I can help you if you'll come with me."

"He's not going anywhere with you maniacs," Rand said.

Parker looked at her watch. "My men have their orders, and soon we will be past the point of no return. I won't be able to stop them." She retrieved her cell phone from her coat pocket and showed it to David. "I can call them off if you'll agree to come with me."

David folded his hands behind his back. "I'm afraid, Dr. Parker, that you have nothing left to bargain with."

Parker looked disappointed. She put the phone back in her pocket. She turned and motioned toward the front entrance. A moment later, the two genetic abominations, Abrix and Mantilla, came through the door.

"Is this how you intend to let it end?" Parker said, turning to David.

"No," David said softly. "This is where it will end for all of you." Without another word, he stepped forward and clasped his right hand around her neck.

"David, don't!" Rand shouted.

Parker felt a pulse of electricity surge through her body. She tried to breathe, but it felt as if her chest was clenched in a vise. Her pulse quickened as her body became starved for air. She felt dizzy.

Abrix and Mantilla rushed forward and grabbed for David's arms. They tried to pry his hands away from Parker's neck, but despite their efforts, he continued to hold on to her, undeterred. Even when both men began delivering powerful blows to David's head and face, he seemed unaffected.

"And now come the answers to all of your questions," David said. He drew Parker closer. Her body went limp in his arms. "Dr. Dana Parker is my first," he said, easing her lifeless body to the floor. "She was filled with many complex emotions: love, hate, and a great quantity of rage for someone who professed to be a champion of reason. Her memories are now mine. Those feelings—all of her emotions— are mine. I will consider her temper first, while it's fresh in my mind. Every irritation collected over her lifetime, every fury she ever knew, I will now turn upon you both."

Abrix and Mantilla charged forward, collided into David, dragged him backward past the pulpit, and pinned him against the wall beneath the tall stained-glass window.

Shullman moved up behind the three combatants.

"What are you doing, Mark?"

"I've got to try to help David." Shullman fired a round over their heads. He rushed forward and punched the back of Abrix's head with the butt of his handgun and quickly followed with a strong kick to Abrix's back. It felt as though he had struck a brick wall. Shullman holstered his weapon and leapt onto Abrix's back. He tried to force his arm under Abrix's neck. "My God!" Shullman screamed. There was a loud crack, and a massive arc of electrical energy exploded out of Abrix, knocking Shullman to the floor. He lay still, unconscious, with his clothes and hair singed and smoldering.

Rand rushed over and knelt beside his downed partner. He felt Shullman's neck. There was a strong pulse. He looked around the sanctuary for cover. On the left side of the worship hall he noticed a small door. He took Shullman by both arms and dragged him over to the door.

Shullman began to stir. "What happened?" He stared up at Rand groggily. "What the hell is going on? This is insane!"

"Do you think you can stand, Mark?"

Shullman leaned on his right elbow. "Yeah, yeah, I think so. Where's Anslem?"

"They still have him pinned against the wall."

The powerful agents, Abrix and Mantilla, continued to restrain David, pressing his body firmly against the wall.

"Jesus!" Shullman said. "What are they doing?" He pulled out his gun and chambered a bullet. "Let's try this again."

"Hold up, Mark," said Rand. "Let's get Plan B in motion first."

"What do you have in mind?"

"First, we take out those two freaks."

"Agreed. And then what?"

"Get Anslem. Call for reinforcements, and try to stay alive until they get here. As soon as we get Anslem, we need to cut the lights. We're defenseless. They can see everything we're doing in here." Rand peered through the lower window at the top of the door. He saw a cement walkway and hedges, but it was too dark to see beyond them. Gun muzzles flashed by the tree line, and an instant later a torrent of bullets shattered the windows above his head. A second volley of shells exploded through the lower door. A single bullet struck Rand in his right shoulder, spinning him to the floor.

Shullman crawled over next to Rand and rolled him onto his side. Rand's back was soaked in blood. "It went straight through," Shullman said. He found the exit wound and applied pressure to the area with both hands.

Rand drew back in pain. "I'm going to bleed to death. You've got to call for backup, Mark. We need more men."

Shullman pulled out his phone. The display was shattered. He touched the screen. Nothing worked. "It's fried," he said.

"Reboot it!"

Shullman fumbled with the phone's power button. "Damn it! Nothing!"

Rand winced. "Use mine. Inside coat pocket."

Shullman retrieved Rand's phone, stared at the display, and then looked at Rand with a worried expression.

"What's wrong?"

"No signal."

"That can't be. It would mean they're jamming us, and that's impossible."

"What's our next move, partner?"

"You've got to try to save Anslem."

"Enough," David said. He pushed forward with all of his strength, forcing Abrix and Mantilla to release their hold on him.

Abrix countered quickly. He stepped forward and unleashed a violent barrage of punches on David's body.

David stood firm, weathering each blow. Abrix continued to strike David. But soon his attack slowed as Abrix realized that his vigorous assault was for naught. Behind him, Mantilla looked on with an expression of awe.

David raised his right fist and brought it down on Abrix's skull, knocking Abrix to the ground. Abrix struggled to get up, but David delivered a second and a third blow, and his foe dropped, broken, to the ground. After a moment, Abrix stood up and staggered backward toward Mantilla.

"I failed," Abrix said. "He's too powerful."

David started to speak but was interrupted by a burst of laughter from high above. In the choir loft David noticed the dark outline of a man perched on the backrest of a church pew. The man slowly stepped down and came to the front row, where the light exposed his long blond hair and obscene grimace full of jagged teeth. The man leaned forward, draping his ring-bejeweled fingers over the railing. He wore a meticulously hand-tailored black coat with a red vest. His shirt was an even darker red with a mandarin collar, held tight by metal fasteners beneath his chin.

David immediately recognized him from Madison Tower. He was the one Bondurant referred to as Galatin, the Golden One. But David knew him more from the recesses of Fain's assumed memories. Galatin was a powerful and malevolent being, a true destroyer, and a destructive force that abhorred all living things—especially Fain and his kind.

Galatin vaulted the railing and landed softly on the floor of the center aisle. No words were spoken as the pale man swept his eyes over the room. He launched himself with inhuman speed toward Mantilla and Abrix. He targeted Mantilla first. The collision was immediate, and the momentum of Galatin's ruthless attack carried his adversary backward, smashing him into a row of long wooden pews. The struggle was over in an instant. Galatin now moved toward Abrix, who was still recovering from his earlier defeat at David's hands.

"What hope could such an ordinary immortal have against me?" Galatin said. "How weak you are. You were born mortal—pathetic— and had immortality thrust upon you. And now I will to take it from you." Galatin leaped forward ten feet, knocking Abrix to the ground. He lifted the downed agent over his head and threw him through the stained-glass window. Fragments of shattered stained glass broke away until the entire upper half of the window collapsed inward, covering the altar with broken shards of glass.

The sound of a helicopter could be heard maneuvering in the dark outside. The aircraft dropped down in front of the broken window and shined its bright searchlight into the worship hall.

Shullman said, "I'm seeing it, but I'm still not believing it."

"I know," Rand said. "It's like some kind of crazy monster's ball."

The sound of automatic weapons fire erupted outside again. The noise moved from the right side of the church toward the front of the building. There was a loud chattering of multiple gunshots, and then the shooting slowed to a handful of blasts. There was final pop, and then, silence.

The helicopter turned from the window and moved up and away from the church.

An instant later, the double doors leading into the sanctuary flew inward, breaking away from their hinges. A man in black came through, dragging Abrix's limp body by his right ankle.

"My God. Are you seeing this?" Shullman said.

"From the well," Rand said. "The man from the well."

"Oerell," David whispered.

Oerell walked down the center aisle, dragging Abrix's broken body behind him. He glanced at David and then looked in Rand and Shullman's direction. "I've been looking for you three," he said. "You were there in the woods that day," he said to David. He released Abrix's leg and rubbed his hands together. "I had to kill a lot of Agent Taft's friends to find you. And now that I am this close to you, I can see that you are like me. Aren't you, David Anslem? I find that to be most intriguing! Who told you that I was buried there? Hmm?"

David didn't answer.

"There was only one other who knew of that dark hole in the wilderness—the one who put me in that deep grave, lo those many years ago. But you weren't there. I would have remembered you."

"No," David said. "I wasn't there, but I saw what you did."

Oerell's eyes widened. "You have Viro's memories. "

"You should leave now," David said.

"Yes," Galatin said, smiling. "You should go now. I'll give you a head start. It would be the fair thing to do."

"And who is this?" Oerell said, turning toward Galatin. "I don't know you, but I know your kind, and I know your black souls hold many secrets. Why don't you come closer so that I may touch you and take that which is inside you?"

"Oerell, it would be unwise of you to engage Galatin," David said. He pointed at the shattered front doors. "You still have time."

"Time?" Oerell said. He glanced at the doors. "Oh, I see. Of course. *Fain.* Isn't that the name he goes by now? He is coming."

"And I doubt that he will be as merciful this time," David said. "He will destroy you."

"Not if I destroy you first."

"You have to believe me when I tell you that I know your power. You can't win against me."

"We shall see," Oerell said. "In time, we shall see." He glanced in the direction of the front doors again, and then left the church through the back of the sanctuary.

"You too still have time to leave, Galatin," said David.

"I'm not going anywhere," Galatin said.

"Time is running out. Fain is very close now."

"But not close enough to save you, is he?"

"Is that why you are here? For me?"

"Of course," said Galatin. "I have to know what makes you worth more than all of his other sleepers. A priest—is that why you were chosen? I'm tempted to let you live, to let you suffer this curse. How well do you think you would fare over time, as death becomes your obsession?"

"I am now set in authority over death," David said.

"Are you now?" Galatin said, laughing. "No, David Anslem, death is your new master. Do you think you will be able to keep those destructive urges in check? Are you strong enough, day after day, with the burden of judgment, and having to decide whom you will allow to live or die? Even the most powerful Relaters become weary, and over time they become corrupted by their hunger. You know it's true. You have but to search your memories—your maker's memories. He was once human and became immortal, and like all the others before him, he has become ruined by his lust for power and consumed by his appetite for mortal souls. Tell me something, David Anslem. Did you choose immortality, or was it thrust upon you?"

David didn't answer.

"Ahh," Galatin said. "I see that the answer has struck you speechless. Is that because you now know what you've lost? Oh yes, immortality can be most appealing at first. But what you have gained is an earthbound rapture, and since you are a man of God, David, I know that you of all people can understand that God's paradise would be far sweeter. But now that is something you will never know, because you can never leave this world, or take in a human breath again. You will never know what was meant for you above. And as time goes by, and your purpose here becomes more obscure, you will yearn for the time when you were a man—an ordinary man." Galatin glanced over his shoulder toward the front entrance. "And then there is Fain."

"What of him?" David said.

Galatin turned back toward David, smiling. "He is here. I sense your new master's presence."

"He is not my master," David said.

"How curious that you would say such a thing. He and I are quite similar, you know. Of course you do, because you are now one of us, and therefore are destined to creep through time like us, always looking over your shoulder toward the past. It was by similar incident that your new master and I were both made. But now, having Fain's thoughts, you know inside you which of us harvests with a more crooked scythe, don't you?"

"You should go now, Galatin," Fain said, coming through the shattered front entrance.

"Viro," Galatin said. "The great life shaker."

Fain swept his eyes over the room and then walked down the main aisle. "What do you want here, Galatin? Why have you involved yourself in my affairs?"

"Your dealings have always been of interest to me," said Galatin. "But most recently I have become intrigued about the government researchers you've been hunting. You know the ones I'm talking about? The scientists' bodies that you've been storing in my old tower? The geneticists who have in their possession the secret of immortality. Don't deny it. I saw it in Bondurant's memories after I cored the brain from his skull."

"And why would you care?"

"Of course I care. Just not in the same way that you do. You can't have rogue collectors out there now, can you?" He turned to David. "Did Fain tell you that he hunts the others of his kind?"

"Fain didn't have to tell me," David said. "I have his memories."

"Yes, but I'm certain that you don't have all of them. I'm sure there are some chapters of his life that he has kept from you. You know that what I speak is true. And why do you think that is? I'll tell you. In this world, Fain has no companions. He has only rivals and conquests, and in the end he will destroy you. He's just like his maker, Pan."

"Is that what it's about?" Fain said, "What it's still about? Pan?"

"I will have him," said Galatin.

"Arrogance has always been your folly, Golden One. Think of the results the last time your kind tried this. Together with the great Malleret and Jusserand, you defied Pan and—"

"And what?" Galatin growled.

"They are gone and you were nearly destroyed. And I would suspect that you have been forever diminished by the encounter."

"Weakened? You would be mistaken to believe that."

"You can't defeat us both," David said.

Fain stepped closer. "You need to leave here, and leave Pan to me. I won't warn you again."

Galatin bowed and leaned in closer to David. "Be glad your maker saved you this night." He turned and moved in a blur toward the front entrance.

Fain retrieved a small black phone and held it to his mouth. "Let Galatin go."

"Is that wise?" David said.

"He may yet prove useful to me."

"Simons didn't show."

"It won't be difficult to find him now. He has nothing left." Fain turned his gaze toward Rand and Shullman. Both men were standing at the front of the church.

"I'll take care of them," David said.

Fain looked satisfied. He turned toward the front entrance and raised his hand. A moment later, a dozen men in black came through the door. "Bring the two Relaters' bodies," Fain said. He departed through the front entrance.

The men in black collected Abrix and Mantilla and followed Fain into the darkness.

Shullman helped Rand over to the front pew. "Hang in there, partner. Do you want to sit down?"

"No, no…I've lost a lot of blood. I need to get out of here. See what's going on outside. See if it's clear."

Shullman walked to the side door and peeked through the shattered window. It was quiet outside. The bodies of a dozen agents lay scattered around the property. Farther out, by the road, he could see several abandoned vehicles and more bodies on the ground.

Rand steadied himself against the backrest. He wobbled as he applied pressure to his injured shoulder. "What the hell is going on, Mr. Anslem?"

David walked over to Rand and examined his wound. The bullet had gone through his lower right shoulder just under the collarbone. "It doesn't appear that any major arteries were damaged," David said. He placed his left hand on the entrance wound and his right hand on the exit wound, and slowly squeezed his hands together like a vise.

Rand felt the painful throbbing subside, and the skin around both injured areas began to tingle. After a moment the bleeding stopped and the soreness ceased altogether. "What have you become?" said Rand.

"Try not to use your right arm for a while," David said.

"How did you do that?"

"It's within us all, Mr. Rand: the spark of life, the force without form, the soul, if you will. It's pure energy." He looked away for a moment. "Life." He walked over to the pulpit and stared up at the broken stained-glass window. "It's internal, external, and eternal."

"What am I supposed to do now?" Rand said, walking up behind David.

"I'm going to ask you to end your investigation into Fain."

"And if I don't?"

"He may take an unhealthy interest in you."

"As long as there are murders, and people keep disappearing, there will be an investigation."

"Then keep investigating. Just leave us out of it. The decision shouldn't be that difficult. You have to understand your quandary. No one will believe the truth of the mystery you have unraveled here tonight, and reporting what you've discovered would effectively end your FBI career. But worse, by reporting what you have seen here, you will gain the wrong kind of attention."

"What do you mean?"

"There are others, Mr. Rand."

"Like Fain?"

"Yes, but much worse. Fain bears no ill will toward man—unlike his rivals."

"But he does kill?"

"Yes, but most often he does so presumptively."

"Do you think that makes it okay?"

"No, not always. But sometimes it is necessary."

"And what should I do about Simons? He's not going to get away with this."

"Simons is alone now. He's out of men and resources, and he will attempt to disappear, to go into hiding."

"There's nowhere he can hide from me."

"Simons is no longer your concern."

Rand frowned. "What about Dana, and what she said about you, and what you said about her after you…. I mean, who's telling the truth here?"

"Parker was deceived."

"And was Simons?"

"From what I can see from Dr. Parker's memories, and what she knew of Simons, it would appear that he has not yet realized the truth."

"And what about you, Father?"

"What about me?"

"What side are you on?"

"I'm on the side of life, Detective."

"And what about the company you keep? Are they on the side of the living? That man, that thing from the well, killed an FBI field agent, a university professor, and all of those students."

"That was a tragedy," David said. "I was not made aware of the incident until after it happened. I am truly sorry. I can offer no consolation for the loss of life, but I will remind you that Fain's involvement tonight did save your and your partner's lives."

"And if you and I had waited that night by the pit for this Oerell's unearthing, he would have killed us all."

"Yes."

"How can you just throw in with these monsters?"

"It was not by choice. There is nothing I can do to change what has happened to me. Now I have to see this through to the end."

"Fain is a killer. He's evil, Mr. Anslem."

"Fain is not evil. The same cannot be said about his adversaries, especially Galatin."

"Galatin?" Rand said. "You mean that blond-haired maniac? Who is he?"

"You wouldn't believe me."

"Yeah, that would be true if I hadn't seen all this tonight with my own eyes."

"I will caution you again, Agent Rand, to keep what you have seen this evening to yourself. From here on you will need to proceed with the utmost caution."

"You didn't answer my question about Galatin."

"He is an old and unholy terror."

"What does Galatin—"

"Forget that you ever saw Galatin," David said. "And if you're lucky, he may forget that he saw you."

"The world's gone crazy," Rand said.

David knelt on one knee in the wreckage of the pulpit.

David closed his eyes and quietly whispered a prayer. "To thee, oh Christ, this tender flock I leave; be you now their heavenly Father when I am no more. Protect them from the beginning of life until its eve has fed thee with the riches of their souls. Feed, protect, love, and then translate them to thy rest above." He continued to kneel in silence.

"Mr. Anslem?" said Rand.

"I'm a poor and deluded creature," David said. He opened his eyes. "I am weak, and without God, I am nothing. I'm the slightest breath sustained only by his grace." He stood up.

"What happens now?" Rand said. The sound of police sirens could be heard approaching in the distance. "Will you help me?"

"I have to go now," David said.

"What if I need to contact you?"

David turned and walked down the center aisle toward the exit. He paused by the front entrance, staring back one last time, knowing that he would never see this place again, but would forever think of the one for whom it was built.

EPILOGUE

Jack Simons awoke in the dark. An alarm sounded—a loud, unfamiliar droning sound. A security alarm. He sat up at his desk. The clock read 11:45 p.m. He had been asleep for an hour and felt dopey from the sleeping pills. Squinting in the dim light, he took stock of his fourth-floor bedroom. The door was locked, and the makeshift barricade of a dresser and stacked chairs was still in place. A secondary interior alarm now sounded. Both warning alarms combined, overlapping in a discordant rhythm.

He got up from the chair and crossed the room to the far wall, where a bookcase concealed a spacious, well-stocked safe room. He moved the shelves to one side and moved forward through the chamber entrance. Three flat-screen surveillance monitors lined the back wall and provided the room with its only light. Each monitor showed multiple views of the rooms throughout the house. There was no sign of an intruder.

He slammed the vault door closed. The electromagnetic seals activated with a loud hum, and heavy mortis locks clanged into place. Finally, three large metal bolts rose from the floor, locking the door from behind.

"The room is secure," a woman's computerized voice said.

Just below the group of surveillance monitors, two small lights flashed red on a metal control panel. *How did they find me?* he thought. He had made no mistakes. He had purchased the townhome in an obscure part of the city, and had acquired the New York property under an assumed name.

Another light flashed on the control panel. The light glowed orange and Simons could see on a monitor that the garage was engulfed in flames. The picture turned to snow and the faint sound of a smoke detector could be heard from the bedroom.

He reached for a metal weapons cabinet underneath the control panel. He sorted through the mix of arms until he came to a modified automatic shotgun. He removed the weapon's traditional circular magazine and replaced it with a bulkier square clip that contained custom electric blue-tipped ammunition.

He went to the back of the safe room, where a small pocket emergency door led to an escape passage. He crouched and looked through a peephole. A single bulb lit the narrow stairwell on the other side of the door. The corridor below the stairwell was filled with smoke.

Simons typed in a security code and pulled the door open. Smoke poured through. He coughed, holding his breath against the fumes as he moved out onto the landing. The stairs descended thirty feet and ended at a T-junction. The left corridor led back into the house through a concealed passageway, and the right hall came out on the street behind the main house. More stairs ran deep into the sewers and were linked by a network of old subway tunnels.

He aimed the shotgun down the steps and squeezed off a round. The electric shell shattered the wall with a bright blue flash, sending bricks and shattered wood in every direction. It was becoming harder to breathe, and Simons could feel the heat from behind the wall. His face dripped with perspiration. He raked a sleeve across his forehead and moved downward.

He reached the first junction and lunged around the right corner. He fired his weapon blindly into the dark. The discharge lit up the stairwell. No one was there. He turned quickly toward the corridor behind him. He saw the silhouette of a man who was standing with his back pressed against the passageway. Simons fired his weapon again. He kept firing. A half a dozen explosive shells caved in the walls on both sides of the hallway. There was no sign of the intruder, but a massive backdraft of flames roared through the breach in the wall and threatened to consume him.

Simons moved quickly down the stairs as burning boards and smoldering bricks tumbling past him. Reaching the bottom, he turned to run, but stopped when he noticed the silhouette of a tall figure concealed in the shadows. The figure was blocking the door ahead of him. Simons leveled his weapon in the man's direction.

"Who are you?" said Simons.

"That gun won't do you any good," a voice said from the shadows. "And at this distance, I assure you that I can remove your head before you can pull that trigger again."

"Who sent you?" Simons said.

"I'll ask the questions," the voice said. After a moment, Galatin emerged from the darkness. His blond hair gleamed in the flickering light, and his head moved from side to side like a predatory animal as he moved slowly toward Simons.

Simons adjusted his weapon, raising it higher. Sweat stung his eyes as he stared up at the bizarre-looking man.

"You don't know me," Galatin said, standing directly in front of him now.

"No..."

Galatin flashed a sinister smile, revealing sharp fangs. "I imagine that your employer Pan has left a lot untold. But that's understandable, since the truth would certainly have compromised his hold over you."

"What are you?"

"What do you think I am?"

"You look like a...like a vampire."

"Vampire?" Galatin mused. "Mmm. Do you believe in such creatures?"

"No..."

"I am Theius Galatin."

"You're not like the others."

"No, I'm not like Fain and his kind, nor was I created in some scientist's lab."

"Like Fain."

"I can assure you that Fain is not the genetic abomination that your employer would have you believe."

"I've seen the research. I've seen the evidence."

"The evidence…" Galatin nodded. "Super soldiers, one-man army, and such."

"It's true."

"No," Galatin said. "Pan's and Doctor Gelder's Lies."

"No!" said Simons. "It's impossible."

"I'm aware that Pan promised Gelder the formula to unlock the secrets of everlasting life, if the two of you served his needs. Where, and from whom, do you think the source of such knowledge came? It wasn't from science."

"What you talk of is unnatural. Supernatural."

"You've been deceived," Galatin said. "And you're not the first man Pan has made the promise to."

"But the data?"

"Tailored to suit the purpose of your collaboration. The mighty Pan gave you Abrix, Mantilla, and the other eternals, with the promises of the science behind their creation. And weren't you all to eager to sacrifice everything and anyone in your pursuit to study and replicate their kind?"

"I did it for my country," Simons said. "And I saw the evidence with my own eyes. I've seen the process at Strategic Labs. The creation of Abrix, Mantilla, and the others were his proof."

Galatin shook his head. "They were not manufactured. They were reborn in their maker's image. And to those contrived, there is a great contriver: Pan. They were tools given to you. And all of you were pawns in a hunt for an immortal."

"Yes, to hunt down and retrieve Fain."

"To probe and measure him. There was never any hope of success against him. You were sacrificed."

"For what purpose?"

"Pan must have Fain back. He must have all those many souls inside him. You see, it was Pan who first hunted Fain, sending out his empowered seekers—others like Abrix and Mantilla—to recover him. But Fain devastated them all, and that was ages ago, during Fain's younger, more vulnerable years. It is now believed that he has grown in power—power that rivals his maker. The hunter has become the hunted. With Fain taking so many souls for so long, Pan must be cautious. Elicit help from someone like you and your governmental post."

"I've lost my position," said Simons. "I've sacrificed my career and all of my resources. Everything."

"Of course you have. And all of the science Pan provided as proof was a lie. Surely you suspected?"

"No. I refuse to believe it."

"It's irrelevant what you believe. I've told you the truth. Pan has no blueprint for everlasting life. He is the design. Pan lives forever. And whether you believe that he accomplishes it by science, nature, or some sinister supernatural force, it is inconsequential. What you must come to understand is that Pan would never allow you to have the secret. There was only one other who was trusted with such knowledge, and that was Fain. He betrayed Pan, and they have been at war ever since. They are destined to destroy one another, and in their ending I will be there to take control of their powerful secret world."

"What do you want from me?"

"It should be clear why I sought you out."

"How could you have possibly found me? I made no mistakes."

"You should have left the city," Galatin said. "You see, when a slayer slays, he becomes what he kills, and there are few things remaining on this world that I haven't killed. Take wild beasts, for instance. When they're destroyed, they offer me something human beings do not. Aside from an overall lack of empathy, animals, especially cats, have acute hearing, dim-light vision, and a finely tuned sense of smell. And bears are magnificent creatures. Did you know a bear's sense of smell is twenty-one hundred times stronger than a human's? It's thought to have the best sense of smell of any other animal on earth. It's true. A bear can smell death and rotting flesh from twenty miles away. When I came upon Abrix and Mantilla days ago, they reeked of you, thus making it the simplest of tasks to find you. But enough about me. I'm sure you're curious about my visit, aren't you?"

Simmons nodded slowly. He struggled to keep the heavy gun leveled in Galatin's direction.

"I must confess something to you," Galatin said. "May I?"

Simmons nodded again, and looked over his shoulder. The fire was getting closer.

"I'm disappointed," Galatin said. "Through Abrix and Mantilla's assumed memories I have seen that Pan dealt with Gelder directly, but there's no sign that he ever met with you. Is that true?"

"Yes. He only met with Dr. Gelder."

"And was there a contingency plan? I was hoping that your trail would lead me back to the one you serve. Will he come for you?"

"He doesn't know where I am."

"When and where will you see him?"

Simons shook his head. "I hope never. My mission is compromised. I'm out of men and resources. And now it would appear I'm out of time." He lowered the gun.

Galatin studied Simons's eyes, measuring the truth in them. After a moment he held out his open hand. "Walk with me."

Simons stared down at Galatin's ring-encrusted fingers. He dropped his weapon on the ground. He didn't want to take the fiend's hand, but he found it impossible to resist. It was as if Galatin's suggestion was planted in his mind, overwhelming his senses. He felt dizzy, intoxicated, and after a moment his hand reached out toward Galatin as if guided by a mysterious force.

Galatin grasped Simons by the wrist and walked quickly into the darkened passageway. They descended a short staircase and emerged in an underground passage where the air was damp and thick with the smell of raw sewage. They turned left and moved through the tunnel in complete darkness.

Simons struggled to keep up. He kept his free right hand forward, trying to feel his away in the dark, but Galatin's incredibly fast pace kept him off balance. They rounded a corner and Simons struck the wall with his shoulder and head. Dazed, he fell to his knees. Galatin continued forward, dragging Simons across the uneven stone floor.

The passageway ended at the base of a short staircase that led up to another tunnel. Simons gained his footing just as Galatin vaulted upward, nearly pulling Simons's shoulder from its socket. They came to a landing where the tunnel widened. A faint light was visible nearly fifty yards in the distance. Galatin released his grip and Simons stumbled backward against the wet bricks, exhausted and out of breath. His head ached, and his body was skinned and bruised. He rubbed his wrist, trying to get his circulation going again. "Just get it over with," he told Galatin.

"Take your life?" Galatin said. "No, I'm not going to kill you." He stepped closer. After a moment, his crazed, jack-o'-lantern smile vanished, his black eyes changed into a warm shade of blue, and his once harsh complexion morphed into that of an handsome young man.

Simons stared up at him, astonished. "How is it possible? You're just a boy."

"You see what I want you to see," said Galatin. "Over time, mortals grow old and wrinkle. I do not age, but the face you saw before is what I've turned into—what I've had to become. That monstrous outward manifestation is the consequences of my life's journey."

"Why spare me?"

"There is a saying: 'The mercy of the wicked is cruel.'"

"I see," Simons said. "And what is the price for this consideration?"

"All will be illuminated in due time. For now, your appointment with me is a simple one. It is my wish that you rearm yourself."

"Rearm? How? I lost nearly everything in the encounter at Anslem's church."

"I'll provide you with the resources," Galatin said. He handed Simons a piece of paper.

"What is this?"

"The address of your new dwelling—a more defensible residence. And I've provided you with a bank account that's filled with money—lots of it. You will keep this meeting between the two of us a secret. Betray me at your own peril. If I discover any disloyalty, I will visit pain and suffering upon you the likes of which there are no words a human tongue can describe. Serve me well, and I'll give you your life." He stepped to the side and gestured at the open end of the tunnel. "You may go for now, but rest assured that I will be waiting and watching."

Simons stared down at the note and slid it into his front pocket. He moved past Galatin, glancing him over warily. After a moment he stopped and turned back.

"Is there something else?" Galatin asked.

"About Pan..."

"What about him?"

"If what I knew about him has all been lies, then who is he, really?"

"No one knows Pan's beginning, save perhaps Fain. The secret of Pan's origin is his power."

"Why would someone so powerful have need of me?"

"You already know the answer to that question. Is it not the simplest of military measures? Isn't it always in the crucial moments of a struggle that the strongest implement the weakest? Your involvement allowed Pan to remain invisible. Fain, on the other hand, maneuvers openly. He has his own resources, but he bested you directly, dismantled your little hidden government venture singlehandedly. His actions are bold and provocative. He would not provoke his creator unless he was confident that he could succeed against him. It is my belief that Fain holds the secret to Pan's destruction. You and I will uncover the secret together. We will use the discovery to destroy them all, and we will begin our inquisition with David Anslem."

The End

26921278R00161

Made in the USA
Columbia, SC
21 September 2018